Eileen Merriman's first young adult novel, *Pieces of You*, was published in 2017, and was a finalist in the NZ Book Awards for Children and Young Adults and a Storylines Notable Book. Since then, she has published another eleven novels for adults and young adults and received huge critical praise, with one reviewer saying: 'Merriman is an instinctive storyteller with an innate sense of timing.' In addition to being a regular finalist in the NZ Book Awards for Children and Young Adults, Merriman was a finalist in the 2021 Ngaio Marsh Awards for Best YA/Kids Book and *Moonlight Sonata* was longlisted for the Jann Medlicott Acorn Prize for Fiction 2020. She has been published in Germany, Turkey and the UK, and five of her young adult novels have been optioned for film or television, including the Black Spiral Trilogy. Merriman's other awards include runner-up in the 2018 *Sunday Star-Times* Short Story Award and third in the same award for three consecutive years previously. She works as a consultant haematologist at North Shore Hospital.

Book 1 of the gritty, fast-paced, thought-provoking Eternity Loop Series.

Promise you will never, ever mess with time . . .

Both Rigel and Indigo are Offspring, born to virally optimised parents. With dire warnings about the possible consequences of time travel, they have been forbidden from even thinking about it. But Indigo is bored — what could really go wrong? She longs for excitement, which she might just find with the mysterious stranger Billy Raven.

Meanwhile, Rigel has an odd feeling that he can't shake off. Is it because his dad, Johnno (aka Phoenix), is off on another dangerous mission? Or is it because of what the Foundation did to his mum, Violet? Or is something else going on?

Only time will tell.

EILEEN MERRIMAN

TIME'S RAVEN

PENGUIN BOOKS

PENGUIN

UK | USA | Canada | Ireland | Australia
India | New Zealand | South Africa | China

Penguin is an imprint of the Penguin Random House group of companies,
whose addresses can be found at global.penguinrandomhouse.com.

Penguin
Random House
New Zealand

First published by Penguin Random House New Zealand, 2023

10 9 8 7 6 5 4 3 2 1

Text © Eileen Merriman, 2023

The moral right of the author has been asserted.

Design by Cat Taylor © Penguin Random House New Zealand
Cover background gradient © Kuro via Creative Market
Front cover image by John Cobb via Unsplash
Author photograph by Colleen Lenihan
Prepress by Soar Communications Group
Printed and bound in Australia by Griffin Press, an Accredited ISO AS/NZS 14001
Environmental Management Systems Printer

A catalogue record for this book is available from the National Library of New Zealand.

ISBN 978-0-14-377867-7
eISBN 978-0-14-377868-4

penguin.co.nz

MIX
Paper from
responsible sources
FSC® C009448

For Maisie, who knows about haiku and tigers burning bright and the power of imagination.

CHARACTER LIST

HOFFMAN-MEHTA FAMILY & ASSOCIATES

Indigo Hoffman (Moon): 17 years old, second-generation virally optimised (G2); daughter of Bruno Hoffman and Harper Mehta

Bruno Hoffman: first-generation virally optimised (G1); former VORTEX member; Indigo's father

Harper Mehta: first-generation virally optimised (G1); former VORTEX member; Indigo's mother

Griffin Lewis: 19-year-old friend of Indigo's residing in 1996 London

Elodie Boucher: 18-year-old friend of Indigo's residing in 1996 London

Billy Raven: a young man of indeterminate age who Indigo first meets in 1996 London

Andromeda: 20-something-year-old Offspring, currently being held prisoner in 2005 Santorini

FLETCHER-BLACK FAMILY & ASSOCIATES

Rigel Fletcher: 18 years old, second-generation virally optimised (G2); son of Johnno (Phoenix) Fletcher and Violet Black

Fox Fletcher: Rigel's 13-year-old brother

Johnno (Phoenix) Fletcher: first-generation virally optimised (G1); former VORTEX member; Black Spiral Intelligence (BSI) agent; father of Rigel and Fox

Violet Black: first-generation virally optimised (G1); former VORTEX member; scientist at Apollo Foundation; mother of Rigel and Fox

Kit Williams: 18 years old, Rigel's friend from high school

Vaughan Johnson: 17 years old, Rigel's friend from high school

BLACK SPIRAL INTELLIGENCE (BSI) STAFF

Rudolph Underwood: Director of BSI/Head of NZ Branch

Rawiri Sullivan: BSI agent and first-generation virally optimised (G1); former VORTEX member

Camilla Chase: Head of UK Division of BSI

Harvey Wu: BSI agent/neurophysicist, UK branch

Brie Morrison: BSI employee

Ci Chang: BSI agent

QUICK FAMILY & ASSOCIATES

Billy Quick (Raven): 16-year-old from 1988 England

Natalie Quick: Billy Raven's older sister

Cedric Quick: Billy Raven's father

Mr Elder: Billy Raven's English teacher

Aurelia Nightingale: a teenage girl whom Billy Raven meets in 1988 England

Catherine Edwards: 16-year-old girlfriend of Billy's from 1988 England

OTHER

Laura Strom: a virally optimised scientist (G1) working for a splinter cell

Callum Templeman: first-generation virally optimised (G1); former VORTEX member

Miles Newton: Eternity Project employee

Grace Newton: Miles's wife

Rua Matipo: Aurelia's friend, lives in the Cook Islands

PART I

ONE:
BILLY

Once upon a time . . . Is that how one starts a tale like this? I have been battling with time all my life; battling and playing with, and conquering.

Once upon a time, I conquered time.

Once upon a time, I was sixteen years old, sitting in a classroom that smelt of aged sweat and Mr Elder's breath.

'Speak up, boy,' he said.

I took a deep breath, trying to chase the bad thoughts out of my head. Hoping my voice wouldn't shake. 'To sleep, perchance to die.'

Elder threw a piece of chalk at me. 'Perchance to *dream*, Mr Quick. Your surname is somewhat of an oxymoron, don't you think?'

I heard titters from behind me, some louder than others. Rubbing my forehead, where I was sure the chalk had left a bruise, I said, 'To sleep, perchance to dream. For in that sleep of death—'

Mr Elder strode forward and brought his ruler down on my desk. I'm ashamed to say I jumped.

'Ay, there's the rub!' he bellowed. Oh, how I hated him then. How I wished it was my English teacher who had slipped into the sleep of death ten days before, rather than my mother.

'A-ay, there's the r-rub,' I stammered. 'For in that sleep of death what dreams may come when we have shuffled off this mortal coil . . .'

Elder held his hands in front of him, his fingers laced. 'Thank you, Mr Quick. I think you've successfully murdered *Hamlet* now.'

More laughter. My whole body felt as if it was on fire. If only I could shuffle off my mortal coil, escape this nightmarish existence forever. All my father had done since Mum had died was drink and cry, cry and drink.

I didn't cry anymore. I just wanted to die.

But I even failed at that.

TWO:
INDIGO

He sneaks into my dreams sometimes. Billy Raven, I mean. In my dreams, we're standing on Tower Bridge, kissing as the river coils beneath us. But then he starts kissing my neck, and it's not long before I realise he's feeding on me, taking my immortality for his own. When I twist away, I see that the river beneath us is running red.

I always wake with the same words clanging through my thought-stream: *What's done cannot be undone. Don't forget.*

If only I could. I'm in so much trouble, not only with my parents (*How could you run away like that?*) but with the BSI, too (*Your hearing will be on 8 January*).

Rigel, or, as the BSI like to call him, Hunter Blue, is about the only person I'm not in trouble with, even though it's my fault he nearly got separated from his body forever, suspended somewhere between the past, the present and the future. And if he blames me for the disappearance of his father, Black Wolf, he hasn't let on.

But I've hardly seen Rigel lately. He's been too busy cuddling up to Brie.

It's a slow, syrupy summer's day, and I'm relaxing by Dad's pool. Perhaps 'relaxing' is the wrong word. I'm hardly relaxed. All I can think about is the hearing tomorrow. I've been charged with unauthorised time travel, which is a direct violation of Black

Spiral rule number two, designed to keep us Offspring, the second-generation products of the Foundation experiments, out of trouble.

'Urrgh.' I slip off the hammock and dive into the pool. The water is a perfect twenty-eight degrees. I flip over, staring up at the cloudless sky. Tomorrow is Friday, a scheduled rain day. It seems appropriate that it will be grey and wet the day I'm sentenced to my punishment, whatever that turns out to be. I just want to get it over and done with.

And then what? I'm meant to be starting my final year of high school. What if I'm not allowed to because of my criminal convictions?

Relax, Indy. It's BSI business. Normals won't hear about that kind of stuff.

I close my eyes, tempted to tell Rigel to get the hell out of my thought-stream, but something holds me back. *That's the problem,* I think-reply. *The BSI could banish me to Siberia and no one would even blink.*

No one's going to banish you anywhere. They're just doing what they have to do.

I stretch my arms above my head, waiting for the pool edge to bump against my fingers. *Is that the kind of stuff you discuss in your BSI meetings?*

It's the kind of stuff I just know.

And what have you been doing? Or shouldn't I ask? I'm trying to block the next image, but it bobs up anyway: Brie greeting Rigel at the airport five weeks ago with a hug and a kiss. Ugh, why am I remembering that?

Rigel's thought-stream blurs, and I realise he's blocking me as well. *Training.*

Is that what you call it?

It's not what you think, he think-says. *See you tomorrow.* Then he's gone, and I'm floating by myself, staring into the blue.

I'm on house arrest, being shuffled back and forth between Mum's and Dad's. At least Dad has the pool. Tonight, the night before my hearing, I'm at Mum's again, enduring a trip through the Virtual Mall to choose my outfit.

'Why am I dressing up for a hearing?' I grumble for what must be the tenth time. 'It's not as though they're going to give me demerit points for looking scruffy.'

'Believe me, first impressions matter.' Mum touches her I-Bio, taking control of the Indigo avatar on the e-screen so she can get the avatar to enter the next shop.

'Is it just me, or is everything in here purple?' I take over my avatar again, spinning her around and into the next store.

Mum frowns at my selection, a pair of white wide-legged trousers paired with a blue shirt. 'You can see your belly-button.'

'What's so offensive about a belly-button?' I'm winding her up and I know it. 'OK, OK,' I relent. 'How about this?' I click on a longer version of the shirt, one that sits on the waistband of the trousers. 'No breasts, belly-buttons or vaginas.'

'I hope you're not going to use that tone at the Tribunal.'

'I'll try my best to be civil.'

'Because if you talk to them like that, I can guarantee your punishment will be worse.' Mum purchases the items. A message flashes up on the screen, promising a drone delivery to our front door within the next ninety minutes.

I slump into the couch. 'I'll be good, I promise.'

'And you need to tell the truth.'

'I've already told the truth. In my debriefing, remember?'

My mother's glare is a mirror-image of mine, I'm sure.

'Excuse me for remembering what happened the last time you promised to tell your father and me *the whole truth*.'

'I was under the influence of a vampire,' I mumble, squirming beneath her gaze. Time's vampire.

But he did love you, a voice inside me insists. *He wasn't lying about that.*

'Because you chose to deliberately flout all the rules that were meant to protect you,' my mother snaps. 'And quite apart from that, how old was this Billy Raven anyway? Do you have any idea how much trouble you're in?'

My anger rising, I say, 'I can't believe you of all people are telling me off for going out with an older man. How old was Dad when you met him? Oh, twenty-five, you say? And you were — what? — my age?' I jump up and retreat to my room, my mother's thought-voice chasing me. *Indigo Hoffman, how dare you speak to me like that . . . wait until I let your father . . .*

'Blah blah blah,' I whisper, blocking her so she doesn't get completely hysterical at me. I'm probably already grounded for the rest of my life anyway, but arguing with my mother is exhausting.

Mum's voice floats down the hallway. 'Get back here Indigo — we haven't chosen your shoes yet.'

'You choose them,' I yell. 'I've got a headache.'

It's not a lie. A headache is exactly what I get every time I think about what happened only five weeks ago. I draw my curtains and lie down on my bed, trying to chase the memory away, but it's still too vivid. All I can smell is blood, blood and the overwhelming scent of cloves.

Do tigers hunt alone? Rigel, Andromeda and I had asked before attacking Billy in tiger form. It was a taipan snake rather than a tiger that had ended his life, though, its venom paralysing him before he bled to death.

He'd told us he was a god, but in the end he died like any other man.

I shudder, turn onto my side. I haven't heard from Andromeda since that day. Maybe she's returned to 2005 Santorini, where Billy hid her. Or maybe she's gone back to 2088, where she came from — although there's no guarantee that the threat she had fled from has now gone.

My headache is getting worse. I pull the covers over my head and escape the only way I can.

If my mother finds out, she'll kill me.

But there are worse things than being dead.

A giant yellow orb floods into my eyes. I am a Tiger Moth, *Arctia caja*, navigating by the light of the full moon, my giraffe-patterned wings outlined in its hypnotic glow.

Billy: What's your favourite animal, Indigo Moon?

I float high above the trees, a celestial calm filling me, one I feel only when I'm travelling. Since I've mastered whole-body *shifting*, it has become almost effortless to travel, unlike when I used to send out my dream-flow and leave my earthly body behind.

Not time-travelling, though. As far as the BSI are concerned, it's unlikely I'll ever be doing that again.

Thought I might find you here, a familiar voice think-says.

If I were in my human form, I might sigh or groan. Instead, I flit around my newly arrived companion, whose wings are equally resplendent in gold, blue, green and pink.

Sneaking around again, Hunter Blue? I think-ask.

It's Rigel to you. My childhood friend — although we're hardly children anymore, now he's eighteen and I'm only ten months away from that, too — settles on a tree trunk.

Aren't I allowed to call you by your BSI name, then? I think-ask, alighting beside him.

You'll call me whatever you want, I'm figuring. A split second later, the moth has gone, and a Rigel-tiger is prowling around the base of the tree.

Show-off, I think-say, cycling rapidly through my favourite moth forms like a model on a catwalk, Hawkmoth-Coffee-Clearwing-Emperor Moth, before changing into tiger form too.

I'm not even going to dignify that with a reply. Rigel sits next to me and starts licking a front paw, his tiger-toes fanned out. *Your moths are pretty and all, but can they bring down a deer?*

Haven't you ever heard of an Assassin caterpillar? If your tiger eats one of those, it'll bleed to death. I stretch out in the long grass, my eyes still full of moon. Is it weird to worship a rock the way I do?

Rigel stretches out next to me. *Remember the time we went travelling as elephants and nearly got shot by those hunters?*

See? Sometimes it's better to be small but deadly. I shudder, remembering that day. *I thought we were going to die.*

Maybe it's not as easy as that, he think-says. *Since we're immortal and all.*

I don't know if you can grow back your head if it's chopped off, though, I think-say, and if we were in human form, we'd probably be giggling. Instead, I ride the pink bubbly wave of Rigel's thought-stream, happy to bask in the glow of the moon with the guy who used to be my best friend, back before I nearly got all of us killed.

I'm still your best friend, Indy, he think-says, as I drift into sleep. *Aren't I?*

Of course, I think-say. *If you'll have me.*

I sense Rigel's thought-stream turn a cryptic blue-green, feel the feline rasp of his tongue on my nose. *You'll be OK tomorrow,* he think-says. *I promise.*

THREE:
BILLY

1988

I walked home slowly, the sun peeking at me through the clouds. It was twenty minutes to the semi-detached house I shared with my father and my older sister, Natalie, if I took the shortest route.

I wasn't interested in the shortest route, though. Intent on spending as little time at home as possible, I cut down to the river and wandered along the footpath, watching the swans slide through the water. A trio of youths in uniforms different from mine watched me with half-lidded eyes, cigarettes dangling from between their fingers. Ducking my head, I traced a semi-wide berth, avoiding them without wanting to look too obvious. I was average-sized, not too fat, not too skinny, but it was easy to get picked on when you were a loner.

Loner. Loser. My eyes stung. My defences, the walls I'd built around myself over the years, were weak, eroded by thirteen months of watching cancer ravage my mother's body. Chasing the self-hating thoughts away, I took a deep breath and looked ahead, down the line of the river. All I could see was an old man sitting on a bench with a newspaper, and a blonde girl in skinny jeans and a long black coat.

The girl was sitting on a curve in the footpath, dangling her feet over the water. When I drew closer, I saw she was older than I'd first thought, maybe by a year or so, with a row of tiny studs below her lower lip that caught the sun when she lifted her chin. Weird. I'd never seen anything like that before. Maybe she was a punk, although she didn't have a mohawk or shaved head to match.

She returned my stare. I looked away first, trying to hurry past her, but her voice caught me. '. . . Raven, right?'

I turned. 'Huh?'

'I said, you're Billy Raven, right?'

'No. I mean, I am Billy, but my last name's not Raven.' The girl had delicate features, with high cheekbones and a tapered nose, and very long, glossy hair. Not punk-like at all.

'What's a punk?' the girl asked.

'W-what?' Had I spoken aloud?

The girl stood up. She was tiny, maybe five foot tall at the most. 'Never mind. Don't you want to know what my name is?'

'Um . . . yeah?'

'Maybe you don't.' The girl began walking away, her hair swinging past her butt. Cute, definitely cute, and *definitely* way out of my league.

The girl looked over her shoulder. 'Where I've come from, you're almost out of *my* league, Billy Raven.'

What? She was obviously mixing me up with someone else, out of her brain on acid or something. But that look she was giving me was making my heart race and my stomach flip. Not just that, but I had the oddest sensation, as if the world was going all blurry around the edges. Maybe I was dreaming.

'What's your name?' I asked, trying to sound confident.

'Aurelia,' she said. 'Aurelia Nightingale.' Her eyes were the bluest I'd ever seen, the colour of tropical island lagoons.

'Lots of birds where you come from,' I said, and her laugh set me aglow, in a good way.

'Walk with me,' she said, as if she were a queen and I was her servant. So I did, and as we strolled further and further from my house, the winter sun dipping below the hills, Aurelia slipped her hand into mine. It was so natural, as if I'd known her for several weeks rather than a few minutes.

In fact, as I'd tell her later, much later, we'd been together for over a century.

FOUR:
RIGEL

I've got no idea what I'm meant to wear for the hearing today, so I dress in my usual BSI uniform; black bamboo trousers and a black V-necked t-shirt with a Rod of Asclepius embossed over the left breast.

The Rod of Asclepius, a snake curled around a staff, was my Uncle Rawiri's idea. When the BSI was formed, they couldn't exactly copy the Spiral Foundation's circular spiral emblem. The Rod of Asclepius is also the symbol of healing, which is the exact opposite of what the Spiral Foundation did to the generation before us, for the most part.

I walk down the hallway, pausing in the doorway of my parents' bedroom. It's eight am, so Mum has left for work already. As for Dad, he left for work seven weeks ago and never returned.

I talked to him, though. Five weeks ago, after blacking out in a bookstore in London.

But where are you? I'd asked.

I'm unstuck, or stuck, I don't quite know how to explain it, my father had said. He'd told me that Billy Raven was a time vampire. *He feeds off people like us, takes our powers and immortality for his own . . . but it's never enough. That's why you have to get Indigo away from him.*

I *had* got Indigo away from him, had destroyed Billy Raven in the process . . . and yet, I'd failed, too.

'We killed him,' I whisper. 'Billy Raven is dead. But where are you?'

I push off the doorframe with my foot. *I'm going to find you*, I promise my father, even though I know it's very unlikely he can hear me.

But first, Indigo's hearing.

At nine am on the dot, we're escorted into a large boardroom on the top floor of BSI Headquarters, one with alternating waveforms in the walls designed to neutralise thought-signals before they can enter or leave the room. The Tribunal are already there, two men and two women at a long table, their backs to the massive windows looking out over the city.

I think they hate me already, Indigo think-says in a closed-comm that only the two of us can hear.

I'm sure that's not true, I think-answer. *They're just old*.

Uncle Rawiri shoots us a *look*, as if he knows Indigo and I are conducting a private convo. *Cut the thought-speak*, he think-says, confirming my suspicions, before nodding at Indigo's parents, Bruno and Harper, who have filed in behind us.

Indigo barely acknowledges they've entered the room. I'm getting the impression that things between her and her parents aren't great; even worse than when her parents split up four years ago and Indigo came to stay with our family for two weeks in protest. She would have stayed longer if Uncle Bruno hadn't come to drag her home, kicking and screaming *I hate you, I hate you*.

Indigo can be pretty feisty. Can't say I blame her, though. I don't think I'd like it if I found out my father had been having affairs with junior doctors either.

Rudolph Underwood enters last, wearing a black suit with

the BSI snake and staff embossed over the left breast pocket.

'Hello,' he says, holding out his hand to Bruno. 'I'm Rudolph Underwood, BSI Director-General.'

'I know who you are,' Bruno says, not taking his hands out of his trouser pockets. Indigo's mum just crosses her arms and looks away.

'Have a seat,' Underwood says, not bothered in the slightest by their hostility, or if he is, then he's not showing it. 'Not you, Ms Hoffman,' he adds, when Indigo goes to follow them over to the seats lined up against the opposite wall. He indicates a red leather armchair to the left of the desk. 'We need you there for the web link. Director Chase,' he waves at the e-screen on the wall opposite her, 'will be joining us from London.'

'Fine,' Indigo mutters, sinking into the chair. She looks so small. Maybe it's the big chair, or the rows of tiny braids in her hair. I sit next to Rawiri, touching the buzzing disc on my wrist.

Brie: How's it going?

I whisper a quick reply — *Just starting, catch you later* — and watch my words appear on the screen before zipping off into cyber-space, or in this case Brie's office on the floor below. Remembering last night, my stomach clenches and releases again.

Was that your first time, Hunter Blue?

Yeah, I'd replied, glad it was too dark for her to see me blushing.

You did just fine, she'd murmured.

Nah, I think I need more practice, I'd teased, and that was exactly what we'd done, even though it was after midnight. No wonder I feel so wiped out today.

Underwood stands to the right of the desk, his hands clasped together. 'Welcome,' he says, as if we're attending a graduation dinner rather than a disciplinary hearing. 'Let me introduce the members of our panel.'

Too distracted to listen, I decide to make up my own names for the Tribunal: the short, shiny-headed man is Bald Eagle, and the very thin woman next to him is the Stork. The pink-haired woman next to *her* is the Peacock, and the hook-nosed man next to the Peacock is the Vulture. None of them look a day under fifty, unlike my mum and Indigo's parents, who don't look any older than me. Immortality has its benefits.

'And I'm sure you all remember Camilla Chase, Director of the UK division,' Underwood continues when a petite woman with a black bob appears on the e-screen. 'Let's proceed, shall we? Indigo, can you begin by telling us when you first started time-travelling?'

Indigo takes a deep breath. 'I guess it was about six months ago. I couldn't sleep one night, so I travelled to London. And I was walking around, wondering what it would have looked like in the 1500s when Henry VIII was alive. Which got me thinking about how cool it would be to go back in time. I thought I'd be a fly, so I wouldn't interfere with anything.'

'You saw Henry VIII?' The Peacock leans forward.

'Not the first time. I only got there on my tenth attempt.' Indigo tugs on the end of one of her braids. 'It took a while to get good at it.'

'And did you always travel as a fly?' the Vulture asks.

'The first couple of times.' Indigo averts her eyes. 'But then . . . I thought it would be fun to take part in some stuff.'

The Vulture frowns. 'Such as?'

'Um, so I went to New York. It was just after the Statue of Liberty had been reconstructed, and I wanted to see the fireworks.'

'That would be two years ago, then?' the Bald Eagle says.

Indigo nods. 'At first I was a seagull, perching on top of the Statue's head.'

'Her head?' The Bald Eagle looks affronted.

Next he'll be asking if you pooped on it, I think-say, and sense a flicker of amusement in Indigo's thought-stream. Rawiri elbows me.

'It was the best view,' Indigo says. 'But everyone looked like they were having such a good time and I wanted to join the dancing. So I *shifted* into human form, and that's when I met Elodie and Griffin.'

'Elodie and Griffin?' The Bald Eagle strokes his shiny head. 'Who are they?'

'Are these the same friends you met in the 1990s?' Chase chimes in from the e-screen. When I look up, I see that she's been joined by Ci, the BSI agent I met a couple of months ago. His hair is in its usual cresting wave formation, although he's dyed it turquoise since I saw him last.

'Yes.' Indigo folds her hands in her lap.

'But I thought you said the Statue had just been reconstructed,' the Peacock says.

'Like I said,' Indigo mutters, 'my direction sense wasn't that good to start with. I was out by about seventy years.' The panel exchange horrified looks. Groaning internally, I lean back in my chair.

'And what happened after that?' the Stork asks.

'They told me they were celebrating the end of their year's OE in London, and were about to go their separate ways. I thought that was a shame, because we had such a great time together, so I decided to travel back to London around the time they first arrived for their OE.'

'In 1996,' Underwood prompts.

'Well, technically it was 1995, but yeah.'

'And how many times do you estimate you did that?' the Bald Eagle asks.

She shrugs. 'I don't know. Maybe six or seven? I was careful,' she adds quickly when the panels' collective eyebrows shoot up, like some kind of freaky caterpillar Mexican wave.

'*Careful?*' The Bald Eagle's tone has changed from incredulousness to — what? Mocking? 'In what way?'

Indigo clears her throat. 'I never spent more than a few hours there each time. I figured that way there'd be a low chance of causing any disruption to — well, history.'

The Vulture grunts. 'I'm not sure how you came to that conclusion.'

'Yeah, well, it was all going fine until I met this guy in a nightclub.'

The Stork's narrow features contract even further. 'By *this guy*, one assumes you mean Billy Raven.'

'Yes. I didn't know who he was, though, not then.'

'Of course not,' Underwood says in a grandfatherly tone.

'And after that?' the Bald Eagle prompts.

Indigo flushes. 'Next time we met was at a Queen concert. And after that,' she lowers her eyes, 'we saw each other a couple more times. Then he came to my house and — well, I guess he kidnapped me. I think you know the rest.'

The Peacock settles back in her chair, her oversized orange cardigan billowing around her. 'I think it would be best to hear it from you, Ms Hoffman, however. From the horse's mouth, as it were.'

Maybe you should shift *into a horse*, I think-suggest to Indigo.

That could be considered contempt of court, she think-fires back, and I suppress a smile. It's not funny, none of this is, but how else are we meant to get through this?

We? Indigo think-says. *I'm the one who's in trouble here, not you.*

I wouldn't be so sure, I think-reply, and jump when Rawiri kicks me on the ankle.

'Ms Hoffman?' Underwood prompts.

Indigo snaps to attention. 'OK,' she says, her voice barely betraying the nervousness staining her thought-stream. 'I hope you're not in a hurry.'

'No hurry at all,' the Peacock says, so Indigo starts talking. I've heard it all before, both from Indigo and as part of the debriefing we had at the London BSI HQ last year. How Billy had handed Indigo over to a Splinter Foundation cell in Norway so they could harvest her stem cells; how he'd stolen her back and hidden her in 2005 Santorini with the mysterious Andromeda, a young woman he'd rescued from an unknown danger in 2088. How Indigo had ended up in nineteenth-century America, about to be married to Billy Raven. How Andromeda, Indigo and I had combined forces to destroy Billy Raven, and then Andromeda had left us, and hadn't been seen since.

'Have you anything to add, Agent Blue?' the Bald Eagle asks me once Indigo finally finishes, which must be at least twenty minutes later.

'Billy Raven called himself Janus,' I say, after thinking of and dismissing several replies, such as *Cut her some slack, will you?* and *Can't you see she's suffered enough?* 'The god of beginnings, time and dualities. He stole my dad's dream-flow and hid it somewhere. He's still out there, but no one knows where.'

The Vulture swipes a tissue beneath his craggy nose. 'Billy Raven, you mean?'

'No, my father,' I say, with a rising frustration. I see glances being passed around the room, all of them disbelieving. I don't get it. Why is everyone around here so closed-minded, so willing to believe my father is dead?

The Bald Eagle, who seems to be the leader of this pack, threads his fingers together on the desk in front of him. 'Well,' he says, as if I had never spoken at all, 'I think we have enough information now to proceed.'

Underwood nods. 'In that case, we will let you adjourn to deliberate and reconvene in,' he checks his watch, 'an hour, to deliver your verdict.'

'Oh no,' the Bald Eagle says. 'I don't think there is any need for that. Do the rest of the panel members agree?'

'We agree,' the Stork says, her voice like gravel rolling down a driveway, and the Vulture and the Peacock nod.

Indigo's dad leaps up. 'What's the point of a hearing, if it was a foregone conclusion?' Harper, Indigo's mum, puts a restraining hand on his arm, but Bruno shakes her off. 'This is a farce, a complete waste of time!'

The Bald Eagle gives him a steely look. 'If we had heard evidence today that would have given us cause to change our decision, then we would certainly have asked for an adjournment. But, as I said, that won't be necessary.' He takes a slim e-tablet the size of a playing card out of his pocket and passes it to Underwood.

Indigo hunches her shoulders, and I tense as Underwood reads from the tablet.

'We, the members of the Black Spiral Tribunal, have considered the evidence before us, and have decided to clear Indigo Hoffman of all charges.' The smile hasn't even reached my eyes before Underwood goes on: 'However, this is contingent on a period of rehabilitation at Black Spiral Headquarters, for a minimum period of twelve months.' And even then, I'm thinking *Well, that won't be so bad* and *Hey, maybe we can hang out together?*, until Underwood delivers the final nail in the coffin, or maybe that's two nails.

Two words.

In. London.

FIVE:
BILLY

1988

Every school day for the next four weeks, I took the long way home past the river. Every day, Aurelia was sitting there, waiting — even when it was cold and drizzly, the autumnal temperature no more than ten degrees Celsius. Every day, at Aurelia's insistence, we sought privacy in a collection of nooks and crannies — beneath a willow tree, under the bridge, and once, the last time, in the rear of an abandoned car that was never going to drive anywhere again.

'Where are you from?' I asked her on that first day, when we were sitting beneath the willow tree. I wasn't getting many clues from her accent, which seemed to be a mixture of English, American and Australian.

'The Cook Islands,' she said, crushing a flaming red leaf between her fingers.

'The Cook Islands?' I wasn't even sure where those were. Off the coast of Australia, maybe?

Aurelia laughed. 'They're in the Pacific, about three hours by plane from New Zealand. My parents were hiding there, trying to lead a normal life, but then the inevitable happened.'

'The inevitable?'

'As in, me,' she said. 'Once I turned thirteen, everything changed.'

Too shy to ask what she meant by that — because if it involved any talk about periods and the like, then I was sure to blush — I asked, 'And how old are you now?'

'Guess.' Aurelia stood up, her hand on the tree trunk we had been nestling under.

I shrugged. 'I don't know, seventeen?'

'Yes . . . and no. It's complicated.'

Gazing up at her, I asked, 'Complicated how?' *Girls* were complicated, as far as I was concerned, and getting more so by the minute.

'Biologically, that's true. But chronologically, I'm both much older and much younger than that.'

'OK . . .' More confused than ever, I pulled my knees up to my chest and wrapped my arms around them.

Aurelia turned a circle, her arms spread wide, her long black coat rising up like a cape. 'What's your favourite animal, Billy?'

'As in a real one, or a made-up one?'

She stopped twirling and sank down beside me. 'Both.'

'My favourite animal for real is a panther. But my favourite made-up animal is a centaur.'

Aurelia's eyebrows drew together. 'That's half-person, half-animal.'

'If you want to get technical, yeah. We're all animals, though, right? It's only been a few million years since we split off from chimpanzees.'

'Interesting,' Aurelia said, and she genuinely *did* seem interested, if the way she was holding my gaze was anything to go by.

'What's *your* favourite animal?' I asked, distracted by the way she kept touching my arm when she spoke, by the way her tongue kept darting out over her lips.

'I like dogs. Especially Siberian huskies.'

'That's very specific,' I said, simultaneously wondering if Siberian huskies had eyes like hers.

Aurelia leaned into me. 'They're usually blue.'

'Huh?'

'Their eyes. And sometimes brown, and sometimes one of each.'

I stared at her. Had I spoken aloud about the eye thing? I was pretty sure I hadn't.

'Relax, Billy,' she said. 'Soon enough, you'll see we're one and the same, you and me. You just don't know it yet.'

I didn't know where Aurelia went in the weekends. All I knew was that I was in agony by the last bell on Monday afternoons, as if in the grip of withdrawal from a powerful drug. After the first weekend, I wasn't even sure I would see her again.

But come Monday, there she was in her long black coat, her blonde locks scooped into a ponytail. She rose from the bench when she saw me approach.

'Hello, Billy Raven.'

'Hello, Aurelia Nightingale.' I'd given up on telling her my name was Billy Quick. Besides, I kind of liked becoming someone else when I was around her. This time it was me who took her hand, rather than the other way around. Her skin was as warm as ever, almost unnaturally so, considering it couldn't be any more than twelve degrees.

'Where shall we go?' Aurelia asked.

'I know a place,' I told her, and took her to my favourite spot beneath the bridge. We had to clamber over rocks and a fallen tree trunk to get there, but that meant there was a low chance of anyone else being there.

Aurelia poked with her foot at a circular arrangement of

blackened lumps. 'Someone's had a fire.'

'And a smoke.' I flicked away a cigarette butt and sat on my bag. Aurelia bent to pick up a rock, and for the first time I noticed the tattoo snaking out of her collar.

'It's a rose,' Aurelia said, noticing my look and touching her neck.

'A rose,' I repeated. 'When did you get that?'

Aurelia threw the rock into the water. 'If I told you, you wouldn't believe me.' She sat next to me, arranging her coat beneath her. 'Where I come from, tattoos aren't such a big deal. Some people even have them on their eyelids.'

'Their eyelids?' I asked, while wondering what she'd do if I tried to kiss her. It wouldn't be the first time I'd kissed a girl, but I didn't know if I was very good at it.

'Oh, Billy,' she said. 'No one ever learned anything without practising.' Then she slipped her arms around my neck, and I was lost in a fizzing explosion of sensations — her tongue darting between my lips, her roses-and-rain scent, her breasts pressing into my chest.

After that, the aching-yearning sensation I got whenever I was away from her was worse than ever. After that, she was all I could think about.

I got braver around Aurelia, telling her I needed to practise kissing as much as possible. And we did, until the following Monday, one week after we'd first started making out, when a groan escaped her, and she said, 'Now that's how you hook a girl. By kissing them just like that.'

Two weeks later, in the rear of the abandoned car, the windows fogged from our ardent breath, Aurelia gave me a hickey on my neck, so I gave her one in return. She didn't even jump when I accidentally bit her, drawing blood. But suddenly my tongue was burning, and my heart was beating very, very fast.

'Oh, Billy.' Aurelia released me, and it was as if she was fading, or maybe it was because my field of vision was beginning to narrow. 'What's done cannot be undone. Don't forget.' Her voice sounded as if it was coming from very far away.

My mouth opened but nothing came out. My chest felt as if it was being crushed from the inside, and I couldn't breathe, could hardly see. The last thing I remember before the darkness flooded in was Aurelia's voice echoing around my head: *See you in a hundred years, Billy Raven.*

When I came to, my heart and head throbbing, a doctor was shining a bright light into my eyes.

'Welcome back, Billy Quick,' he said. He told me I'd had a cardiac arrest two weeks ago, and had had to be shocked back to life. He told me I'd been in a coma ever since.

I gaped at him. 'I— Aurelia,' I croaked.

His forehead furrowed. 'Aurelia?'

'My girlfriend.' She must have been with me when my heart had stopped, was probably the person who'd called for help. And surely she'd been to visit me — hadn't she?

'I'm sorry, I haven't seen your girlfriend.' The doctor pressed over my wrist, and I felt my pulse bounding beneath his fingers. 'Tell me, do you remember taking any drugs before or after you got into that car?'

I could have told him that the only drug I'd taken was Aurelia's blood, which I could still taste on my tongue. I could have told him that Billy Quick had died when my heart had stopped that day. I could have told him, but he wouldn't have believed me.

I knew, because I could hear every thought in his head.

'Call me Billy Raven,' I'd said. 'Everyone else does.'

SIX:
INDIGO

We have a family dinner the evening before I fly out to London. It's not just dinner with my parents, which would be excruciating, since they don't want to live with each other anymore. No, it's dinner at Auntie Violet's with Uncle Rawiri, Rigel and Fox. Pity Brie was invited as well.

As if sensing my disapproval at his girlfriend crashing our family affair, Rigel tells me, *Mum invited her, OK?* He imparts this to me once we're all seated around the table, in thought-speak of course, since Brie is sitting right beside him, hanging off his arm.

None of my business, I think-reply, although in a way it is, considering it's my leaving dinner and all. Rigel, of course, has escaped any punishment, since his use of time travel, although not entirely sanctioned, was primarily to try and find me. Blocking him, I take in the familiar surroundings instead — the driftwood light-shade hanging above the table, and on the wall the giant photograph of the looming red cliffs and deep crevasses that form King's Canyon. Rigel's mum always says that even though she was a prisoner for most of the time she was in the Northern Territory, Australia, the scenery is some of the most breathtaking in the world. I'm not sure if photographs of prison experiences are something I need to see right now.

The BSI prefer to call me an intern, an agent-in-training, as if I had a choice in the matter.

Don't think of this as a sentence, Underwood had told me after the hearing. *Think of it as a unique opportunity to undergo training in one of the top academies in the world, a chance to hone your abilities. Once the twelve months are up, there is no obligation to join the BSI.*

'. . . want some?'

I blink at Violet, who is offering me a dish lined with cheesy potatoes. 'Sure,' I say, mustering a smile. 'My favourite.' Across the table from me, I glimpse Brie planting a kiss on Rigel's cheek. Her blonde locks are scooped up high, her horse micro-tattoos rearing up at me every time she bats her eyelashes at him. Maybe he should get a tattoo above his right eyebrow to mirror the one above his left, although this one would say *I love Brie* in Japanese characters rather than *Black Wolf*.

Don't be a bitch, I think-tell myself, and ward off a waft of amusement from Fox, who is sitting to my left. Damn, I need to keep a better lid on my thought-stream if even a thirteen-year-old can pick up on my discontent. Besides, I shouldn't be joking about something like that, even to myself. Not when the Black Wolf, Rigel's father, is still missing, presumed dead.

Mum, who is sitting at the head of the table, holds up her glass. 'Can someone pass the bottle of red down this way?'

'That went down fast,' my dad observes from the other end of the table. I'm pretty sure they have some kind of telepathic tiff after that, because my mother practically sculls her next glass of wine, and Dad starts having a loud conversation with Rawiri about his new Swedish girlfriend — Dad's girlfriend, not Rawiri's. Gross. I spear a carrot and push it into my mouth, even though I've lost any appetite I might have had.

'I've been meaning to ask you,' I hear Violet say to Brie, her voice soft, as if she doesn't intend for anyone else to hear. 'Do you happen to own a pink bra with black straps?'

Brie freezes, momentarily, before her face relaxes into a

sheepish smile. 'Um, yes. Did I leave it somewhere?'

'It fell out of Rigel's sheets when I went to wash them.' Violet sounds casual, but her thought-stream is blue with worry.

Jeez, Mum, of course we're being careful, Rigel think-says, and I catch a snatch of Violet's next think-comment, something to do with *Riva virus* before they close out the other telepaths in the room. Riva has been all over the news ever since I returned to New Zealand, a sexually transmitted virus that causes ovarian damage in females, and something called orchitis in males.

I remember Billy Raven telling me about Riva virus; about how it had led to a dramatic fall in birth rates in the future and how he, too, was infertile as a result. But as far as I know, Violet and her lab are working on a vaccine, which she thinks will be ready by next year. Also, Billy told me lots of things that later proved to be untrue.

I'm going to put a baby in you, my darling.

Remembering that, I cringe, and that's it, I can't put another scrap of food in my mouth.

'Excuse me.' I escape into the bathroom, where I sit on the toilet lid, my head in my hands. As much as I'm glad to have escaped Billy Raven, part of me misses the heady excitement of that first flush of attraction, the way he made every nerve in my body spark. Billy Raven, the two-faced god who promised to love me forever. Now I'm going to spend twelve months across the other side of the world, being indoctrinated by the BSI . . . and for what?

'Indigo?' It's Mum already. I've barely been in here for five minutes.

Ten, actually, she think-says. I don't even have the strength to give her a telepathic eye-roll in return. Instead I burst into tears, and next thing everything is blurring and tilting and I am—

Walking on ice, my white paws crunching through the snowy crust. To my left, I see more ice floating past, sea ice, and my gut clenches at the thought of the food that might be swimming beneath the surface.

Food. Seals. My mouth waters. I've been here before, more than once, although usually I seek warmer climates. The Arctic is one of the few places on Earth where icebergs still exist, although it's nothing like the huge land mass of last century. I'll be lucky to see another polar bear, since they're almost extinct and all. Today the sub-zero temperatures are a welcome relief from what I've just left. All I want is to freeze my thought-stream, leave behind the punishments for time-travel violations, my parents fighting over anything and everything, and Billy Raven, *fucking* Billy Raven.

I stroll to the edge of the ice and slip, effortlessly, into the sea. The water closes over me and I am under, eyes wide open, and everything is clear and blue and cold.

I sense him before I see him, his male body a larger version of my own.

You make a good polar bear, Indigo. Pity they can't clone you.

Piss off.

I would, but the olds sent me to make sure you didn't do anything stupid. Rigel swims beside me, intermittently bobbing up for air.

I've done things a lot dumber than this, and you know it. Spotting a shadow to my right, I lurch after it, and clamber up onto an ice floe — but the seal has gone as quickly as it came. *Shit.* My fellow polar bear climbs up beside me and we sit in silence for a few minutes, watching the swells move past us.

I'm sorry, Rigel think-says, eventually.

You're *sorry?* I squint at him. *If it weren't for me, your dad might still be alive. You've said it yourself.*

His eyes darken. *I never said that.*

But you thought it. And I don't blame you. I slump down, resting my head between my paws.

Rigel adopts a similar position, his flank warm against mine. *It's not your fault my dad disappeared, it's Billy Raven's. And I think my father would have come into contact with him sooner or later, no matter what. Dad was trying to flush out a splinter cell, the same splinter cell that Billy gave your stem cells to . . . right?*

I guess.

And he is still alive, he think-says. *I know it.*

I believe you. I watch a tern arc overhead, its wings spread wide. *So what are you going to do?*

Um, it's classified.

By who? The BSI?

He think-laughs, cheerlessly. *No, just me.*

Oh. I'm too tired, too strung-out to think of the implications of that. I want to warn him against doing something stupid, but what good did that ever do anyone? Besides, who am I to lecture him?

Rigel's breath wafts over my nose. *Indigo?*

Yeah?

We can still meet up like this once you've gone . . . can't we?

I sit up. Stare into his eyes. *Won't she get jealous?*

Rigel stares back at me. *Well,* he think-says, his thought-stream running slow and syrupy, like molasses, *there are some things that normals would never understand. Right?* And I know exactly what he means, because for Offspring, to travel, to *shift*, is akin to dreaming, and if you can't dream, then you are nothing.

So I say, *Yes, Rigel, we can still meet up like this.* If polar bears could smile, that's what we'd do, but instead we push our noses together and *shift—*

And I am in the bathroom once more, but instead of my mum, it's Rigel cradling my head in his lap, his hands still arctic-cold.

'You're OK now,' he whispers, swiping my tears off my cheeks. 'You're OK.'

Both of us are ignoring the thought-stream on the other side of the door, which is Brie trying to figure out whether she needs to be worried that her boyfriend is locked in the bathroom with a time-travel criminal.

I could tell her what I know, which is that Rigel's thoughts aren't exactly legal either, and they have nothing to do with me. But that would be breaking Offspring rule number two, which is that a fellow Offspring's secret must be kept, so I sit up and say, loudly and clearly, 'Rigel, please, I just need to be alone.'

Rigel gives me a nod, stands up and opens the door.

'Fine,' he says, even as his thought-stream closes me out, along with the other prying telepaths. 'Can't say I didn't try.'

A necessary lie, for all sorts of reasons.

SEVEN:
BILLY

1988

Things weren't the same when I returned to school after my near-dying episode. Perhaps it was merely that my demeanour had changed, my new confidence intimidating those who'd once ignored or bullied me. Perhaps it was that they sensed something else about me, an other-wordliness.

In fact, I knew it was a combination of those things. I knew it, because I'd plucked it out of their minds. Was it in my stature? Had my eyes really always been that dark, my skin really that smooth? For the first time, people were actually drawn to me rather than indifferent, and they didn't even know why.

I wasn't sure I completely understood why either. But I can't say I didn't enjoy it.

My new ability to dive into people's thoughts, along with their memories, was both enlightening and disturbing. On my first day back at school, I sat in English class, dipping in and out of my classmates' thought-streams when we were meant to be doing the ten minutes of 'free reading' that always marked the start of our lessons. Paul Berthelsen, the acne-ridden guy who sat in front of me, was having pornographic thoughts about Catherine Edwards, the petite girl with doll-like features across the aisle from him. Catherine, on the other hand, was enjoying the Sylvia Plath book she'd borrowed from the library.

I could see why Paul was in lust with Catherine. She was very pretty, and smart, too — and way out of his league, considering she hung out with the popular kids, while his idea of a good time was playing *Dungeons and Dragons*. I lingered on her thought-stream for a moment, and found a second current running beneath, one that told me she was very unhappy at home. Her parents had separated last year, and her brother had recently gone away on a gap year. Catherine was as lonely as I was, her so-called friends more interested in boys and make-up than poetry and the state of the world.

'Mr Quick.' Mr Elder's voice was soft, deadly. 'Perhaps you'd get more reading done if you stopped eyeing up the opposite sex.' He was thinking I was a lazy bastard, a mediocre student who'd never get far. He was thinking that he couldn't fault my taste in girls, though, and that it had been a while since he'd kissed a sixteen-year-old — six months, in fact.

'I guess it's something most of us grow out of,' I replied, and Elder shot me an odd, discomfited look. Oh yes, he had something to hide, a secret that would ruin him if anyone ever found out. Dirty bastard.

'Watch yourself, Quick.' Elder's voice was laced with venom, but I could see the yellow-orange colour of his fear. In that moment I experienced a thrill, a surge of something I'd never felt before.

Power.

Still, it was a couple of weeks before I plucked up the courage to approach Catherine. Also, I guess I was waiting to see if Aurelia would come back. But it seemed she'd left me for good. The yearning-ache hadn't left me, though. I needed something, someone, to fill the hole inside me.

I waited until Catherine was alone, having already gleaned

from her thought-stream that she had hockey practice after school. I'd lingered in the library, selecting a book I thought she'd be interested in, before tucking it under my arm and leaving at the exact moment I sensed her mind-hum draw close.

It was damp outside, her fellow team members scattering in opposite directions. Catherine's bag was slung over her shoulder, her hair freshly permed, a silver chain around her delicate neck. Her head was down, her mind already on the depressing scene she'd encounter when she got home — a supermarket meal heating in the microwave, a table set for two.

I lengthened my stride, falling in beside her. 'Hi, Catherine.'

She looked up. 'Oh. Hi.' Her tone wasn't overly friendly, but I was relieved to read that she didn't dislike me. No, her thought-stream was more an uninterested shade of blue.

'I, uh, think you dropped this.' I held up the poetry book, and she frowned.

'I've never seen it before.'

'It was lying on the ground over there.' I gestured behind us. 'I guess I just thought it was yours because you're probably the only other person I know who likes to read poetry around here.'

Catherine looked at me properly this time, her thought-stream flickering. 'You like to read poetry?' And I heard *his eyes are so dark*, and *he's quite good-looking, in a brooding sort of way. Why have I never noticed that before?*

'Of course,' I said. It wasn't a complete lie, at least not as of thirty minutes ago, when I'd stumbled across a poem that had given me an eerie sensation. *Déjà vu*, I guess you'd call it. I'd already more or less memorised the poem, something I'd never have been able to do as easily before my heart stopped.

My brain had been doing all sorts of weird things since then, even in my dreams.

'Yeah?' I could tell Catherine thought I was only trying to chat her up. 'What's your favourite poem?'

'Hmm, let's see.' I rolled my eyes towards the slate-grey sky. 'There are so many to choose from. But I think it would have to be one by Edgar Allan Poe.'

Catherine slowed. 'What's it called?'

'"The Raven",' I said.

A week later, Catherine and I sat on the couch in her tiny lounge. She was gazing into my eyes, spellbound, as my lips moved, and when I said the part about shutting my eyes and everyone in the world dropping dead, Catherine had replied with the next line. I chose that moment to kiss her for the first time, knowing that Sylvia Plath would have approved, since we'd been quoting her poetry at each other and all. I kissed her the way Aurelia had taught me, soft at first, brushing my lips over the corners of her mouth, then her neck and earlobes, until Catherine let out a soft groan and kissed me back, her mouth open and wet and warm.

And really, I was the perfect gentleman, touching her so gently, and always it was Catherine wanting more, more. Aurelia had taught me well, although it wasn't so hard, considering I could read exactly what Catherine wanted, could proceed at a pace that I knew she'd be comfortable with.

It was a relationship that lasted for three months. I think I was in love with her, too, or at least that was what I told her, but here's the thing about love: at first it's all shiny and exciting and new, but then the weight of expectations and baggage begins to drag you down. When that happens, it's time to move on.

So, I did, over and over, until, twelve months and five lovers later, even that started to bore me. It was time to move on again, but in a very different way.

That was when I started searching for *her*, Aurelia, the young woman who had changed my life in a heartbeat.

It was a search that would last for one hundred years.

EIGHT:
RIGEL

I'm running through the desert, ducking and diving as my attackers loom in front of me — salivating German Shepherds, gun-wielding soldiers, balls of fire, a wild-eyed woman with a knife. My breathing is short and my muscles are screaming, but quite apart from the potential inconvenience of dying, I'm determined to get to my final destination.

After somersaulting over a cluster of jagged rocks that are sharp enough to slice through my shoes, I scramble to my feet just in time to escape a rattlesnake preparing to strike. And I'm close, so close, the Twin Pyramids in view when something hits me from the side—

My vision fragments and dissolves . . . into darkness.

'Shit.' I yank the earpiece out.

'So close,' Rawiri says, his blue top-knot swimming into view once I've removed my Virtual Contacts.

After dumping the contacts in the tube Brie is holding out, I bend over, my hands on my knees. 'What the hell was that?' I ask, once I've got more breath in my lungs.

'Kamikaze drone.' My uncle sounds positively delighted.

'Screw your kamikaze drone.' I sink into the grass, casting my eyes across the field. In the distance, maybe two hundred metres away, a pair of agents are sparring with moves that look like a mixture of karate and judo, although I'm no expert.

We'll train you up soon enough, Rawiri think-says, picking up on my thought-stream.

Whatever. I flop backwards, staring up at the sky. 'You're enjoying this, aren't you?' I say aloud, so Brie can hear us.

He smirks. 'Pleased to see that *Death Sim* is still challenging, even for an Offspring.'

'No one has ever got that far, though,' Brie says. 'Or that rapidly.' She sits beside me.

'That's what all the girls say,' I tease, flinching when she whacks me on the arm.

'Don't say you didn't ask for that,' Rawiri says. 'I'll see you at lunch, hey?'

'Wait.' I sit up. 'Don't I get to try again?'

My uncle's forehead creases. 'You need to rest first.'

'That was my rest. I'm recovered, see?' I stand up, flexing my arms.

'You'll be slower this time,' he insists. 'Believe me, I've been doing this Sim with agents for years.'

I push the earpiece in. 'Not this agent, you haven't.' Hunter Blue. Blue Hunter.

Brie holds out the tube containing the Virtual Contacts. 'I'll give you a tip, shall I?'

'What's that?' I take a contact out and balance it on the end of my finger.

'Think like your uncle,' she says.

'But that would be cheating.' I slide my eyes towards my uncle. He just shrugs and crosses his arms.

Brie glances between us. 'What's that saying? Good guys finish last?'

'Got it.' I slip the second contact in, and the field is replaced by sand dunes and cloudless sky.

My uncle doesn't even ask if I'm ready. Sensing a hum to my right, I flatten myself in the sand, narrowly escaping being decapitated by a discus-shaped blade. While lying on my front, I check my wrist-disc for my coordinates, then take off in a NNE direction, where I know the pyramids to be located. My Offspring muscles have recovered already, something my uncle hasn't taken into account, since he's never worked with Offspring before.

Stop gloating, Rawiri think-says. Ignoring him — I don't need that kind of distraction — I vault over a mound in the sand, which could be an ant hill, but could also be a landmine. As I run, I take a virtual Attack Cylinder out of my trousers pocket, ready to fire it at any human or animal who tries to kill me. The bullets are made not just of lead, they also contain rubrimide, a chemical that paralyses muscles within seconds, including those controlling breathing.

An arm hooks around my neck from behind and I react instantly, pushing the cylinder into the assassin's armpit and firing. She lets out a strangled cry and collapses, twitching a few times before going completely still. Grinning, I go on to take out a rabid dog, a wolf and a pair of scum with army assault rifles. Over the jagged rocks, past the ants, and there they are — the twin peaks of the pyramids, their colour and size similar to Uluru. My heart speeds up as my subconscious registers the threat and I—

Angle my thought-stream sideways and out, hooking into *him*, Rawiri, rapidly accessing the answer. I leap up rather than duck to avoid the drone heading for me at knee-level, then veer off to my left, away from the illusion and towards the real pyramids, an agonising five kilometres and fifteen minutes away.

As I burst through the door to the Pyramids' interior, my

lungs burning, I hear a dry voice say *well played*. My vision explodes into stars. I sprawl onto the ground, my arms above my head, my eyes closed, and feel my earpiece being tugged out.

'Congratulations, Agent Blue,' Brie says, and kisses me on the lips.

'So much for *you'll be slower this time*,' Brie says that evening. We're lying on the roof of BSI Headquarters, our skin still glistening from our swim in the rooftop pool. There's no one else around, which is no surprise, considering it's almost eleven.

'Not sure I'd have got there if I hadn't used your tip.' *Think like your uncle*, a smart move. Why not harvest the mind of the creator, given the chance? I stretch, my elbow joints popping. 'He didn't even seem angry.'

'Like I said, good guys finish last.'

I grin and roll onto my elbow, gazing down at her. 'Am I a bad guy?'

'As long as you're my bad guy,' she says, pulling me down for a kiss. 'Hey. You should consider getting a place of your own.'

'Yeah. Perhaps I should.'

'You don't sound convinced.' She traces a line down my breastbone. 'I'm sure the BSI is paying you a good wage, no?'

'More than enough.' I turn onto my back. 'It's just . . . I don't think it's such a good time to ditch Mum and Fox, you know?'

'You'll still see them. It's not as if you're moving cities.'

I sit up, reaching for my t-shirt. 'I'll think about it. In the meantime, we can hang out here, right?'

'Of course.' Brie pouts. 'You're not leaving, are you?'

'I'm really tired.'

'So, come back to my room.' She touches my thigh. 'I'll leave you alone, I promise.'

I smile, give her one last kiss. 'I believe you. But seriously, I'm not going to be very good company. I'll see you tomorrow, OK?'

Her waves of disappointment follow me all the way to the street. It's at times like this that I really hate being able to read other people's minds.

I'm just grateful that she can't read mine.

The house is in darkness when I get home. I climb into bed, even though sleep is the last thing I'm planning on doing. My dream-flow is already swirling, prepared for the magnetic pull of *her*, my best friend.

Thought you'd never show. Indigo's thought-voice is purple with impatience.

Isn't it daytime over there? As in, early afternoon?

Yeah, because obviously I've got something better to do.

I give her a thought-grin, one designed to wind her up even more. *Sarcasm gets you everywhere, Moon.*

Cut the crap. Where do you want to go?

I yawn. *I don't know, you choose.*

Indigo barely hesitates. *Let's fly.* Soon enough, we're soaring above the white-capped peaks of the Himalayas, a crescent moon riding high above us. I breathe in the snowy air, let out a cry and Indigo echoes me. We swoop and dive, scavenge and feast, and when we've eaten our fill, we perch on a cliff ledge, watching the clouds form and break apart below.

How's it going? I think-ask her, as I do every night, and Indigo think-says *Don't ask*, but she lets me into her short-term memories, and I see that she and the others are undergoing training very similar to mine.

I nailed my Death Sim *today*, I think-say.

Congratulations, Agent Blue. What happens now? Do you get sent out into the field?

I think-snort. *Doubt it. Uncle Rawiri's probably working on the next level as we speak.*

Did you find out what they're doing with your DNA?

I turn my head a hundred and eighty degrees and stare into her eagle eyes. *I think they've just stored it in case I need it.* Haven't they? No one has mentioned it since the day they cored my pelvis and took what they needed, right before I flew to London to try and find Indigo and my dad.

Do you believe that?

I don't know. I ruffle my feathers, suddenly feeling cold. *I can ask, see what they say.*

Don't expect them to tell the truth, Indigo think-mumbles.

Rawiri won't lie to me, I think-say.

He can't lie if he doesn't know, she answers. I don't know what to say to that, so I launch into the air again. Indigo follows me and we play for another hour or so, dipping and whirling until the mountains glow orange-red in the sunset.

See you tomorrow, Indigo think-says.

Tomorrow, I promise, and I *shift—*

And wake in the morning glow of my own room, my I-Bio buzzing with a message from Brie.

Have a good sleep?

The best, I reply, and go to have a shower.

NINE:
BILLY

Looking for Aurelia. What was I thinking? She'd vanished, as if she'd never existed in the first place. Perhaps I was going mad. Perhaps she'd been a figment of my imagination, something I'd dreamed while in a coma. Except she'd left traces of herself — a tiny scar at the base of my neck, blonde strands of hair on my jacket, an ability to read minds.

The latter, I realised, was something Aurelia had been doing all along. All those times I'd wondered if I'd spoken a thought aloud, or given away something with my body language — what an easy catch I must have been. I played the conversations with Aurelia over and over in my head, rewinding and fast-forwarding to see if I could get any clues as to where she'd come from and where she might be now.

Biologically, that's true. But chronologically, I'm both much older and much younger than that.

We're one and the same, you and me. You just don't know it yet.

Where I come from, tattoos aren't such a big deal. Some people even have them on their eyelids.

The old Billy, Billy Quick-yet-slow, had thought she was playing with him, trying to sound mysterious. But the new Billy, Billy Raven, was starting to piece it all together — Aurelia with her unusual piercings and rose tattoo, Aurelia with her strange turns of speech and slang I'd never heard before. I'd thought it was because she'd come from a different country, but the truth was setting in now.

Aurelia wasn't just from a different place. She was from a different time.

A time at least one hundred years in the future, probably more.

See you in a hundred years, Billy Raven.

Had she returned to her own time? When and where was that? Did Aurelia literally mean a hundred years when she'd said that? If so, how could I follow her? And if I did, what if I met the future version of myself? What would happen then?

I had no idea.

At night, in bed, I'd entertain fantasies of reuniting with Aurelia and reigniting our passion. By day, I was working on the new, improved version of myself — starting with moving out of home.

'What do you mean, you're leaving home?' My old man was sitting in front of the TV, balancing a beer can on his gut. 'Your job at the supermarket won't pay your rent. And what about school?'

I shrugged. 'I'll be finished in two months.'

My father snorted. 'Well, don't think you'll be passing your A levels with the amount of studying you've been doing.'

'I've been studying.' Only not in the traditional sense. My newfound ability to mine the memories of my teachers, along with my seemingly limitless capacity to retrieve and retain everything I saw, read or heard, meant I was guaranteed to ace my exams. Not just that, but to gain entry into any course, any university I wanted.

The world, as Grandma would have said, was my oyster. I

preferred to think of it as my kingdom, one that I could mould to fit my desires and expectations.

So many desires. So many expectations.

But first, money. I began to frequent clubs and then casinos. It was easy enough to obtain a fake ID, stating my date of birth to be one year earlier; even easier to sift for tips in the minds of experienced gamblers sitting nearby. It wasn't long before I had won enough cash to pay not only for designer suits and shirts, but for an inner-city London apartment with a view over the River Thames.

'We never see you anymore,' my father complained on one of the many calls I let go straight to answer phone.

'Are you dealing drugs?' my sister asked.

'Never touched drugs in my life,' I told her, knowing that Natalie thought I was lying. Whatever. She could believe what she liked. As for me, I was quite enjoying myself once more, even if I'd come no closer to finding the elusive Aurelia. I had no trouble attracting women with my smart dress sense, Hollywood good-looks and boundless charm. It wasn't hard, when I could read their minds to find out exactly what they wanted.

As my fortune grew, I began to travel, first to Europe and then further afield — the Bahamas, India, Africa, Australia. Then, five years after I'd first met Aurelia, I travelled to a small island nation I'd only ever noticed as an afterthought on maps and globes. New Zealand, Aotearoa, the land of the long white cloud.

It was there that I *shifted* for the first time . . . and made my first kill.

In my defence, it was an accident.

TEN:
INDIGO

It's day eight of my three hundred and sixty-five-day sentence, and I'm bored out of my brain already.

Ten minutes ago, I was delivered to a testing laboratory along with Ci, a BSI agent with weird hair. I'd sooner have stayed on the transport, which is like a rollercoaster without the loop-the-loop bit. Perhaps I should suggest a loop-the-loop to Uncle Rawiri next time I get to talk to him in, like, a year's time, since he was the one who designed it.

The testing lab is small, about the size of our kitchen at home, and located on the fifth level below ground. I'm sitting in a glass box around the same size and dimensions as the car I just got out of, feeling like a chimpanzee at those horrid zoos they used to have in the old days.

'Indigo.' The voice coming through the headphones is that of my instructor, who is in a room remote from here, watching me through a camera I can't see. All I can see is Ci, who is sitting at a desk opposite my box, tapping away on the tablet he carries everywhere with him. I don't know what he finds to write about all day. If he really wanted to record everything, why doesn't he video me?

'Indigo,' Harvey Wu repeats, not without a note of impatience.

'I'm here,' I reply, not without a trace of sarcasm.

Where else would I be?

'Physically, yes. And now I need your concentration.' I bite the inside of my cheek, listening as he gives me my first instruction. 'Tell me what happens when you're about to time-travel.'

'What *happens*?'

'Let me put it another way. I don't want you to actually time-travel' — he emits a little chuckle, as if to say 'we all know what happened last time you did *that*' — 'but I want you to lead me up to the moment when you're about to travel. Don't talk. Just assume that state of mind, if you can.'

I could refuse. I could fake it, too. But part of me wants to see what will happen. Hell, maybe I could even let it go a little too far and *actually* time-travel, tell them it was a slip-up. So I close my eyes and coil my dream-flow tight, the way I always do before I travel. I'm thinking of the last time I went to New York. I'd ended up in a speakeasy in the 1920s, listening to jazz and trying to make sense of the conversation around me. Zeppelins? Hayburners? Shebas, what? Never mind, the dancing was fun.

I'm super-coiled, in that split second before I fling out my dream-flow, when I hear, 'Open your eyes.'

Huh?

'Hold that if you can,' Harvey says, 'and open your eyes.'

Irritated, I do as he says . . . and freeze.

'Hold it,' Harvey repeats, and I stare, my dream-flow quivering, at the world surrounding me. I can't see the glass box anymore, or anything outside either. All I can see are colours, green and purple and blue, flowing all around me as if I'm drifting in a slow-flowing river.

A river, I realise, that is a computer's interpretation of my mind.

'Extraordinary,' my instructor says.

'How is a bunch of colours extraordinary?' I ask, and just like that, the kaleidoscope river disappears.

'At least I got a screen shot.' Wu sounds as though he's talking to himself. 'Trust me, in the world of neurophysics, that was—'

'Out of this world?'

'Yes,' he says, sounding slightly rattled that I've somehow finished his sentence. 'We already know that you and your parents access parts of your brain that we normals cannot, but that was something I haven't seen before. The signal I was picking up came from deep within your hindbrain, which is the part essential for—'

'Respiratory rhythm, motor activity, sleep and wakefulness,' I say, noticing that Ci is listening intently, his fingers still for once, poised above his tablet.

'You have a good memory of your biology lessons, yes,' Wu says. 'And yet, those are all essential activities that happen without your conscious awareness, unlike the time-travelling.'

'So what are you going to do with that information?' I ask. 'Train other BSI agents to time-travel?'

'Perhaps,' Harvey replies, vague now. 'We'll return to this another day. For now, I'd like to move on to the next activity.'

'Fine.' I slump into the chair. 'What do you want me to do next? Balance a ball on my nose? Shoot fire out of my nostrils?'

Ci snorts, his lips twitching upward. Harvey, seemingly unphased by my sarcasm says, 'That could be interesting, but no. You can read the thoughts of others, obviously.'

I don't even bother to answer that one, instead rolling my eyes towards the roof of my glass box, knowing he'll be able to see me on camera.

'But,' he says, 'have you ever tried to *control* the thoughts of others?'

I sit up straight. 'As in take over their thought-streams?'

'That's right.'

'No.' I frown. 'I don't even know if that's possible.'

'But you've never tried.'

'Well, no. I don't think most people would like that.' I glance at Ci, who is fidgeting, his eyes darting towards the ceiling. He's nervous, I realise, but why? The realisation hits me milliseconds before Harvey says, 'We have a volunteer for you.'

'Ci?' My gaze meets that of the BSI agent. I wonder how much he gets paid for something like that.

Ci licks his lips. 'Ah, yeah, I . . . Will it hurt?'

'I have no idea.' My tone is steely. I'm half-hoping Ci will refuse, although I'm not entirely sure why. What am I afraid of?

'I don't know why it would,' Harvey says. I wonder how he can be so sure.

Ci stands up, his fists clenched. 'You know what? I don't like the sound of this.'

'Remember how I said you'd get a bonus? Double it.' Wu clears his throat. 'Unless you think it's beyond your capabilities, Ms Moon.'

My thought-stream, I'm sure, is glowing hot red. 'I never said *that*.' I stand up and press my palms against the glass. 'Do we have to stay in here?'

Harvey hesitates. 'Where do you want to go?'

I shrug. 'Outside.' Surely they're not worried about me escaping from this prison that apparently isn't a prison?

'Courtyard,' Wu says. 'I'll see you in five.'

'The courtyard?' Ci asks after we've left the room. 'What are we going to do there?'

'I haven't decided yet.' We jog down the stairs to the monorail below, where I use my I-Bio to summon a car. After getting in, we pull the harnesses over our heads and are whipped around three corners, each tighter than the last, before being propelled up to ground level.

A couple of minutes later, we exit into a large courtyard surrounded by centuries-old buildings made of brick and stone. The Tower of London is disturbingly close. I never did get to speak to Henry VIII when I travelled back to the 1500s, although I managed to glimpse him at court, and had no idea what all his wives saw in him.

I shiver. 'It's freezing out here.' The sky is thick and grey, the damp air clinging to my face. I wouldn't be surprised if it started snowing.

'*You* wanted to come out here,' Ci points out, his breath puffing in front of him.

'It won't take long.' Hearing the scrape of boots on cobblestones, I turn to see Harvey Wu, who is dressed more sensibly than us in a black jacket with the fire emblems on the sleeves that indicates it's lined with heating coils. The wind is cutting straight through my jersey. Never mind. Soon I'll be distracted enough that I won't feel anything.

'You'll need to remove your blocker,' my instructor reminds Ci. Wu cuts me a wary gaze, obviously wondering if I have an ulterior motive. I don't blame him.

'Hold still,' I say in a soothing voice, reaching for Ci's thought-stream, which is green with anxiety. Ci is thinking that I might be about to make him do something really embarrassing, like take off all his clothes. As if. He may be annoying, but I don't want to be responsible for a case of hypothermia. Besides, gross.

I wander around the courtyard, partly to keep warm and partly so I can concentrate on Ci's thought-stream. He's still worrying about what I'm about to do, but beneath that is another subcurrent which is mostly centred around a guy named Joel. A romantic interest, from the hue of the undercurrent, although not really a happy one. Joel has no idea that Ci's interested in him, and Ci hasn't yet worked up the courage to ask him out.

That's when I know what I'm going to do, or at least attempt to do. I focus on the undercurrent, trying to get familiar with the rhythm of it, inhale-exhale, ebb and flow.

'Would you hurry up?' Ci gripes. He's shivering, his lips tinged blue. Wu is hanging back, his arms crossed, his gaze inscrutable behind his Smart-Glasses.

'Certainly,' I say, sinking to the ground. The cobblestones are so cold that my teeth start chattering, too, but I barely have time to register that before I'm—

Staring at my body, which is slumped over, my eyes closed. The outline is blurred, too, in a way I'm used to seeing right before someone *shifts*. No time to distract myself with that though. I lift my — Ci's — wrist, and run my finger over his I-Bio, finding his contacts with two swipes of the screen.

Hey Joel, I type. *Wondering if you're free for the theatre tonight? I've got a spare ticket. Ci.*

After pressing send, I release the undercurrent, and my view of the world changes within a single beat of my rapidly fluttering heart. I am *Attacus atlas*, the largest moth in the world, my multi-coloured wings spread wide. How is it that I've *shifted* while simultaneously taking control of Ci's thought-stream? Below, I see Harvey and Ci looking up at me, their mouths open. I entertain myself by flying a circuit around the courtyard before *shifting* into my body once more, which is now shivering so hard I can barely concentrate. So perhaps I'm imagining the whisper I hear in my thought-stream, the one that says *What's done cannot be undone. Don't forget.* Shaking my head, I sit up, casting around for the owner of the voice, but it has gone as quickly as it came.

No. That can't have been Billy Raven. He's dead, poisoned by the most venomous snake in the world. That was an auditory memory triggered by the *shift* . . . wasn't it?

'Maybe better luck next time,' Wu says as we return to the climate-controlled underground interior of the BSI compound.

'What do you mean, better luck?' I'm watching Ci, who is walking in front of us, his head bent over his I-Bio.

'Shit,' Ci mutters, shooting me a dirty look.

'Did he reply?' I ask.

Ci's cheeks turn as pink as his thought-stream. 'Yes,' he says, and we all three halt, Harvey glancing between me and Ci.

'Bring him flowers,' I tell Ci, before giving Harvey a triumphant smile and leaving them there. The hour's up, my lesson over, and I do believe I've exceeded my instructor's — and my — expectations.

It's only once I reach my room, looking forward to a half-hour break before the next lesson, that I realise I heard something else before, something that can't have been an auditory memory. It can't have been a memory, because he said something else, something I've never heard before — something that's only coming to me now that my dream-flow is fully centred once more.

Don't you know that time vampires are forever?

If I'm not mistaken, Billy Raven has returned.

I sit upright and pluck my own blocker off the bedside table, then shove it deep into my ear.

'What's done cannot be undone,' I whisper . . . and start to shake.

ELEVEN:
BILLY

1993

The woman who stamped my passport had warmly toned skin and an accent that reminded me of Aurelia.

'Welcome to New Zealand, Billy Raven,' she said. 'I hope you enjoy your stay.'

'I'm sure I will,' I replied. It had been two years since I'd legally changed my surname, a move that might have disgusted my father or sister if they'd heard about it. It had been three years since I'd been in contact with either of them, however, and I had no intention of seeking them out ever again.

As the taxi drew away from Auckland Airport, I pressed my nose to the window, taking in the wide, open spaces and clear blue sky. It was early morning, only eight am, and the January sun was already high in the sky. Even the air smelt fresh, like pine and something else. Perhaps it was the peppermint on the cabbie's breath, which I could smell even from the rear seat, or the apricot kernel scent of her moisturiser. There was another smell, too, one that was making my heart race and my belly flutter; like scraped knees and bloody noses and my lower lip when my five-year-old teeth went through it after falling off my bike.

'Are you from England?' the cabbie asked. She was young, twenty-five years old according to my fossick through her subconscious.

I wondered if she tasted as good as she smelt.

'How did you guess?' I shrugged off my denim jacket, watching how her eyes flicked towards me and away, but not before she'd taken in my toned biceps and broad chest.

Her glossy lips curved upwards. 'Not hard, with that accent. Got snow over there at the moment?'

'I think so,' I said. 'But it's been months since I was last home. Tell me, where's the best place in New Zealand to hear good music?'

The cabbie's eyes met mine in the rear-vision mirror. 'Dunedin's where it's at, so I hear.'

'Dunedin?'

'Yeah, it's in the South Island. Heaps of bands get their start down there. Like Straitjacket Fits, ever heard of them?'

I nodded slowly, filtering through her memories to get the answer I needed. '"She Speeds" is one of my favourite songs.' Another lie. I'd never heard the song in my life, but I was humming it now, having directly mined it from the cabbie. 'How about tonight? Where should I go?'

'There're plenty of bars and nightclubs in the city. My favourite's a joint called Pink Lady on K Road.' She raised an eyebrow at me in the mirror. 'They get all sorts in there, if you're into that kind of thing.'

I could have innocently asked *what kind of thing?* The old Billy not-so-Quick wouldn't have had a clue what she was referring to, nor picked up on the way the cabbie's gaze lingered a few seconds longer than was polite.

'Actually,' I said, 'perhaps I am into that kind of thing. Don't know if I want to wait until tonight, though . . .'

The cabbie smiled. She turned off the meter and indicated right, heading away from the city, where my hotel was located.

'Good,' she said. 'I know a quiet spot.'

Several more twists and turns later, we parked outside a vacant lot. 'The windows are tinted,' my would-be lover said, placing a shade across the windscreen before joining me in the rear of the cab.

We hadn't been kissing for long, less than thirty seconds, when I moved my lips to her neck. She moaned, then jumped when my teeth broke through her skin, but it was too late — my vampire glamour was clouding her thought-stream, sending her to giddying new heights of passion.

'I think I'm in love,' she said, her words slurred.

'I think you are,' I murmured, wishing my teeth were sharper, that I could taste more than a few droplets of her intoxicating essence. If only I had canines like a wolf or a panther, I thought, and that's when it happened; when I felt a tug, a wrench, followed by a blur and a sickening *shift*.

My panther-teeth sank through her tender human flesh, bypassing the slow flow of the jugular vein and tearing straight through the rapidly pulsing carotid artery. Oh, but the scarlet liquid jetting into my mouth was like coming home.

As for what happened next, like I said, that was an accident. Next time I'd be more careful.

I never even knew her name.

TWELVE:
RIGEL

I'm playing chess with a faceless opponent. We're sitting opposite one another on a cliff ledge, ravens and vultures circling above. In the gorge below, a river runs thick and red.

'Black or white?' my opponent asks, his voice lacquer-smooth.

I dare to look at the blurry outline of his head. 'Black,' I say, and he laughs.

'So predictable, Hunter Blue. Perhaps,' he advances a white pawn two squares, 'if you win this game, then I might give you a clue.'

My heart is racing, and it has nothing to do with the blood river or the birds waiting for a chance to peck out my eyes. 'A clue?' I mirror his move with my own black pawn.

'Yes, a clue as to the whereabouts of your sire, the Black Wolf. Or have you forgotten your father already?' His features, although still blurred, are shifting like clouds moving across the moon.

My heart accelerates so fast I feel as if I'm going to pass out. 'No,' I say. 'You can't be — that's not possible.' We paralysed him with taipan venom, then let him bleed to death.

My opponent moves his knight in an L configuration. 'Come on, Rigel or Hunter or whatever you like to call yourself. Do you really think you can kill a time vampire?' I can see him properly now, the person I thought I'd never see again — Billy Raven, with his pupils like black holes, threatening to suck me in. He'd had me believe he was Janus, the two-faced god — the god of beginnings, gates, transitions, times. The god of duality. The god of lies.

'The god of *you*,' Raven taunts. It's all I can do not to leap up and wrestle him to the ground, but I know if I do, then I won't get my clue.

Gritting my teeth, I move my bishop in a diagonal. 'So, he *is* alive then?'

'If one can call his current state alive, then yes.' We keep moving the chess pieces, faster and faster, until our hands are a blur. Pawns fall, along with bishops, rooks and knights.

'What about his body?' I ask, trying not to imagine what horrors my father is enduring. 'Where is that?'

Raven's teeth glint at me. 'You haven't won yet, Mr Blue.'

'Really? Check.' I glance up. Raven attempts a retreat, and I make my final move, trapping his king once and for all. 'Mate.' I straighten up. 'Give me the clue.'

'Certainly.' Raven's smile turns into a smirk. 'You want to know where your father's body is? Why don't you start by asking your boss?'

'My boss?' I scowl at him. 'Who are you talking about?' Rudolph Underwood? Camilla Chase?

'Come on,' he taunts. 'It wouldn't be a clue if I gave you the whole answer.' The next thing I know, I'm flying over the ledge, clutching at rocks, tree roots, anything, but I'm—

Falling—

And I—

Wake twisted in my sheets, the darkness flooding into me.

I'm so terrified that I don't know what to do with myself, so I have a shower. This is possibly the dumbest thing I could do if I'm worried about being ripped out of my body by a time vampire, but it's as if I need to wash his poison off me. Has Billy Raven really resurrected himself, or was that just a very vivid nightmare?

I should call the BSI, or at the very least, Rawiri. But can I really trust them?

You want to know where your father's body is? Why don't you start by asking your boss?

There's no reason why Raven should tell me the truth anyway. He could be playing with me, cat and mouse, before he shreds me or sends me into the same purgatory Dad is in.

No. Surely it was a dream.

I turn off the tap and reach for my towel. The house sounds very quiet. My heart is still racing. Once in my room, I lie on the bed, open my dream-flow and contact the person I most need to talk to *right now*.

She answers straight away.

What were you meant to be achieving anyway? I think-ask once Indigo has finished telling me about the mind-control exercise.

I guess it could come in useful, knowing a BSI agent can control the minds of enemies.

I get off my bed and peer through a gap in the curtains. The street is empty, the street lamps casting an insipid glow onto the footpath. *And did it work?*

Well, I got Ci to send a message to someone.

A message?

Yeah, so he could hook up with this guy he's got the hots for.

Right . . . I yank the curtains shut again.

You don't believe me?

Of course I believe you. I hope Ci was happy with that.

He will be. She takes a deep breath. *But I'm not sure I should have gone outside to do the mind-control exercise.*

How come? I think-ask, and that's when Indigo tells me about the voice she heard.

My pulse jumps. *Billy Raven? Did you tell the BSI about that?*

Indigo's frustration glows red. *They said they'd look into it. But when I said I could help, they told me no way, that I was still a minor. They said that it was probably just a flashback anyway, and not surprising after the trauma I've been through. Maybe they'll take you more seriously.*

Maybe . . . I turn my bedside light on again and pace the room.

You don't trust them, do you?

I trust Rawiri, I think-say. *But as for the others . . .*

Yeah. I can almost see Indigo sagging back against her pillows. *Me, too.* Her thought-stream is still running red. It reminds me of the river in whatever-it-was I had before — the nightmare? Premonition? Did that really happen?

It wasn't a dream, Indigo-think says. *Was it?*

No, I don't think so. I thud down on the end of my bed, massaging my temples. *What are the chances everyone tells me I had a flashback, too?*

Pretty high, I'd say.

I think for a moment. *Maybe we're going to have to go it alone.*

To do what?

Find my dad. Work out a way to get rid of Raven, once and for all.

Indigo's reply is swift. *No. If Billy Raven really is still alive, we'll need all the help we can get.*

Yeah, sure, but it sounds like the BSI need more evidence. Either that, or we're telling them something they already know and want to keep to themselves. Maybe it's even got something to do with why they asked for a sample of my stem cells. Either way, they'll likely shut us down and then what?

Then we're done for. Indigo sounds less fiery now.

I stand up again. *You know what? They're right. You shouldn't be dabbling in this kind of stuff. It's way—*

What are you saying, Rigel? That I'm too young to handle this?

No, I didn't—

I think about Uncle Johnno every day. About how he wouldn't be trapped or dead or whatever if I hadn't been so stupid. At the very least, I could help you find him. And as for Billy, well . . . She trails off.

Well, what? I think-ask, but it's coming through anyway, a wordless communication that sets my heart racing again. *No. That's insane, are you kidding?*

It'll work, she think-says. *I know it.*

How *do you know that?*

He fell in love with me once. Her thought-stream is glistening silver, as sharp and deadly as a scalpel. *I'm sure I can make him do it again. What's that saying? Love is blind?*

No, there is no way you're— It's too late, she's blocking me.

'Damn it.' Giving up on sleep, I tug on a pair of shorts and go to make myself a very strong coffee.

THIRTEEN:
BILLY

1993

I guess I was lucky to escape murder charges after the death of that cabbie, although I suppose the police would have been looking for a crazed dog rather than a shape-shifting man. Truth be told, that episode had both energised and terrified me. I hadn't meant to bleed her dry. All I'd really wanted was a taste, but something about her scent had driven me a little crazy.

I don't know if it was because of the cabbie's blood-essence that I gained the ability to shape-shift, or if it had been a natural evolution in my transition to becoming superhuman. Or was I less than human?

Both, perhaps.

Initially I only *shifted* into panther-form, taking care to leave my earthly body in a safe place when I did so. After that first time with the cabbie, I restricted myself to hunting and killing animals — cats, rabbits, domestic chickens, wild pigs.

Then, one night as I lay sleepless in my hotel bed, I visualised myself as my namesake, a raven. It didn't happen straight away. In fact, I may have fallen asleep. But the next thing I knew, I was soaring high above the harbour, gazing down at the choppy swell below.

My reach had extended, a world with no boundaries. Over the course of the next few months, as I worked my way through a series of Antipodean lovers, I learned how to *shift* to countries as far and wide as India, Africa and the Arctic Circle.

And still, I didn't find Aurelia.

I masqueraded as a banker, with an office on the fortieth floor of a skyscraper looking out to a dormant volcano. I wore Armani suits and drove a black Lamborghini; heads turned everywhere I went, which suited me just fine. One weekend I drove the length of the North Island to Wellington, where I drove my car onto a ferry and crossed Cook Strait before completing the long drive to my final destination.

It was June, and snow was dusting the hills when I drove into Dunedin. I parked my car in the Octagon, noting the Robbie Burns statue and the students roving in drunken packs. Glad I'd swapped my suit for designer jeans and Doc Martens, I strode into the nearest pub and ordered a pint of beer. It was half-past ten in the evening, late enough for it to be elbow-room only at the pub, early enough to know that the night had only just begun.

I'd nearly finished my pint when I felt an arm brush mine. My hairs were standing up on end even before I turned my head. Perhaps it was her scent, a foreign perfume I'd never come across before. Perhaps it was the way she sized me up, as if I was the prey rather than the hunter — a feeling I hadn't had since I'd met Aurelia. Her hair was an unusual colour, too, blonde shot with silver, although she didn't look any older than twenty. When I went to delve into her thought-stream, all I got was a blank. *What the hell?*

The girl-woman smiled briefly at me, then glanced at the barman. 'I'll have a gin and tonic,' she said as I tried to read her again, only to come up against something solid and steely.

Had someone put something into my beer, rendering my mind-reading abilities useless? Yet when I homed in on the barman, I could read him loud and clear: he thought the woman was attractive, too.

I inhaled again, detecting vanilla, jasmine, lily of the valley and the musky undertone of an animal I'd only ever encountered in Africa. The girl-woman swung her eyes towards me, and I saw her irises were a very odd colour, the same amber shade as the beer in front of me. I'd never seen eyes like that in any human. A memory-voice from years ago reverberated through my head: *We're one and the same, you and me.*

Lowering her voice, she said, 'I can still smell the wolf from *your* last *shift*.' She lifted her chin, sniffing the air. 'And pig blood. A good meal, was it?'

'It was adequate,' I replied, daring to hold her gaze. Her irises were still lionesque, and her thought-stream was intermittently visible now, like the sun emerging from behind the clouds.

'Billy Raven,' she said. 'Right?'

'Right,' I replied, sliding my hand over hers. She didn't even flinch. 'Let me guess. We're one and the same, you and me, correct?'

The girl tilted her head to one side, her hoop earrings swinging. 'Oh no,' she said. 'Compared to me, you're merely an amateur.'

I narrowed my eyes at her. 'Who *are* you?' Was this Aurelia in a new incarnation? I wondered, right before she sliced into my thought-stream, making me jump.

Leave yourself wide open like that, and you're going to get hurt, Billy Raven. She leaned forward, her lips brushing my ear. 'Do you like to dance?'

'I like to dance,' I said, my stomach tumbling in a way it

hadn't done since I'd met Aurelia. The girl-woman swivelled her hand in mine until our fingers were threaded together, and led me onto the dance floor, where students were jostling and jiggling and making out. It wasn't long before we were dancing, the girl-woman coming tantalisingly close to me before pulling away, her hand still in mine.

'Where are you staying, Billy Raven?'

'I don't know yet,' I replied, my head whirling.

'Then come with me.' She led me out of the pub and down the street to a musty-smelling room in a small hotel.

Holy hell, I thought-said, once we'd locked the door behind us, *I don't even know your name.* I pressed my lips to her neck, nipping her with my teeth.

The mysterious girl-woman extracted herself from my embrace, blinking, as if she'd just woken after a long sleep. *The name's Andromeda*, she said, rising to her feet. *I — I've got to go.*

Where have you come from? I think-asked, but she was already beginning to distort and blur, as if I was viewing her underwater. *Don't go*, I pleaded. I'd be lonely again, seeking an answer for which I wasn't sure I even knew the question. Not to mention we hadn't finished what we'd started.

The next thing I knew, I was lying in the hotel bed, staring up at a mildew-stained ceiling.

'That wasn't a dream,' I whispered. 'That can't have been a dream.' I closed my eyes and breathed in, out, in, out; thinking of Andromeda's willowy body and her sinewy limbs; evoking the scent of vanilla and jasmine and musk—

And *shifted*—

Out of that world, and into the next.

FOURTEEN:
INDIGO

I wake with a rapid pulse of adrenaline in my chest, a stark contrast to the I-can't-be-bothered lassitude of the previous morning. Checking my I-Bio, I see that it's quarter to midnight. Damn it, I've only been asleep for an hour, yet I feel wide awake. At home it'll be late morning, the sun high in the sky. If I weren't stuck here, I'd be at the beach or lounging by my father's pool with an e-book.

Sighing, I touch a button on the windowsill to remove the virtual blinds before peering into the darkness. My room may be four levels below ground, but the periscopic windows mean that I have the same view as someone standing directly above me. My eyesight is hyper-acute, sensitive enough that I can pick out the bird circling overhead. It looks like an eagle — a golden eagle, if the distinctive hum of Rigel's thought-stream is anything to go by.

If this is some way of you trying to keep watch over me, then I'm telling you now that it's not going to work, I think-say.

Just scoping the place out, Rigel think-replies, right before the eagle disappears and I feel the mattress sink beneath me. I turn, scowling at the guy lying on my bed with his arms behind his head.

'You could at least have put a shirt on.'

'I just got out of the pool.' He sits up. 'Wow, you've got your own bathroom and everything.'

'It's better than a bucket in the corner, I suppose.' Wary of who might be listening in, I lean against the wall and switch to think-speak. *Did you speak to the BSI about Billy Raven?*

No.

So you went to work like nothing had happened?

Not exactly. I called in sick. His eyes flick around the ceiling, as if checking for cameras and microphones. *And I had a chat to Brie.*

A chat to Brie? I stare at him. *Wait . . . about this? I thought you said you hadn't spoken to the BSI.*

Rigel's gaze settles on me. *Sure, but she's someone we can trust.*

Someone you *can trust.*

Relax, will you? You're forgetting that I can read her — she doesn't wear a blocker like Underwood. I'd know if she were lying to me. And Brie's got higher-level security clearance than me, because she's been working there for longer. She said she'd see what she can find out about my stem cells and what they might be doing with them. Also, I want her to relay my message to them.

Message? What message?

He flexes and extends his fingers, as if limbering up for a fight. *That I've got the flu. That'll give me a week, at least.*

To do what?

To help you, of course. He stands up and starts pacing the way he always does when he's agitated. *Look, I'm not that happy about you using yourself as bait.*

Bristling, I think-say, You're *not happy? What are you, my dad?*

He rolls his eyes at me. *I'm acting as your friend, Indy. But speaking of parents, maybe we should talk to them, see if they can h—*

No way. I leap off my bed and nearly fall over, because one of my legs has gone to sleep. Massaging my calf, I think-say, *They'll lock me down, even worse than I am at the moment. There are rooms here with blockers in all the walls. I won't be able to talk to anyone or travel or do anything, just because everyone thinks I'm still a kid.*

Rigel sighs. 'No one thinks you're a kid, Indy,' he says, and for some reason his tone makes me feel like crying.

'But that's exactly how everyone has been treating me!' My voice wobbles. *And you know we're better equipped to deal with this than anyone*, I continue in thought-speak. *No one else has as much experience with time travel as me, and you and I are the only ones I know who can whole-body shift.*

Apart from Raven, Rigel think-says.

I give him a slow nod. His mouth twisting, Rigel moves towards me and clasps my wrists.

OK, he think-says. *Here's my plan.*

A couple of minutes later, we lie on my bed, our thought-streams weaving together. It's dark, but I can see the outline of Rigel's jaw, the flutter of his eyelashes. Sometimes, lately, I wonder if I am borrowing my senses from other animals even while retaining my human form — my wolf-smell, my owl-eyes, my bat-hearing. I can even hear Rigel's heart beating, tripping a little too fast for my liking.

It's fine, he think-says, as my thoughts filter through to him.

I think you should get it checked out after what happened to your mum. And their friend Ethan, remember him?

Don't stress, I'm not going to die of a heart attack anytime soon. The doctor in London said they couldn't find anything wrong with my heart. Rigel exhales. *So.* Slaughterhouse-Five.

Yeah. Have you read it?

He shifts onto his side, propping himself up on an elbow. *Of course. I read it through twice after we returned to New Zealand, hoping I'd be able to contact Dad again, but nothing ever happened.*

Huh. So much for that. *What are you going to do, then?*

I'm going to travel back to the day Dad left for London, see if I can get any clues from him as to where he was going.

Do you think he would tell you, if you asked?

No. His eyes gleam at me. *But I'll see what I can get from his thought-stream.*

Unsanctioned time travel. What do you think your punishment would be?

I don't want to know. The mattress jiggles as he rolls onto his back. *Who should go first?*

You can. I move my arm until it is contacting his. *Rigel?*

Yeah?

Does Brie know you're here?

No. Does it matter?

No, I think-say, knowing that neither of us believes that.

His thought-stream is stained a defensive grey-green. *I don't want to get her in trouble.*

Of course not. I hesitate. *How will I know if you need me?*

I'll call for you, he think-says. *I'll tell you the Hunter has fallen. How about you? What will you say?*

I swallow. *I'll say, Blood Moon.* I don't know where that came from, any more than I can explain this crushing feeling inside my chest, as if I'm about to lose something I never knew I had in the first place. *You should leave your body here. In case something happens.*

Rigel turns towards me. *I'll be back before you know it,* he think-says, and his breath smells sweet, like chocolate. I have to block him, then, before my unbridled thoughts escape.

Then he's gone, leaving me to watch over his earthly body. I nudge a lock of hair off his forehead, brush my fingers over his eyelids.

Stay safe, Blue Hunter, I think-whisper. If I didn't know better, I'd think he was dead.

FIFTEEN:
BILLY

2088

I was standing on a street corner, dwarfed by shiny buildings that reached high into the sky. Even higher than that, oval objects were zipping around, sometimes landing on top of the buildings. If I squinted, I could make out people stepping in and out of them. What were those — helicopters? Could they even be called helicopters when there were no rotor blades?

I started walking, veering left and right to avoid people. They were dressed in clothes such as I'd never seen before; with weird suits that finished at the elbows and knees, boots that came to mid-calf and elaborately styled hair dyed in a variety of colours. The street signs were in English, but with unfamiliar street names, such as Southwalk Street and Blackfriars Road. And why was everyone looking at me as though I was naked?

'Shit.' I ducked into an alleyway. All I was wearing was my Y-fronts, and it was a miracle I was even wearing those. What had happened before? One minute I was lying on my bed, thinking of Andromeda, and the next—

And the next thing, you were here. A woman with silver-blonde hair took me by the elbow and tugged me into a doorway.

'Andromeda.'

'Ssh.' She was fidgeting, her eyes darting over my shoulder, as if she were worried about being seen with me. *It's not you I'm worried about*, she thought-said, waving her palm over a shiny rectangle on the outside of the building, which resembled a plaque without the writing. A section of wall appeared to dissolve, revealing a revolving door. 'This way.'

I followed her inside, blinking at the shiny foyer. Pods were travelling up and down internal shafts around the periphery, each one carrying one or two people.

I'm feeling kind of conspicuous here, I think-muttered.

Relax, we'll sort you out soon. Andromeda stepped into an open pod, beckoning me to accompany her. We shot upwards, stopping seconds later. When the sliding doors opened, we exited straight into an apartment.

'Whoa.' I moved over to the window, staring out at a view that was familiar, but not. Was that Big Ben? And the River Thames? Which meant that I must be in London, but not like any London I'd ever seen. For one thing, there was a gigantic circular object suspended above the ground, as tall as a skyscraper, with capsules slowly circling around the outside and a creepy image of a gigantic eye in the centre. The whole thing was glowing blue and pink. Was it real, or merely a holographic image? 'How many floors up are we?'

'This is the thirtieth floor.' Andromeda slipped into the next room.

I turned, surveying the pristine kitchen and lozenge-shaped couches. 'Nice apartment.'

She reappeared, pushing a bundle of clothes at me. 'It's not mine.'

'Right . . .' I clasped the bundle, wondering if the clothes belonged to her father, a brother maybe . . . or a boyfriend? Is that why she was so twitchy? 'What year is this?'

'Guess.'

'Um . . . 2020?'

She let out an odd sound, like a cross between a grunt and a laugh. 'Wash your mouth out.'

'Huh?'

Andromeda shook her head. 'Never mind. Add another sixty-eight years to that.'

My mouth fell open. '2088?'

'That's right. Do you think those will fit?'

I looked down at the white t-shirt and yellow linen trousers. 'Not quite my usual style, but sure.'

'I hate to tell you this, but your usual style is a little dated.' She held up a hand, halting my movement towards her. 'We don't have time for that.'

'You seemed pretty keen ninety-five years ago,' I mumbled, pulling the t-shirt over my head.

'Because no one knew where I was.' She crossed her arms, watching me fasten the magnetic-like dome on the trousers. 'How did you do that?'

'How did I do what?'

Andromeda peered out of the window, then back at me. 'Travel here.'

'Just like you travelled to 1993, I imagine,' I said.

She frowned at me. 'But you were born in the 1970s?' I sensed her nudging into my memory banks, and some instinct had me closing her out. She recoiled, and before I could blink, Andromeda had gone, or at least the human Andromeda had.

Watch yourself, Raven. Andromeda's lion form prowled around me.

I could say the same of you. My *shift* into wolf-form wasn't quite so effortless. *Where's your earthly body?* I think-asked, knowing that my own human form was still lying on a motel bed in 1990s

Dunedin. At least, that was how it had always worked when I'd *shifted* before.

The lion bared her teeth at me. *Let's just say that my shape-shifting is more evolved than yours. Where have you come from, Raven?*

You know where I've come from, I think-replied, and we circled each other, our gazes locked.

I know when *you've come from, but I don't know how. The first virally optimised humans were created just over fifty years ago . . . so tell me how you fit in.*

I leapt onto the bed, peering down at her from my vantage point. *How about I ask you a question?*

Fire away, Andromeda think-said.

Do you know Aurelia Nightingale?

Aurelia Nightingale? Is that what you call her? she asked, then froze. I went very still, having heard it, too — a faint hum. It was growing louder. *Take me with you*, she think-said.

Take you where?

Anywhere, as long as it's not here. Please. They won't let me get away so easily next— There was a whistle, a stirring of air, and the lion crumpled to the ground, jerking a couple of times before its eyes closed.

'Oh, Andromeda, after all we've done for you,' a voice said, and I realised that we were no longer alone. A young man was standing by the window, his iridescent suit glistening in the sunlight. 'Hello,' he said, aiming a metallic cylinder at me. 'I don't believe we've been introduced. My name is Miles, Miles Newton.'

SIXTEEN:
RIGEL

I'll be back before you know it. I disentangle my thought-tendrils from Indigo's and concentrate my dream-flow down, down, until it reaches infinite density.

Billy Pilgrim has come unstuck in time, I think, recalling the phrase from *Slaughterhouse-Five*. *Billy Pilgrim has come unstuck in time.*

A *whump-whump* sounds deep within me, like a vintage helicopter's rotor blades.

Billy Pilgrim is— *No, wait, Black Wolf is stuck in time.*

Like an echo, I hear: *And I asked myself about the present: how wide it was, how deep, how much was mine to keep.*

I am reaching, searching, grasping, but the voice is slippery, elusive. Instead, I pluck out a memory and focus on the scent of freshly ground coffee, the feel of the floorboards beneath my feet, the morning glare of the sun in the periphery of my vision—

And *shift*, travelling back to two months ago.

My father is going on another mission. I know, because he's going through his usual ritual, which involves shaving, drinking strong coffee and listening to his favourite band, Rabid Monkeys. I stroll into the kitchen and pour myself a coffee, so black and thick it's like tar.

What's up? I think-ask when Dad leaves the bathroom, frowning at his I-Bio. Our thought-streams intersect, briefly, and I detect what he has just read on the disc screen: that his flight to London has been delayed by an hour.

'Ah well.' Dad straddles a stool and reaches for his coffee cup. 'At least I found out before I left for the airport. Want a lift to school?'

'I've finished, remember?' I say, and now I am diverging from the memory, from the script I have in my future brain, because I have returned to November 2066 and I need to try and save my father's life. *What do you know about this cell you're tracking?* I think-ask.

I sense the startle in the flicker of my father's thought-stream. *It's not something I can share*, he think-answers, and there is the block, one that used to be impenetrable to me. But this is the older and wiser Rigel, the Hunter, and I am getting a glimmer, a glimpse of something. A name. An image, one that flashes up and disappears again as my father realises what I'm doing and intensifies his block. Billy Raven. Shit.

Dad gives me one of his steely looks. *Curiosity killed the cat.*

No, it will kill you, I think-reply and his expression changes to one of confused concern.

Since when did you get so worried about me going off to work? he think-asks. How I wish I could tell him the real answer, but I don't want to do something that will screw up time, even though I probably have already.

If you come across someone called Billy Raven— I begin.

Dad clutches his coffee cup. *Where did you hear that name?*

I can't tell you. Just stay away from him. Don't let him in. Before I can tap my head to show him what I mean, a wave of nausea hits me so hard I double over. Everything has gone blurry. There is a ringing in my ears. *Please*, I think-say, trying desperately to hang on, *tell me what you know about him. So you can help us to help you.*

My father's words are barely audible, even in think-speak, over the rushing of blood in my ears. *Time vampire . . . Eternity Loop . . . not even the BSI . . . but you mustn't . . .*

And I feel a great wrench, as if I'm being forcibly removed from the past and catapulted into the present — and I *shift*—

And I'm lying on Indigo's bed, gasping for air as if I've been dropped from a great height.

'What happened?' Indigo's worried eyes drill into mine.

I inhale. 'Nothing.' Frustrated, I sit up.

'Nothing?'

'I don't know.' Switching to think-speak, I say, *As soon as I tried to warn Dad about Raven I started feeling really awful. It's like time knows we're interfering with it.*

Indigo huffs through her nose. *Time isn't a person.*

Isn't it? I massage my throbbing temples. *Maybe time is god, did you ever think of that?*

You're making my *head hurt now. Did you get any other clues?* She touches my wrist as I let my short-term memory flow through to her and my skin tingles. *Eternity Loop*, she think-says, seemingly oblivious to my body's reflexive response. *What do you think that means?*

I try to focus. *Maybe that's what Billy Raven has created. A time vampire in an Eternity Loop.*

But what's an Eternity Loop?

What you create if you keep travelling back and forth in time?

Do you think your dad was time-travelling?

I raise my head. Indigo's features are barely visible, but I don't need to read her expression. Her thought-stream is golden-yellow, as if she has come to a conclusion I have yet to make.

Maybe, I think-say, as my hindbrain goes *Well, of course he was.*

And if so, do you think he was tracking Billy Raven?

I frown. *But why did he need to fly to London to do that?*

Perhaps, Indigo think-says, *he was putting the BSI off the scent.*

Why would he want to do that? Even as I say that, the answer is obvious: my father didn't trust the BSI. And if he didn't trust them, then how can we assume that either of us is safe?

I guess there's only one way of finding out, Indigo think-says.

Please, I think-say, knowing that it's futile, that she has already made up her mind. *Please don't go near him. You mightn't make it out alive.*

I think you're underestimating me, my best friend think-says.

So I do the only thing I can think of that might delay her, that might sway her.

'Indy,' I say. 'Please. I don't think I could stand to lose you, too.'

And kiss her.

There is a fundamental difference between kissing a human and kissing a fellow Offspring, and it is this: I can't hide anything, and nor can she. As Indigo's lips soften beneath mine, I feel something inside me unspool, spilling out all the forbidden emotions I've been trying to squash since I last kissed her. How it felt to hold her close. The memory of her bare skin against mine. How, the last time I kissed her, I was Rigel-in-Billy's-body, but now it's me, only me, and she's not pushing me away.

I don't tell her I'm in love with her, not in words, but there it is, my inner self laid open for her in that moment. Here we are, lying in each other's arms. Here is my hand on her hip, my heart pounding against hers. And we could take it further, we could, but there is something between us, and her name is Brie.

I'm sorry, I think-say, rolling off her. Indigo is silent, but her palms are pressed over her eyes, her thought-stream an explosion of colour. 'I'm sorry,' I repeat, aloud this time.

'Are you going to tell her?' Indigo asks.

'Not right— I'm sorry, OK? I didn't mean . . .' What *do* I mean? What have I done — not just to Indigo, but to Brie, too?

Indigo sits bolt upright. Great, she's blocking me, her voice hard. 'If you think I'm going to be manipulated by another male, then you're wrong.'

'I *wasn't* trying to manipulate you.'

'Really? Because that's exactly how it seems to me.' She's trembling. And oh, I almost wish I hadn't kissed her, because then I wouldn't know how she is in love with me, too.

Indigo is in love with me, too. How could I not have sensed that before now?

'Please.' I try to touch her, but she shrinks away. 'Please. If you'd stop blocking me for one second, you'd know I wasn't— Indy, this has turned out all wrong.'

'You're damned right it has,' she snaps. Before I can reason with her, before I can show her that what I feel for her isn't a lie, she is *shifting*. If I could go after her I would, but she's still blocking me. She could be anywhere, anytime, but one thing is certain: she's gone straight to Billy Raven.

There's nothing else to do but wait, to safeguard her earthly body until she returns. And if she doesn't?

'Then you will hunt,' I whisper.

Hunter Blue. Blue Hunter. Indigo Moon.

And an internal voice says *Black Raven, Black Raven, Black Raven*.

SEVENTEEN:
BILLY

2088

Resisting the urge to hold my hands up, I said, 'Who the hell are you? And what have you done to *her*?' From the slow-sluggish waveform of Andromeda's thought-stream, I was picking that she was either heavily sedated or dying. As for Newton, I was getting nothing, a blank.

'Merely a sedative, as you've deduced,' Newton said. 'And as for who I am, that's a more complicated answer.' He was still pointing the cylinder at me.

'You're a mind-reader, too, I see,' I said, still trying to act cool.

'A telepath, yes. But as for you, well, I'm still trying to work that one out.' He freed his hand to smooth his hair, which was dyed in rainbow stripes. 'Almost,' he said, as if I'd spoken aloud. 'Apart from purple. I'm not really a purple person.'

I shook my head, irritated. 'Stop doing that.' I felt as though my mind had been plundered, my thoughts and memories exposed for him to see and exploit. What had Andromeda said to me when we'd first met? *Leave yourself wide open like that, and you're going to get hurt.* Somehow, both Andromeda and Newton had managed to shield their minds from me. I needed to learn how to do the same.

'My apologies, Mr Raven.' Newton glanced at the lion, which was blurring and *shifting*, transitioning from animal to human once more. 'Or do you prefer Mr Quick?'

'Billy Quick is dead,' I said, experimenting with throwing up my first block. Almost immediately I sensed a retreat, although I feared it wouldn't be long before this Newton person found a way around my clumsy defences.

'Interesting.' He nodded towards Andromeda, who was struggling into a sitting position. 'Tell me how you two met.'

I couldn't read Andromeda, not while my block was still in place — at least, not then — but her pleading expression told me all I needed to know.

'Let's just say we go back a long way,' I said, debating whether I should retreat into my earthly body, the one I'd left in 1993.

Newton narrowed his eyes at me. 'I'm intrigued, Mr Raven. Would you like to continue this conversation over a drink? Are you partial to Ozone?'

'What about Andromeda?' I asked.

'Well,' he said, not even turning to see who was coming through the front door of the apartment, 'she's going home. Aren't you, Andromeda?'

There was a blur of movement, another whistle, and Andromeda collapsed once more.

'You need to be faster than that,' Newton said in a conversational tone as a pair of men in black jumpsuits loaded her comatose body onto a stretcher. 'How's your shape-shifting, Mr Raven?'

'Funny you should ask,' I said.

We had our drinks, which Newton assured me didn't really contain ozone, on the fiftieth-floor balcony of a bar a few doors down from the apartment. Androgynous wait staff, all of whom looked disturbingly similar, with their blonde hair and brown eyes, buzzed around tables, dispensing colourful drinks, at least one of which was on fire, and bar snacks and pipes with elaborately curved stems.

'What are they smoking?' I asked.

'There's no smoke.' Newton twirled a metal swizzle stick in his cocktail. 'They're inhaling Baccus, a synth compound which is free of carcinogens and gives a much better buzz than tobacco.'

'Is it addictive?'

Newton's teal irises rested on mine. 'All good things are addictive. How do you like the Ozone?'

'It's good. Let me guess, the alcohol is synthetic, too?'

He smiled. 'Oh, it's not alcohol. No one drinks that anymore.' Before I could ask what was giving me the floaty feeling, in that case — but perhaps I didn't want to know — he think-said, *Before you closed me out, Mr Raven, I detected something very interesting.*

Interesting how? I think-asked, while struggling to maintain my block.

That you have travelled here from the twentieth century, for one thing.

I traced the rim of my glass. *And?*

And that you were born as a non-virally optimised human, a normal. True?

I don't even know what virally optimised is. I watched a pair of women at the other table, who were holding each other's gaze a beat longer than was socially polite, who were unconsciously mirroring each other's gestures in an age-old mating ritual. At least *that* hadn't changed.

As I thought. So how, Mr Raven, did you come to acquire these abilities?

I met a girl, I think-said, my fingers on my neck. *She . . . changed me.*

Infected you, you mean?

My brain was whirring, trying to make the connection. *Is that what you mean by virally optimised? As in, she gave me a virus?*

M-fever. Or a variant, yes. But you . . . He was regarding me as if I was some kind of zoo specimen. *You,* he carried on, *are more advanced than a first-generation virally optimised human; more like an Offspring. So you,* Newton patted his lips with his napkin, *don't make sense. Not at all.*

I could have told him about the taxi driver, but something held me back. Because what I'd gleaned from him already was that somehow I had evolved since Aurelia had infected me — which presumably meant that maybe I could continue to do so.

I sipped on my drink. *What's an Offspring?*

It's the genetic product — the child — of two virally optimised humans. These Offspring are evolutionarily more advanced than their parents. For instance, they can shift not just as animals, but in human form, not to mention being able to time-travel without placing a huge physiological stress on their bodies. He coughed, his fist over his mouth. *Like you.*

Right. My brain continued to leap, to make and solder connections. Was it something to do with the taxi driver? It was only since I'd drunk her blood, her essence, that I'd been able to start shape-shifting. As for the time travel, that was only something I'd done since I met Andromeda. Had I tasted her blood?

Andromeda, I think-said, my blood singing a new tune in my veins. *Tell me about her. Is she second-generation?*

Yes — which, for reasons I'll enlighten you on later, is actually very rare and sought-after.

And you?

I'm second-generation, too, the child of a virally optimised couple. He leaned forward. *Would you believe I'm thirty-six years old?*

You don't look a day older than eighteen, I think-answered, swirling the stick in my now-empty glass, and at that moment I sensed the locus of control shift, ever-so-slightly, in my direction. Unexpected, but gratifying, too.

Newton smiled, gestured at my glass. *Will you have another?*

I do believe I will, I think-said.

EIGHTEEN:
INDIGO

I am suspended in the past-present-future, or rather my dream-flow is. Maybe it was foolish to leave my earthly body in the company of the two-timing Rigel Fletcher, but it isn't as if I have much choice.

Finding Billy Raven is easier than I thought it would be. My dream-flow hasn't forgotten the visceral tug I felt whenever I was near him, the heady intoxication of his scent, cloves and oak and danger danger danger. Yet I'm not looking for present-time Raven, whatever that means. No, I'm looking for a memory, his memory, the one I accessed when in Santorini — the one where he met Andromeda for the first time.

I don't know if this will work, have no idea if the skills I learned from my lesson with Harvey Wu are going to translate into this next step. If I get it wrong, then I could— What? I have no idea, but I need a clue, more than I have now. So I focus on the darkened room, the clink of glasses, the loud music and—

There is a ripple, a sickening *shift*, and I am—

Oh. There he is, as disturbingly handsome as ever, his cloves-and-oak scent too strong to be anything but real. He is sitting on a bar stool, his arm brushing mine, and I am peering through eyes that are not my own. Andromeda's thought-stream flares and flickers, then grows dull as I weave mine through, reducing hers to an undercurrent.

I give Billy a quick smile, then glance at the barman. 'I'll have a gin and tonic,' I say, because that's what Andromeda had said. Feeling a nudge, I realise Billy's trying to access my — our — thought-stream. I block him, but not before I hear what he's thinking: *I've never seen eyes like that in any human. Could it be that she's like me? Has she* shifted *into animal form recently?*

Lowering my voice, I say 'I can still smell the wolf from *your* last *shift*', just as Andromeda had last time. I lift my chin, inhaling. 'And pig blood. A good meal, was it?'

'It was adequate.' His eyes are dark, holding me fast. I should feel revolted, but even now, after all that's happened, I am being drawn in.

'Billy Raven,' I say. 'Right?'

'Right.' His hand is on mine. My stomach triple-somersaults. 'Let me guess. We're one and the same, you and me, correct?'

I tilt my head. 'Oh no,' I say. 'Compared to me, you're merely an amateur.' The music is louder now, some song about God shuffling his feet, which is oddly appropriate.

Billy's narrowing his eyes, trying to read me again. How can I block him while trying to read his mind? How am I going to get access to the information I need about this Eternity Loop?

You know how, I tell myself.

I don't want to do it.

But then again, another part of me does.

'Who *are* you?' Billy asks.

Leave yourself wide open like that and you're going to get hurt, Billy Raven, I think say, before opening up a closed comm. *Do you like to dance?*

I like to dance, he think-replies, and as I lead him to the dance floor, which is packed with sweaty, drunk students, I get a glimpse of a sub-thought, *his* sub-thought: *Aurelia?* It's accompanied by a deep blue longing.

Aurelia? The only Aurelia I know is the icily beautiful woman we met when Billy and I time-travelled to the Grammy Awards that time.

'Who's Aurelia?' I ask when he draws me close, and he jerks a little.

'She was my first kiss,' Billy says. 'But not my last.' He lowers his mouth onto mine, and for a few seconds, a mere few seconds, I have unlimited access to his memory banks. It's not Andromeda he's thinking of. No, he's remembering his first kiss. He's remembering Aurelia, with her glossy blonde hair and a rose tattoo.

Oh, Billy. What's done cannot be undone. Don't forget.

His memory unspools further, and I'm glimpsing what happened next: the crushing chest pain, the loss of vision, a near-death experience. In his memory, Aurelia is leaving him, forever: *See you in a hundred years, Billy Raven.*

Billy pulls away, and the door to his memory slams shut. 'I think we should take this somewhere else, don't you?'

'Yes,' I whisper, the all-too-familiar craving upon me. If I don't leave now, I know, then I may never escape. 'Yes,' I say. 'Let's take this somewhere else,' and I disengage, *shifting* with lightning speed and I—

'Billy Quick?' Rigel is crouching beside me, his palm on my forehead. 'Who is that?'

I sit up, pushing him away from me. How did I end up on my bedroom floor?

'You've been out for hours,' he mumbles, flushing when I look him in the eye. 'You barely even had a pulse.'

'Did I say you could touch my body while I was gone?' I snap, then wish I hadn't. 'Sorry.'

'I was just checking you weren't dead.' He stands up, passing his fingers through his hair.

'Pretty hard to kill an Offspring.' I struggle to my feet, wincing at the stiffness in my limbs.

'This is Billy Raven we're talking about.' He crosses his arms. 'Or Billy Quick.'

'How did you hear that?' I move into the bathroom and fill a glass from the tap.

'That's what you were thinking when you came to. And before you say it, I wasn't trying to invade your privacy. You were just really loud.'

I drain the glass and turn around, swiping my wrist over my lips. 'I don't know why I called him that.' I frown, trying to remember. 'But I think maybe I got it from him. From his memory.'

See you in a hundred years, Billy Raven. But the boy who'd kissed Aurelia had called himself Billy Quick, hadn't he?

'He let you into his memory?' Rigel is leaning against the doorframe, and all I can think about is how his lips felt on mine a few hours ago. Stop it, there's no time for that now.

Besides, he already has a girlfriend.

Pushing the intrusive thoughts away, I say, 'Of course he didn't *let* me in. Just like your dad didn't *let* you in.'

'Do you think that's his alter-ego? An alias?'

'Maybe. Or maybe he stole someone else's identity.'

'Billy the vampire,' Rigel murmurs, glancing at me from beneath his eyelids, so I let him have it, the full memory of what just happened.

'I didn't sleep with him, if that's what you're wondering.'

'Thought never even crossed my mind,' he says. Both of us know *that's* a lie.

There is a rap on the door, making both of us jump.

'Indigo? Are you up yet?' It's Joy, one of the fitness trainers. 'Boot camp starts in five.'

I hesitate, then call out, 'Sorry, I must have slept in.' *Go*, I think-tell Rigel. *I'll talk to you later.*

Later, he think-replies.

Don't even think about it, I think-add, glimpsing the edge of his next thought.

If you don't want to know then you shouldn't be looking, he think-snipes in reply, and leaves in true Offspring style, with a whole-body *shift*.

NINETEEN:
BILLY

2088

After a brief sojourn to check on my body in 1993 Dunedin and pay the hotel for another week's stay, I *shifted* back to 2088 London once more. That makes it sound easy, but in reality it left me feeling weak, drained. I was worried that I wouldn't be able to effect a *shift* back quite so easily. Could it be that the abilities I'd gained from feeding off Andromeda were fading already?

The restaurant Newton had chosen was in another elevated location. On this occasion, however, we sat in a self-contained capsule that rotated slowly around the outside of the circular eightieth level of a building called the Needle, owing to the pointy spire on top. From time to time we would dock, barnacle-like, on the outside of the building and a waiter would enter the capsule to exchange dishes or fill our glasses.

'Tell me,' Newton said once we'd consumed our starters, oysters complete with a complimentary black pearl in each, 'have you ever heard of Riva virus?'

I sipped on my drink. 'Is it different from M-fever?'

He nodded. 'Far worse. It doesn't kill its host, but it spreads like — well, like a coronavirus. We have vaccines now, of course, but the damage was done before they could be rolled out on a large scale. And every time Riva mutates, a new vaccine has to be made. In the meantime, it wreaks new damage.'

I rolled my pearl between finger and thumb. 'What sort of damage?'

'It leads to death of eggs in females, which, as you may or may not recall, are already present in the female ovaries at birth. It also causes a marked reduction in the male sperm count.'

'Oh. Shame.' I considered that for a moment. 'So, mass infertility, then?' And yet there seemed to be plenty of people buzzing around. 'When did this happen?'

'First case was detected about twenty years ago.' Newton smoothed his rainbow ponytail. 'You're going to ask how come there are so many young people around here.'

I twisted a ring around my left pinkie, a chunky platinum one that I'd bought on a recent trip to Ireland. 'You read my mind.'

'If only.' He arched an eyebrow at me, a gesture that pleased me. My newfound blocking ability was obviously working, then. 'Take a look at the wait staff and tell me what you see.'

'Well,' I said, 'I hate to say this, but they all look kind of . . . similar. I can't even tell if most of them are male or female.'

He smiled. 'That's a fairly accurate observation. They're pleasant enough, of course, which is what you want in the service industry, and they're easy enough to generate en masse.' We docked again and the doors slid open to admit our waiter, who deposited large plates containing artfully arranged food in front of us. 'Enjoy your meal,' it said, before leaving us alone once more.

'Wait.' I stared after the waiter. 'Do you mean they're — what, clones?'

'Exactly, Mr Raven. Laboratory-bred. They're not capable of anything too intellectually taxing, and of course they're just as infertile as the rest of us, but they've revolutionised the service industry.'

'But what happens when you need more than semi-intelligent clones?' I asked. 'As in scientists, doctors, IT programmers and the like? Or have you replaced them all with artificial intelligence?'

'We have quite a lot of AI, but that's not enough.' Newton gazed out of the window. We were orbiting the Needle once more. Capsules zipped around the air space above and below us, often passing each other with only millimetres to spare.

'And you?' I asked. 'Were you also infected?'

He grimaced. 'Unfortunately, yes. Very few of us were spared, the females worse than the males. In fact, only a couple of Offspring females have been found to be fertile, and it's amazing they were born at all.'

'Such as Andromeda?' I asked, recalling last night's conversation. *Very rare and sought-after.*

'Such as Andromeda. Which is why we'd like to use her stem cells for further research. Unfortunately, she has been less than cooperative to date.'

'Which is why you're keeping her prisoner?'

'Now, now, that's a bit strong.' His nose wrinkled. 'Let's just say that we're protecting her from other parties who'd use far less gentle methods of persuasion. Do you know how much a frozen embryo fetches on the black market these days? Let alone stem cells capable of curing a whole generation of infertile females?'

'Do you know for sure that they can do that?'

Newton raised his drink. 'This is the best part,' he said, clinking his glass against mine. 'We already have. I'll introduce you to the recipient tomorrow, if you like.'

'I would like that.' I pushed salad onto my fork. 'And Andromeda? Will I get to see her again?'

'Of course, Mr Raven. In fact, I think she may already be a little bit in love with you. For a generous fee, I would like to turn that attraction to our advantage. What do you say?'

I swallowed my mouthful. 'Let's talk some more.'

Newton said, 'Perhaps, after your meal, you'd like to come back to my apartment for a night-cap.'

'Oh, I do like night-caps,' I replied.

As for Andromeda, I had other plans for her, and they had nothing to do with curing infertility.

TWENTY:
RIGEL

'Oh stink, are you still sick?' Brie looks the complete opposite of sick, if the cheerful image on my I-Bio is anything to go by.

'Yeah, summer flu is the worst,' I rasp, emitting a pathetic cough.

'Poor thing. Can I bring you anything?'

'I don't think you want to catch this. Thanks anyway.' I blow my nose. 'Sorry, got to go. My throat is killing me.'

I'm scuffing down the hallway to the shower when my brother intercepts me. 'Faker.' Fox tosses a tennis ball at me. I swipe it out of the air, then chuck it at his head.

'Piss off,' I growl. Swearing, Fox ducks before hurling himself at me. We both *shift* at the moment of the tackle. Then we are snarling and biting and tumbling, hair and foamy saliva flying, until a painfully loud thought-command brings us to a standstill.

Stop that right this minute!

I roll onto my side, blinking. Our mother is standing in the doorway between the hall and the lounge, or at least the white wolf version of her is, ready to discipline her unruly cubs.

Sorry, I think-mumble, *shifting* back into human form. Fox doesn't even bother to change, just slopes into his room with his tail between his legs.

'Fox is right,' Mum says, after a rapid *shift*. 'You don't look very sick to me.'

There's no point lying to my Mum, (a) because she's likely to pick it up from the colour of my thought-stream, and (b) because she can sniff out injuries and sickness through brick walls.

Speaking of which . . . I frown. '*You* are though,' I say, and she gives me one of her intense looks, one that makes me feel as if I've been turned inside out.

'What do you mean?'

'You've got a fever.' I move closer and touch her forehead. 'I'm guessing about 38.5 degrees.' Her eyes are bloodshot, too. Has she been crying? Her thought-stream is radiating worry rather than sadness, though.

'Rigel . . .' For some reason, my mother seems more concerned with the fact that I can *detect* her fever, rather than why she has one. 'Don't.'

'Don't what?'

She moves away. 'Don't try to heal me. It's dangerous.'

I follow her through the lounge and into the kitchen, where she extracts a thermometer from the cupboard above the fridge. 'Just because I detected your fever doesn't mean I can heal,' I say, but in my head, I'm thinking *What if? What if I could heal my mum's heart?*

'In my experience, it goes hand-in-hand. And it didn't go so well for you last time, remember?' Mum pushes the thermometer into her ear. When it beeps, she looks at the reading, then shows it to me.

I shrug. 'See? I was wrong.'

'By point one degree.' She stares at the digital read-out. '38.4.'

'Guess that explains your scratchy throat and eyes,' I say, unable to resist showing off my new ability. 'And since when did I heal anyone?'

'Your heart rhythm went crazy immediately after you visited

Indigo in Norway last year,' Mum says. 'When she had that head wound, remember?'

'Billy Raven had just kicked me out of his body,' I argue, remembering how I'd woken up in hospital, blood streaming out of my nose and my heart leaping all over the place. 'It's not surprising I nearly had a cardiac arrest.'

'Did you ask Indigo what happened to her head wound after you visited her?'

I hesitate. 'No.'

'Well, maybe you should.' Mum checks her temperature again, scowls at the thermometer. 'Guess I need to stay home.' She glances up. 'What's *your* excuse?'

'Mental exhaustion,' I say, blocking her and going to have my shower. When I get out, there's yet another message from Brie: *Hope you're feeling better soon. Missing our nights together x*

'Shit.' After retreating to my room, I flop onto the bed and stare up at the ceiling, having an internal debate with myself.

I can't keep doing this.

Doing what?

Lying to Brie.

It was just a slip-up. It's hardly the end of the world. And Indigo basically told you to piss off, so it's not as if it's going to be an ongoing thing.

If it was just a slip-up, then why do you keep replaying that kiss over and over in your head?

Groaning, I sit up and throw my towel at the wall. I know what I should do, but I'm not looking forward to it. I get dressed, check the time. Five past ten, five minutes into when Brie normally takes her tea break. Suddenly I have an urge to get it over and done with, to spill the beans and take the consequences, whatever they might be.

'Here goes,' I whisper, before selecting her last message and tapping on the call icon.

'Hey.' Brie's smile disappears almost immediately, as if she knows what I'm about to say. 'What's up?' Her voice is as stony as her expression.

'Um, I . . . there's something I . . .' I blow out a breath. 'Look, I need to tell you—'

'That you've been cheating on me?'

My chest tightens. How could she know that? Or is it a calculated guess? 'I'm sorry,' I say. 'It was only once, a kiss. But I don't think . . . No, I *do* think that I have feelings for . . . someone else.' Could I be any less articulate? Why can't I just come out and say—

'That you've been spending more time with Indigo Moon than your own girlfriend?' I've never seen Brie like this before; her voice dripping acid, her eyes flashing. I suppose I can't blame her.

'I'm sorry,' I repeat, frowning when her image blurs. A bad connection, maybe?

'I suppose I shouldn't be surprised,' Brie says, and suddenly, inexplicably, her voice is soft again, her face, too. 'Look. Mistakes happen, OK? Have a think about what you really want. Because I really think you and I have something special. And you and I both know Indigo will never love anyone the way she loved Billy Raven, right?'

'W-well, I . . .' I stutter, flummoxed by her rapid change in tone. 'She and Billy are over. She hates him. And I'm sorry, but I don't think I can carry on with this. With us.'

Brie's face hardens again. 'What if *I* don't want to break up?'

'What if *you* don't want to break up?' I repeat. What? Do I have to explain the rules of breaking up to her? As in, if one of you wants it to be over then it's over, unless they're some kind of psychopath.

Her image blurs again, but not so much that I can't see the look on her face. Whoa. She really hates me.

'You might think this is over, Rigel,' Brie says, 'but believe me when I say it's not.'

'I'm sorry,' I say again, before ending the call. What just happened there? I need to speak to Indigo. No, actually, maybe I need a guy point of view, Kit or Vaughan, although it's been ages since I hung out with either of them.

I'm contemplating contacting Rawiri, in case he has any more experience with crazy ex-girlfriends than I do, when Mum's thought-voice stops me in my tracks for the second time that morning: *Rigel, Fox, you need to stay home. You're under quarantine until further notice.*

What? I stride into the lounge, but she's not there. *Why? What have we done?*

It's not what you've done, it's what I've potentially given you, or you've given me. When I rang in sick, I was asked to come and have a test, and now I'm in isolation.

A test? For what? I think-ask, but the answer is already flowing through to me. *Riva? I thought that was an STD.*

Believe me, that's not how I got it. Stay home, but expect a nurse to turn up soon to test you both.

What? Fox's thought-stream is jagged with panic. *There's no way I'm letting anyone stick a swab up my Johnson.*

Jesus, I think-say, at the same time as Mum interjects, *It's a blood test, silly.*

'Urrgh.' I take the thermometer off the bench, where Mum left it, and stick it in my ear.

'What are you doing?' Fox is glaring at me as if it's my fault our house has suddenly become a leper colony.

'My temperature's normal.' I lean against the bench. 'But you, my friend, have a fever.'

'What?' Fox snatches the thermometer off me. 'Oh,' he says, right after it beeps. 'What does that mean?'

'38.7 degrees,' I say. I peer more closely at him. His eyes are slightly bloodshot, just like Mum's were. 'I think you've got Riva. And a high chance of . . . crap.'

'What are you doing?' Fox asks when I grab his hand.

'Tell Mum about this,' I say, leading him into the lounge, 'and you'll be sorry for eternity. Now sit down and shut up.' I drape my palm across his forehead. He might be a pain in the butt, but he's still my brother.

TWENTY-ONE:
BILLY

2088

The morning after my dinner with Newton, I woke to the smell of brewing coffee. For a few minutes, I lingered in bed, taking in my surroundings. I was in the guest bedroom at the apartment he shared with his wife, which was rather spacious by modern-day standards. There was even a painting on the wall opposite my bed.

'Who's that?' I'd asked last night, unable to take my eyes off the two-faced man. He had leaves in his curly hair, like someone from Roman times.

'That's Janus,' Newton had said. 'The Roman god of beginnings and endings. One face looks to the past, the other to the future.'

'Fascinating,' I'd answered. Now, I had an eerie sense that this Janus had been watching over me all night, which of course was impossible.

I climbed out of bed and donned the dressing gown hanging on the back of the door before strolling down the hallway. When I entered the kitchen, Newton was standing at the window, looking out over the city below. He pivoted, gesturing at the tall, dark-skinned woman standing by the fridge.

'Billy, this is Grace,' he said. 'Grace, this is Billy, Billy Raven.'

Grace set a bottle of orange juice on the counter. 'Hi, Billy. Sleep well?'

'Very well,' I said, already registering her thought-stream, which was completely open and unguarded. 'Thanks to Miles.'

Grace smiled. 'Miles says you've come to check out the project?'

'The stem-cell project, yes,' I replied. 'I hear you're the project's first success. Congratulations.'

Blushing, Grace put a hand on her belly, which still looked pretty flat to me. 'Only nine and a half weeks, but the scans look promising.'

'The scans look fantastic.' Newton cupped her shoulder. 'Would you like a coffee, Billy?'

'Love one.' I perched on one of the stools by the kitchen counter.

'Let me know if you need anything,' Grace said, giving me a cursory smile before drifting away.

She's kind of pissed off, Miles thought-said, inserting a metallic cup into the side of the fridge. At least, I thought it was a fridge, but probably it did everything from make coffee to a three-course dinner as well.

No kidding, I thought-replied, following Grace's thought-stream as she entered the bathroom, closing the door firmly behind her. *Up to all hours drinking . . . God knows what else they got up to . . . why this Billy guy couldn't have just stayed at a hotel . . .*

'She's a normal,' Newton said softly, once we heard the shower running.

'Lucky for you,' I said, watching the coffee jet into the cup.

'Maybe, maybe not,' he said, ignoring my insinuation. 'If this pregnancy is successful and the next, then we could turn our attentions to . . . other ventures.' He decanted the coffee into a mug and set it in front of me. 'Milk's right there, oat or almond, whatever you prefer.'

'Thanks. Other ventures?'

'There are some who would pay anything to be like us.' He leaned against the sink. 'Do you know what my wife is most scared of?'

'Heights? Spiders?' I was playing with him, and he knew it. The answer was at the forefront of his mind. 'Ah. I see.'

'She already looks older than me. It's subtle, but it bothers her. In another ten, twenty years, the differences will be quite stark.'

'The fountain of eternal youth . . .' I said. 'That's where Andromeda comes in, right?'

'Apparently.' Newton narrowed his eyes at me. 'At least, that's what I thought until I met you.'

I sipped on my coffee. 'I'm not sure I could replicate what Aurelia did with me.'

'I'd rather you don't try and feed on my wife.' His tone was cool. 'Besides, she's immune to the M-fever variant, which presumably is the source of your abilities. Our population have all been vaccinated, because of the high death rate.'

'Pity,' I said, and Newton emitted a low, animal-like growl.

Pretending I hadn't noticed, I said, 'Don't suppose I could borrow some clothes off you?'

'Funny you should ask that,' he said. 'Those were my clothes you were wearing yesterday.'

'The ones Andromeda gave to me?'

Newton raised an eyebrow at me. 'Andromeda used to stay here quite often,' he said, stressing the 'used to'. 'She and Grace are quite good friends.'

'Ah. Hence the willingness to donate her stem cells?'

'To Grace, yes.' He dumped his cup in the sink. 'I'll leave some clothes on your bed,' he said, and left to join his wife in the shower.

We took the Underground route to the research facility, although it was far different from the twentieth-century London Underground. The trains had gone, replaced by pods that zipped around on tracks on multiple levels. Each pod appeared to be capable of sitting up to four people, and was programmed once the occupants stepped inside.

'The trains were inefficient,' Newton told me. 'And contributed in a large way to the spread of the last three epidemics. This system was built using a model designed by Black Spiral.'

'Black Spiral?'

'An intelligence organisation fronted by people like us, mostly. They were formed in the thirties after the Foundation was driven underground, although in a more figurative sense.' He touched the door and a screen lit up, showing what appeared to be an electronic newspaper. 'The Foundation are the people who designed M-fever.'

'To create people like you?'

'To cut a long story short, yes.' He swiped his finger across the screen, and I watched, fascinated, as the text changed. *Skilled workforce crisis deepens*, a headline announced. *Hospital waiting lists grow as ageing doctors retire*, the subheading read. 'It's all very well to have more babies,' Newton said, 'but the crisis is now.'

I gave him a slow nod. 'Hence the need for a non-ageing workforce.'

'Exactly.' He swiped to the next page, which at first glance appeared to be an advertisement for Coca-Cola. When I peered closer, I saw that it had been rebranded as Coke-X. Before I could ask what was so different about Coke-X, we were whipped upwards and sideways, and came to a halt outside what must have been at least the tenth level of a mirrored building. 'Welcome to the Eternity Tower. This way,' he said, think-adding, *And if you tell anyone what you're about to see, I may not kill you, but believe me, we have ways of controlling people like you.*

Such as? I think-asked. I didn't like his tone. Perhaps I'd teach him a lesson, later.

I'm about to show you, he think-said, passing a hand over a section of wall to reveal a hidden doorway. *Starting with Andromeda.*

'Is she asleep?' I asked a couple of minutes later. We were standing in the corridor, peering into a room in which a woman with silver-blonde hair was lying in an elliptically-shaped pod, her eyes closed, her chest barely moving.

Newton crossed his arms. 'Sedated is probably a better word for it.'

'So that's how you got the stem cells for your wife?'

He had the gall to look shocked. 'God, no. Do you think we're animals? As I said, Grace and Andromeda are friends. Andromeda felt sorry for her. Yet when we began trying to discuss other ventures, such as the Eternity Project — well, you've seen how that went down.'

'As in, Andromeda time-travelling into 1990s New Zealand?' I watched Andromeda's eyelids flutter, sensed a flicker in her thought-stream. Did she know I was here?

'That's right. We managed to haul her back — with difficulty, I might add — and you saw first-hand what happened after that.'

'You shot her,' I said, employing my newfound ability to block so Newton couldn't sense my train of thought. Andromeda was quite enticing, perhaps even more so than Aurelia.

'With a Tranq Gun, yes,' he said. 'No permanent damage done.'

I turned my head. 'And she's the only one of her kind, you say?'

'As far as we know.'

'So Andromeda is your only hope.'

'Pretty much.' He laid his palm, flat, on the glass. 'As I intimated before, I wonder if you could be more persuasive than us. If you could make her see reason.'

'As in, win her over through my powers of seduction?' I asked.

'Well, yes.' He was blocking me, too. 'It seems to be an area in which you excel.'

'Indeed.' I peered at Andromeda again. 'And what do I get out of this?'

Newton spread his hands. 'Name your price, Mr Raven.'

TWENTY-TWO:
INDIGO

It's almost noon when I'm summoned to the director's office. The message arrives during an Advanced Physics lesson, where I'm contemplating informing the instructor that the current laws of thermodynamics are obviously wrong. At least, they are if you're virally optimised or Offspring.

Energy cannot be created or destroyed. That's where they're wrong. We're creating new energy all the time, especially when we *shift*. Maybe that's why we couldn't destroy Billy Raven.

What's done cannot be undone. Don't forget.

I jump. Ci, sitting next to me, gives me a strange look. 'Your I-Bio is buzzing,' he says, clearly oblivious to the voice that just crept into my thought-stream. I turn my wrist over to read the message: *Please report to Director Chase's office at 1200 hours.*

I show Ci. 'What do you think that's about?' I ask, earning a dirty look from one of the young women sitting in front of us. There are only four other BSI agents-in-training in our class, and they're all geeks, as far as I'm concerned.

He shrugs. 'As long as it doesn't involve using me as a puppet, I don't really care.'

'Come on, I did you a favour,' I murmur.

Our instructor, a leathery-skinned professor who looks as though he was preserved a few hundred years ago, says, 'That'll do for today. Tomorrow we'll move on to special relativity, so make sure you've read chapter twelve in your online text.'

'I can't wait,' I murmur, sidling out into the corridor. Camilla Chase's office is located at the other end of the compound, although with the monorail everything seems close. Prof has already told us how he refuses to use 'that thing', saying it makes his bones rattle, confirming my suspicion that he's closer to a fossil than a living being.

The door to the foyer slides open as soon as I step out of the car, revealing a black-and-white tiled floor with a large desk at one end flanked by two leather couches. A woman with tight black curls is sitting behind the desk, using both hands to manipulate the images in front of her. There's no need for screens in here with the BSI's virtual technology, which is yet another one of Rawiri's inventions.

'Hello, Indigo,' the woman, whose name I can't remember, says. 'Director Chase said you can go straight in.' She gestures at the wall behind the desk, causing a revolving door to come into view.

'Thanks.' I stroll through the door and into Camilla Chase's office, with its thick black carpet and white leather chairs. Chase is sitting at a marble desk, her yellow cardigan the only spot of colour in the room.

'Have a seat,' Chase says, shutting down her virtual screen with a sweep of her slender hand. I take a seat next to the fire, my gaze drawn to the periscopic view to my left, where flakes of snow are swirling around the courtyard. 'How are you settling in, Miss Moon?'

'OK, I guess.'

Chase nods, her scalpel-sharp bob swinging past her ears. 'Good, good. And your quarters, how are they?'

My quarters? I stare at her. Is that some sort of reference to my butt or something?

'Your rooms,' she says, obviously noting my confusion. 'How is your suite?'

'Oh. Yeah, it's fine.' I look out of the window again, watching the snow swirl in the wind, as if it has taken on a solid form. If I squint, it could almost be a bird. Is Rigel coming to visit me again?

Chase's voice drills into my ears. 'We were just noticing . . . Well, perhaps we weren't clear enough when you first arrived. You do know about the no-visitor policy?'

I look back at her. 'No visitors?'

The director folds her hands. 'That's right. This is an academy, and, of course, you're still a minor. Although we can turn a blind eye on this occasion . . .'

I could say *what occasion*? I could, but of course I know exactly whom she's referring to.

Fighting to keep my voice even, I say, 'Perhaps you could have told us we were under surveillance.'

'We prefer to use the word *security*.'

'I bet you do.' They know Rigel has been visiting me. How many words did we speak aloud? Too many, I realise. Far too many.

Chase gives me a manufactured smile. 'It's only natural you might want your boyfriend to visit.'

'He's *not* my boyfriend.'

Nodding in an I'm-humouring-you kind of way, the director says, 'And, of course, we've been *very* clear that there is to be no more unsanctioned time-travelling.'

My brain makes several rapid cross-checks, reasonable assumptions and calculations before I answer. 'I wasn't time-travelling.' They can't prove it. All they saw, as far as I can tell, was me going into some sort of fugue state while Rigel watched over me. 'I just went to sleep and had some really weird dreams.'

'Really weird dreams,' Chase repeats, even as a very familiar, very unwelcome voice whispers, *What's done cannot be undone. Don't forget.*

'I get them all the time,' I say woodenly. 'Rigel was trying to comfort me. That's all.'

'And Billy Raven?'

Thin is the line between civilisation and savagery, the voice whispers.

I know what you want, I dare to answer, and sense a hesitation, followed by a retreat — a retreat that I'm pretty sure will be temporary. I could tell Chase that Billy Raven has returned, and perhaps she would believe me. I could ask her for help, and she would say *sure, of course*, even if that means treating what she thinks is merely post-traumatic stress disorder. But I don't trust the BSI any more than I trust my vampire ex-lover, not anymore.

Meeting Chase's gaze, I say, 'We killed him two months ago. Is there anything else you need to know?'

'No,' the director says. 'I believe that will be all. You are dismissed.' As I go to leave, she adds, 'But if I hear that Rigel, or should I say, Hunter Blue, has been paying you unauthorised visits again, we will have no choice but to move you to a room with blockers in the walls, or, failing that, insert a blocking implant into *you*. Obviously that isn't preferable for either of us, since we'd like to give you the chance to optimise your abilities while you're here. But if you force our hand, that's what will happen. Do you understand?'

Through numb lips, I say, 'I understand.'

As I stride into the corridor, I send a rapid, urgent message to Rigel: *I need to talk to you right now.*

The last thing I expect is an answer from his kid brother.

Um, he's kind of out of action at the moment, Fox think-says.

What? How did you hear me just now?

I was trying to get through to him, too, to see if he was OK. And then I heard you.

Cross-conversations, I think. It happens sometimes. But that's not what I'm worried about. *What do you mean, he's out of action?* I think-ask, directing the monorail car to take me down four levels to my room. There I lock the door, kick off my shoes and lie on the bed.

He's in a really deep sleep. Fox's thought-stream is a worried shade of blue, his memory flowing through in the seconds it takes for me to send my dream-flow outside, where I *shift* into a tawny eagle.

He healed *you?* I launch into the air. *But where did the Riva come from?* I think-ask, even as I recall Billy telling me: *It started off as a sexually transmitted disease. People didn't even know they had it.*

As if, Fox think-says, disgust rippling through at the mention of sex. *Mum reckons she might have caught it from a sample she was handling at the lab.*

Did Rigel try and heal her, too?

No, he's been out to it ever since he tried to heal me, or did heal me. My test was negative.

I circle above the compound, watching a pair of tiny figures — at least from my perspective — cross the courtyard below. *Before or after Rigel tried to heal you?*

After. I had a fever before Rigel healed me, but when the nurses at Apollo took my temperature it was normal. So either I'd cleared it already, or he really did heal me.

And Rigel? Did they test him? Leaving the BSI buildings behind me, I fly above the city — above the Tower of London, above the ruins of Buckingham Palace and out to sea.

Yeah. He's negative.

So where is he now? Rigel's thought-stream is faint and so slow I can't get a fix on it.

He's at the Apollo facility, in one of their isolation rooms.

I thought you said he was negative.

They said they weren't taking any chances. They're wearing full-on gowns and helmets and everything. Fox's thought-stream flares. *Wait. You knew this was going to happen?*

Not to you. I mean, I knew the Riva epidemic was going to happen, but I didn't realise it was going to be so soon. Mind you, Auntie Violet contracting Riva is hardly an epidemic. *Is he going to be OK?*

They think so. Mum's going to give him a roasting when he wakes up, though.

I bet. I stare at the snow swirling around me. For the second time that day, I could almost swear it was taking shape. *Got to go,* I manage, before snap-*shifting* back into my body so fast it feels like I've got knives in my belly.

'Urrgh.' I reach for my blocker, go to put it in my ear . . . and hesitate. Because there it is again, a voice, *his* voice: *Yes, my darling, that was a raven you saw just now. Don't think you can—*

I jam the blocker into my ear, dive beneath the covers and pull them over my head. It won't be long now. Soon, I know, Billy will come for me. And this time, I fear, he won't let me go.

TWENTY-THREE:
BILLY

2088

It didn't happen straight away. Gaining Andromeda's trust, I mean. But over the course of the next two weeks, I visited her every day.

'Why are you here?' Andromeda asked on the third day, after two days in which she refused to communicate with me at all. We were sitting in a room lined with neutralising waveforms to stop any telepathic signals coming in or going out, and to stop Andromeda *shifting* elsewhere. An effective method, Newton had told me, and less messy than implanting blocking devices, which subjects often tried to remove in all sorts of gory ways.

Subjects, I'd said. *Don't you mean captives?* Newton hadn't answered, choosing to ask whether I'd like another glass of Poison instead.

'Why do you think I'm here?' I leaned into the couch, which was blue leather with white polka dots. Not really my taste, but beggars couldn't be choosers. Not that I was intending to *beg*. And as for choices, they were all mine. It was just that no one else knew that yet, especially the Eternity Project.

Andromeda, who was sitting in a complementary armchair, white leather with blue polka dots, regarded me warily. 'You're going to talk me into rolling over like a good dog, is that right? To donate my cells and my soul for the good of the human race? Well, here's my answer: piss off.'

'No one said you have to sell your soul,' I replied, while simultaneously think-saying, *Yes, that's right. I've been sent to gain your trust by seducing you.* The blocker-lined room didn't stop us having a thought-conversation within its confines. Handy, that.

Andromeda crossed her long legs, flicking her slinky hair over her shoulder. *Are you kidding me?*

No, I'm giving you the truth. Just don't let them know I told you that, huh?

She narrowed her eyes at me. *What sort of game are you playing, Billy Raven?*

I tilted my head to one side. *One where we both get to win?* Aloud I said, 'Perhaps we could have dinner together, get to know each other a bit better?'

'Go screw yourself,' Andromeda said, draping her arm over the side of the chair, while think-replying, *Give me one reason why I should trust you.*

Mirroring her, I crossed *my* legs and draped *my* arm across the top of the couch, while admiring the clothes I'd plucked out of Newton's wardrobe — tight-fitting trousers made of a fabric I'd never come across before, bamboo or lotus or something, and a white shirt with sleeves that came to below my elbows. *Quite frankly, I don't give a toss about treating infertility or helping a pack of image-driven rich people achieve eternal youth,* I think-said.

Andromeda gave me a look that reminded me of her lion-self, fierce and regal and very, very dangerous. *What do you care about, Billy? And don't say it's me.*

That's not true, I said, giving her a crocodile-worthy grin in return. *I think we can strike a mutually beneficial arrangement resulting in your freedom.*

She lifted her chin. *What could I possibly give you that you don't already have? Don't think we'll be repeating what happened in 1993.*

That's not what I was going to ask for, I think-said, although I wouldn't have been averse to that possibility. *Why did you travel there anyway?*

For the first time, Andromeda sounded uncertain. *That was a mistake. I was trying to escape — I almost did — but then you—* She swallows. *I don't know how that happened.*

I could tell her that I knew exactly how it happened. If she'd never come across a vampire before, then she wouldn't know about my growing ability to inspire lust and desire in all manner of humans, both old and young. A glamour, some would call it. I was blocking her, though, much as she had activated her own partial block. Lions circling each other, waiting to pounce as soon as a weakness was exposed.

I could still taste her blood from our last encounter, could still feel it thrilling through my veins. Did she realise what she'd done by letting me in like that?

And, strangely enough, there was something about her that did make me want to help her, almost like *déjà vu*.

Shaking my head, I stood up. 'I'll return tomorrow.' For the benefit of anyone watching on the security cameras, I touched her shoulder. 'If that's OK.'

'I suppose that would be OK,' she said, her thought-stream opaque.

I slipped Newton's jacket on. *There's just one more thing.*

Yes?

I never mentioned what my end of the deal was. I fasten the second button on the jacket, admiring the detail on the wrists, almost like the Celtic runes on my pinkie ring.

Go on, then. Her tone dripped acid. I couldn't help but admire her feistiness.

You said you know Aurelia Nightingale . . . correct?

Andromeda's expression was stonier than ever. *Maybe. If you help me escape, that is.*

Done, I think-said, moving forward to kiss her. Andromeda was curiously resistant to my glamour that time, her revulsion staining her thought-stream black. I didn't really care. The deal had been struck. What was done could not be undone.

If I knew then what I know now, perhaps I'd have left well enough alone.

TWENTY-FOUR:
RIGEL

I need to talk to you right now.

Indy? I sit bolt upright, my head swimming.

Careful. It's my mother's thought-voice.

Where's Indigo? That *was* her I heard a minute ago, wasn't it?

I swivel my head. *Where am . . . ?* Oh. There's a heart monitor to the left of my narrow bed; to the right, a metal pole with a bag of IV fluid hanging from a hook. I'm alone, sort of. My mother is still lurking in my mind, her thought-stream alternating between angry and concerned. But . . . what about Indigo? Did she think-speak to me just now, or was that a thought-echo, a memory of a time gone by? And if so, when? A few minutes ago? A few hours?

I warned you, didn't I? Mum's directing my attention to the monitor, which is spitting out peaks and valleys, hills and spikes. *You're fortunate you don't need an ICD as well.*

Indignation bubbles in my gut. *If that's the price I have to pay to preserve Fox's man jewels, then I'll take it.* My mother's implantable defibrillator, which delivers a shock if her heart goes into a dangerous rhythm, was inserted before I was born. It seems to have done a pretty good job so far, although, admittedly, she hasn't healed anyone since my dad nearly died when he was twenty and Mum was seventeen.

Rigel . . .

Did they test him for Riva? Did they test me? I prod at the IV tubing feeding into the vein in my wrist.

Of course they did, my mother think-says.

And?

You were both negative, with no signs of infection. No fever, no conjunctival injection—

No what?

The red eyes, she think-says. *It's a classic sign.*

They were red yesterday, I think-say, remembering. *Before I healed him.* I glance around the room. There are no windows, no clue as to what time it might be.

It's seven-thirty.

I frown. *At night?*

No, in the morning. You've been unconscious for almost twenty-four hours.

And my heart?

Mum seems reluctant to part with the information, if the haziness in her thought-stream is anything to go by. *It's OK. But there have been a few runs of supraventricular tachycardia — rhythm disturbance.*

But nothing in the past twelve hours, I think-say, having gleaned enough to know I don't need to spend another minute here. I start pulling electro-dots off myself, wincing at the auto-wax job I'm doing on my chest hairs.

I guess Mum has a pretty good idea of what I'm up to, because she think-says, *Rigel, stop! You need to wait for the doctors to clear you.*

The doctors? Seriously? I swing my legs over the side of the bed. *Come on, you of all people would know if there's something wrong with my heart, just like I know your fever has gone.* I hope I'm right about that. I'm kind of new to this healer/empath thing.

Yes, the symptoms were very short-lived, my mother think-says. *But I'm not allowed out of quarantine until I return a negative test. This morning's test was still positive.*

Quarantine where? Here?

Apparently. She shows me a thought-image of her room, which is sparsely furnished, with a single bed, a desk and a chair. *Along with everyone else who has been at the Apollo facility or anywhere near me in the past week. And . . .*

And? There's no need to log into a newsreel or turn on the e-screen, not when I can get it straight from Mum's mind. *Oh. Crap.* New cases of non-sexually transmitted Riva have been detected not only in Auckland, but in Rotorua and Wellington.

Yes, my mother confirms. *It's everywhere. Turns out I may not have contracted Riva off one of my samples. It's just as likely I picked it up from going to the same supermarket as an infected person. More so, in fact, because I wasn't wearing gloves and a mask in the supermarket.*

Damn. I can't even begin to imagine all the implications of that right now. Probably it's better I don't, because as far as I'm concerned Riva is currently an inconvenience; something to get in the way of what I'm really meant to be doing.

Something's nagging at me, though. Something kind of major.

When Mum's thought-stream turns pink, I know she's read exactly what I was thinking. *No*, she think-says. *We can't. Sure, we might heal a few people before the healing itself kills us . . . but we can't cure a whole epidemic or, God forbid, a pandemic.*

I grit my teeth. *OK. What about me and Fox then? Can we go home?*

Not until you've returned another negative test. The incubation period is about five days, so you've got to stay for at least that long.

I groan, rest my head against the pillow.

And hear a voice think-say, very distinctly, very clearly: *The only way to beat Billy Raven is to play him at his own game. Do you understand what I'm saying?*

I jump.

What's up? Mum think-asks. I glance at the heart monitor, which of course is no longer registering anything since I removed the electro-dots. I bet she can tell my heart is beating triple-time, though.

The voice is still there, a whisper deep within my dream-flow: *There is someone else you need to seek*.

Nothing, I think-say, blocking her, while wondering why my father is communicating with me rather than my mum. Or is he? Maybe it's just another memory-echo, my mind playing tricks on me after my first-ever healing attempt.

Correction, second-ever, if Mum is right about me healing Indigo's head back when she was being held in the research facility.

Someone far, far worse. The echo has turned into a reverberation, shaking me to my core. Resisting the urge to clutch my head, I think-say, *Do you think it'd be OK for me to have a shower?*

I don't see why not. I'll check in with you later. My mother's mind is already moving on to other matters, most of which have the word *Riva* associated with them.

Which is lucky for me, because I'm damned if I'm going to stick around here for another five days. If I do, then I could lose both Indigo and my father forever.

I stand in the shower for ten minutes, listening out for any more messages, trying my best to send one back to my dad, if that's who it was: *What do you mean someone far worse? Where are you?* But there's nothing, the echo gone.

Damn it, I need to talk to Indigo. Not only that, but I need to be there to protect her against Raven, or whoever else might be hunting her. I sit on the tiles, slowing my breathing while I focus on my destination. The *shift* this time is easy, almost effortless.

What I'm not expecting is to get socked in the face the second I appear.

'Jesus.' I stumble backwards, my hand clamped to my nose, which is streaming with what I'm figuring must be blood, although it's too dark to see. I know Indigo was mad at me when I last saw her, but this is a bit extra. Has she been talking to Brie?

I hear a muffled curse, followed by *You could have warned me that you were coming*. Indigo clamps her palm over my mouth. *Ssh. They'll hear us.*

Who?

The BSI. I got a major telling-off today for you being here. And then — oh, gross, are you bleeding?

Um, yes? I duck into the bathroom, where I try to clean myself up, which isn't easy in the dark. From what Indigo has just said, it sounds like turning on the lights would be a very bad idea. *How do they know I was here?* I think-ask. *Hidden cameras?*

Or, at the very least, hidden microphones. Indigo's thought-stream is green with remorse. *I didn't break it, did I?*

I prod the bridge of my nose. *I don't think your right hook is that good. Maybe you should tell your instructors that you need to work on that.* Feeling a wet flannel touch my cheek, I take it from her. *Who did you think I was?*

Who do you think? I thought my blocker had stopped working. I don't know why I'm bothering with that, though. Billy knows exactly where I am.

I want to ask whose fault *that* is, but don't really feel like getting whacked again. *Let's go somewhere else for a bit*, I think-say. *I need to talk to you.*

Such as where?

Somewhere safer than here. I show her what I'm thinking.

Indigo gives me a thought-shrug. *Guess it's not as if I could get in any more trouble. What do you think the chances are of us ending up in the same time and place, though?*

Maybe if we, uh, you know, hold each other, then we won't get separated?

Perfect, she think-answers, obviously choosing to ignore the self-conscious ripple in my thought-stream. She wraps her arms around my waist, her head nestling beneath my elbow because I'm still holding my nose. Sliding my free arm around her, I rest my chin on top of her head.

Ready? I think-ask.

Ready, she think-answers, as our thought-streams plait together, as our dream-flows merge and we *shift—*

Out of the compound, out of 2067, and into November 2066.

TWENTY-FIVE:
BILLY

2088

A week later, I sat in a capsule orbiting the Eternity Tower. Across the other side of the table was Andromeda, dressed in an iridescent blue dress that matched her current eye colour — which, as I'd learned, changed most days.

'They're Fun-Lenses,' she'd told me. 'You can have any colour or pattern you want. Wait until you see the Spirals.'

Tonight was the first time that the Eternity Project had deemed her safe to leave the Eternity Tower — as long as she was under my watch, that was. I'd had to work at persuading Newton on that one, but he was remarkably pliable once I'd managed to convince Andromeda to give one more sample of stem cells. I had a Tranq Gun stowed in my trousers pocket in case things got out of hand, but I was pretty sure I wouldn't have to use it. Not when Andromeda had so much invested in our relationship.

Just one more sample, I'd told her. I promise. The infusion would be enough to boost me until I carried out the last step in my plan, not that Andromeda knew where her stem cells had ended up. The Eternity Project, understandably, had been a little iffy about transfusing the next sample of precious cells into my veins, but I'd reassured them that there would be plenty more coming their way.

We were dining at the same restaurant Newton had taken me to when we first met. I drank Ozone, collected black pearls from salty oysters, held Andromeda's hand and gazed into her eyes as she told me what I needed to know.

'She's not Aurelia yet,' Andromeda said, once we'd finished the main course.

'What do you mean?'

'Exactly what I said.' She sucked Coke-X through a glass straw. 'The girl you're looking for is Katerina. Her friends call her Kat. She's currently seventeen years old.' She slipped her hand out of mine. 'You're going to stir up all sorts of trouble, though.'

'Really?' I murmured, glancing at the pod to my left, where a boy who looked like a younger version of the clone-waiters was dining with a pair of middle-aged women.

'Really. If Newton finds out, he'll probably want to kill you.'

'Is that right?' I stroked her thigh. 'I'm intrigued.'

Andromeda slapped me away as if I were a mosquito. 'If I were you, I'd be very, very careful.'

'Newton told me he didn't know who Aurelia was.'

'That's right,' she said, her thought-stream rippling with annoyance. 'Like I said, she's not Aurelia yet.'

'So who is Kat to Newton, then?' The door behind me hissed open, and I leaned back to let a waiter deposit our dessert in front of us. The Hell Pudding was my favourite.

Once the waiter had lit the dessert, and the flames had died down, Andromeda said, 'Did Miles ever tell you where he grew up?'

I shrugged. 'I just assumed it was around here.' His accent was similar to mine.

She scooped a piece of poached pear onto her spoon. 'Wrong.'

'How did I know you were going to say that?' It certainly wasn't through reading her mind. Her block was granite-solid.

Ignoring that, Andromeda said, 'He was born to a virally optimised couple residing in the Cook Islands.'

'The Cook Islands.' I stared at her. 'But . . . that's where Aurelia is from.'

'Exactly.' She gave me a joyless smile. 'Katerina's surname is Newton.'

My mouth fell open. 'Kat is Newton's sister? But . . . you said she was seventeen. He's thirty-six.' At least, that was what he'd told me.

'Big age gap, yeah. Kat was a surprise pregnancy, especially after Riva swept around the globe. Kat's led quite a sheltered life.' Andromeda's eyes glittered at me. 'And she's insanely jealous of her older brother, or she was.'

'Why?'

'Because they share the same father, but not the same mother. Her mother is a normal, and Kat hasn't inherited the same abilities as Miles. She can read the thoughts of others, but that's it. No shape-shifting, and definitely no time travel, as illegal as it is.' She twirled her straw in her glass. 'What's the most valued commodity here, Billy Raven?'

'Fertility,' I said. 'And immortality.'

'That's right.' She pushed her plate aside. 'Miles loves his little sister. He promised her a very special gift for her eighteenth birthday. What do you think that was?'

It didn't take my newly charged brain long to work that one out. 'I think I can guess,' I said. 'But if he loves her so much, why can't he give her a sample of his own stem cells?'

She shrugged. 'Didn't work — probably because *his* father is half-normal as well.'

'So you're the purebred, then?' So much for only using Andromeda's cells for Grace so far. I wondered if there was anyone else who'd benefited from Andromeda's first stem-cell collection.

'A dubious honour, I'm sure.' Andromeda raised an eyebrow at me. 'Still want to meet her?'

And I said, 'More than ever.'

TWENTY-SIX:
RIGEL

Indigo and I are hanging out in her bedroom, eating chips while pretending to study. I'm lounging on the floor, half-listening to the drum of rain on the roof, half-listening to her tell me for the umpteenth time why she's not going to university. And yet, something is . . . off, in a way I can't explain.

Not until Indigo leans forward and says, 'At least your nose isn't bleeding anymore.'

'Wh—' I gape at her and then *whoosh*, the future Rigel has woken up and is redirecting past-Rigel's thought-stream. Indigo is sitting cross-legged on her bed, while I'm in the usual spot, sitting on a large cushion on the floor, leaning against the wall. 'It worked.'

'Of course it worked.' Indigo swings her legs over the bed. She's wearing tiny shorts and a bikini top that leaves uncovered her pierced belly-button, just like last time we were here. It's not usually the sort of detail I'd remember, but I remember *that* day.

Blocking her from the direction my thought-stream's veering in, I say, 'What do you think the chances are of us returning to exactly the moment we left?'

Indigo hesitates, shakes her head. 'I'm not sure. I mean, I'm getting better at this but . . . time's a bit wobbly, you know?'

'Yeah.' I push my fingers through my hair, which has reverted to its native ash-blond colour. 'I know.' The rain is coming down faster than when we first arrived. I move to the window, staring at the water sliding down the street. 'Did it flood last time?'

'No.' She's standing beside me now. 'Fox said you healed him.'

'I hope so.'

'Are you OK?'

I glance at her. 'Kind of. My heart went a bit crazy but it's . . .' I hesitate. I was about to say, *it's OK now*, but it's not. Not when she's standing so close, her jasmine scent driving me to distraction. I'm remembering the last time we were in this room, in this moment. I'd been plucking up the courage to kiss her, or failing that, at least ask her out, when she'd lobbed her grenade.

We've been hanging out in bars and clubs all over London . . . Last night I hung out with this guy who bought me top-shelf Champagne and danced with me as if I was the most beautiful girl in the world.

'I broke up with Brie,' I say.

'Oh.' She moves away slightly, putting a thin slice of air between us. 'How did that go?'

'Badly. As in, *really* badly.' Anxious to change the subject, I say, 'What are we going to do?'

She perches on the windowsill. 'Billy Raven's coming to get me. There's nothing we can do about that.'

'We could hide you.' I roll my lower lip between my teeth. 'Take you to another time. Isn't that what he's done with Andromeda?'

'Yeah, but then what? I leave you to try and fight him by yourself? I don't think so.' Indigo goes silent for a moment. 'I need him to think I'm sorry for what I've done. I need him to think I'm ready to surrender myself to him, so he doesn't even know what's coming when we go to do it again.'

'What? Kill him? He's already shown us *that's* impossible.' The rain has eased up. All I can hear is the dripping of water off the spouting outside. That, and the erratic beating of my heart. I tell myself it's because I'm standing too close to her. The alternative — that my heart might have sustained permanent damage — is both too scary and too inconvenient to contemplate.

'Only because we didn't do it right the first time. It's something to do with this Eternity Loop, right? If we break that, then maybe we can break him.'

I sink down beside her. 'Do you think it's anything to do with this Aurelia girl you saw in Billy Raven's memory?'

Indigo rubs her arms. 'A boy called Billy Quick kisses a girl who says she'll see him in a hundred years . . .' Her head snaps up. 'That's it, isn't it? This girl Aurelia, whoever she is, travelled back in time and somehow turned him into Billy Raven.'

'So she's some kind of time vampire, too?'

'She must be. So maybe if we get rid of her, then he'd have never been created in the first place.'

'You make that sound so easy.'

'Of course it won't be easy. I'll have to get more clues from him so you can track her down.'

'So *we* can track her down, you mean.'

Indigo sighs and moves back to her bed. 'No, Rigel, *you*. I'll be with Billy, remember?' She gives me a sad smile. 'Do you really think he's going to let me go that easily?'

'But . . . that's insane!' I explode.

'Rigel, what planet are you on? I told you he's coming for me. There's nothing I can do to stop it. And even if there was, I wouldn't, because I'm his weakness — potentially his *only* weakness.'

'But how are we going to communicate with each other?'

She spreads her hands, think-says, *Like this?*

'But what if we can't? What if he traps you in another time, another dimension even?'

Impatience fizzes through her thought-stream. *'What if, what if.* No one ever got anywhere by saying *what if.'*

'How about this *what if?'* I ask, opening up my dream-flow so she can see the memory of the last time we were here. *Here you go, Indy, have it all. This is what I wished I'd done, what I wished I'd said.*

Indigo goes very still. 'Are you serious?'

'No,' I say. Then: 'Do you think I would *joke* about something like that? Do you know—' I shake my head, blocking her again. No, I can't say that. I can't tell her that I feel guilty for not telling her about my feelings for her sooner; that if I had, then this whole Billy thing might never have happened. How do I know she'd have felt the same way anyway?

'Rigel,' she whispers, moving back towards me.

'Forget it,' I mumble. What am I thinking? This is the girl who's been seduced by a vampire, the girl who had businessmen buying her top-shelf Champagne and—

Oh. I tense, then relax as her arms come around my neck, as her lips settle on mine.

I'm sorry I was angry with you the other day, she think-says. Me, I'm lost for words, even in my mind. Because the kiss is happening just the way it should have two months ago, except two months ago is *now*. The second I think *that*, something weird happens, like a *click* in my head, and the off-kilter feeling I've had ever since we arrived in this room disappears.

I kiss her back, a groan escaping when she nips my lower lip with her teeth. *Sorry*, she think-says, and I say *Don't stop*. So we *don't* stop, because we both know this could be the last time we ever see each other — no, don't think that — and soon enough, we're lying on the bed. I can't help thinking that this isn't the first time I've been in this position with Indigo, although last time I was in Billy Raven's body rather than my own, my actions beyond my control.

'Stop thinking,' Indigo murmurs.

'I will if you will,' I say, kissing the side of her neck before think-adding, *I think that's what my English teacher used to call a double entendre.*

Indigo laughs, then sucks in a breath when I move my lips to the hollow between her collarbones. I loosen the strings on her bikini top, cup the curve of her breast. *I love you*, I think-say. *No matter what happens next, I'll always love you.*

Always, she think-replies. The rain intensifies, like our breathing, like our heartbeats. Soon enough, we've removed the rest of our clothes. Soon enough, we're moving together, at last, at last. All I can think is *This is what was meant to happen, this was always meant to happen*, and we don't stop. No, we don't stop until it's over and we're lying, skin-to-skin, our breath mingling, our thought-streams running clear.

'Oh God,' Indigo says and starts to cry. I guess that's when it finally hits her how much we both have to lose if it goes wrong.

'It's OK,' I say. 'It's OK, it's OK.' Because that's what you say even when everything is hopeless.

We stay there for a few more minutes, lying in each other's arms, before she says, resignedly, 'I guess we'd better go back, huh?'

'Yeah,' I say, knowing the BSI have probably got a search party out for me even as we speak. We hold each other tight, concentrating our dream-flows down, then set our course.

I'm mid-*shift* when it happens — a pain in my chest, followed by an explosion in my head.

I never even saw it coming.

TWENTY-SEVEN:
BILLY

I was greeted at the hotel by a chorus of workers singing and playing ukulele. A lei was draped around my neck, a fruit mocktail brought to me on a tray.

'Kia orana,' the skinny Cook Islands porter said. He was wearing a blue uniform and walked with a limp. The badge on his breast said *Sunny*, like his smile, like the sun-drenched lagoon just outside the window. 'How was your flight?'

'Very comfortable,' I said, although whole-body *shifting* meant I'd never have to set foot on a plane again.

'No suitcase?' Sunny asked.

'It's coming,' I lied. I didn't need a suitcase, not when I could *shift* back to my London apartment within seconds. My stem-cell transplant was working well, although I had no idea how long it would last.

Once in my room, I spent a few minutes taking in my surroundings — white sand, turquoise sea, a line of white-tipped waves on the reef that rimmed the island. Rarotonga. Paradise. She was there, I knew it. I could smell her from here, roses and rain.

After a brunch of pancakes with mango and papaya, I strolled along the beach, my feet splashing through the shallows. The sun sparkled across the water. I saw purple starfish, tubular sea slugs, bone-white coral. *Her* scent drew me on, towards the next resort, which I knew was run by her family. I was approaching a couple sunbathing on towels when *it* happened, a blurring-tilting. I tasted Champagne. I heard my own voice: *You know I never miss a Grammy awards event*, and a woman answering, *No, you never do.* Another voice, one I'd never heard before, said *I'm happy we're alone now*, and in the periphery of my vision, I saw bright lights, an oversized Ferris wheel.

I stumbled and went down on one knee. Blink. The lagoon returned. All I could see was blue sea, white sand, palm trees. All I could hear were mynah birds, waves spilling onto the sand, the wind stirring palm fronds. What had happened then? A hallucination? Or was it a memory of something that hadn't happened yet, a time echo?

'You all right, mate?' a tanned youth said from behind me. He was with a slender girl with very long blonde hair and a tapered nose. Roses and rain, a rose tattoo on her neck, and her eyes, her eyes.

The bluest I've ever seen, the colour of tropical island lagoons.

I stood up, brushing sand off my knee. 'Yes, I just tripped over a rock,' I said. 'I wasn't watching where I was going.' Her nostrils flared, and I realised she had sensed me, too. I opened my dream-flow, letting the memory of her own voice echo at her: *We're one and the same, you and me.*

The girl let out a squeak. Her companion's forehead creased. 'What's up, Kat?'

'Oh, I think I — stepped on a shell.' She sat in the sand to massage her non-injured foot.

She was blocking me by then, but I could still detect the magenta hue of her thought-stream; surprise and confusion and something else, too. It was the golden glow I got from most women once I directed my smile at them, but with Kat

I didn't even have to do that.

I moved forward and knelt beside her. 'Do you want me to have a look?'

'Are you a doctor or something?' Her companion sounded less friendly now. No surprise, considering I was about to seduce the girl he was secretly in love with.

'I used to work as a paramedic.' I took her foot onto my thigh. When I ran my thumb over the pearly sole of her foot, I sensed her quiver, detected the naked twist of her thought-stream.

Who are you? she think-asked.

I'm your destiny, I think-answered, having already discerned that her friend was a normal, an island boy named Rua.

'Just a scratch.' I released her foot and helped her up. 'Enjoy the rest of your walk.'

'You, too,' Rua mumbled, taking off so fast that Kat had to jog after him.

Wait, Kat think-said to me, even though to the outside world she had already forgotten me, having caught up to Rua, who was busy telling her how she needed to be careful about 'the paedo creeps who sift around here'. *When will I see you again?*

Tonight, I think-said. *Eleven pm. I'll meet you right here . . . and everything will become clear.*

She didn't ask for my name. She didn't need to.

That evening I sat beneath a palm tree, watching the silver-tipped waves crash into the reef. The moon was riding high and full. My heart was beating a crazy rhythm. *Her* scent was driving me mad, even though she was still a kilometre away, preparing to sneak out of her room.

I had a partial block up, so that the only person I could communicate with was Kat. I'd picked up on the hum of her parents sleeping close by; her virally optimised father could stop us meeting in a heartbeat.

I could hear that, too — *her* heartbeat. I stood up, clenching and unclenching my fists. I was wearing a white short-sleeved shirt that showed off my tanned skin, shorts, no shoes. The girl walking towards me was wearing a white sleeveless dress that came halfway down her thighs, a thin silver chain around her ankle.

Kat slowed when she saw me, twisting her hands together. I didn't blame her for being wary. Staying where I was, I thought-said, *What's your favourite animal, Kat?*

She halted completely, her thought-stream wavering. *I like dogs*, she think-said. *Especially Siberian huskies.*

Imagine if you could shift *into one*, I thought-said, and heard an intake of breath as I did just that. I sat on my haunches and held up a paw. *Don't be frightened. I won't hurt you.*

Her eyes glittered at me. *My father could hurt* you, *though. I could call for him right now.*

Of course. Do you want to?

No. She curled an arm around a tree trunk.

I tried to regulate my breathing, unable to remember the last time I had been that nervous. *Does the name Aurelia mean anything to you?*

'Where did you hear that name?' Kat asked.

'Where did *you* hear that name?' I countered, after *shifting* back into human form.

She wrapped her arms around herself. 'She's like my . . . alter-ego. The person I dream of being if I ever get off this island.'

'Off this island?' I raked my fingers through my hair. 'If you can *shift*, then you can travel anywhere you please.'

'I can't shift yet. Anyway, it's way too dangerous.'

'Because . . . ?'

'Because I might come across people who want to hurt me, exploit me.' Her thought-stream flared.

'People like me?' I bit my lip. 'Who do you think I am, Kat?'

'I don't know. But sometimes, in my dreams . . .' Trailing off, she sat next to me. 'I feel as though I've met you before. As if this has all happened before.'

'It's called fate.' I wasn't lying. This had to happen, had already happened. *See you in a hundred years, Billy Raven*, past-Aurelia whispered in my memory. But not too fast. I couldn't risk her bolting, couldn't risk her running to her parents. 'Tell me something about yourself, Kat,' I said. 'Something no one else knows.'

Kat was silent for a moment. Then she said, 'I wish I could escape myself. I wish I could become someone else.'

'Yes,' I said. 'I know exactly what that's like.'

She turned to face me. 'How old are you, Billy Raven?'

'Well,' I said, slowly, carefully, 'when I first met you, I was sixteen years old.'

'And now?'

'It's irrelevant.' I dared to trail a finger down the side of her cheek, felt a tremor ripple through her. 'Age is irrelevant for people like you and me.'

Her eyes fixed on mine. 'I feel as though we've done this before.'

'We have,' I said. 'But this will still be your first kiss . . . right?'

Kat didn't answer, but she let me tip her chin towards me, let me lower my lips onto hers. Her mouth was soft and sweet, like a plum, and she tasted like Aurelia, just like Aurelia.

'Oh,' she whispered when I moved my mouth to her earlobe, her neck, the pulse at the base of her throat. Our thought-streams were winding together, so close that her waves of ecstasy were becoming mine.

'Welcome back, Aurelia,' I said, lowering her into the sand.

Her blood was just as sweet as the rest of her.

TWENTY-EIGHT:
INDIGO

___

I realise something is wrong as soon as we arrive back in my room at the BSI. It's dark, but Rigel is gurgling, as though he's about to choke.

'Oh my God.' Not caring who might see us, I leap off the bed and flip on the light. There's blood trickling from his nose — my fault, yes — but also from the corner of his mouth.

Indigo. It's Violet, her thought-stream sparking with panic. *Is Rigel with you? Is he OK?*

Yes, I think-say, and then, as he begins to fit, his arms and legs jerking in a horrid rhythm: *No. No, we need help* right now. I fling open my door, yelling 'Help!'

It seems to take forever for anyone to arrive, even though it's probably less than a minute; Harvey and my fitness instructor, followed by one of the research doctors.

'Holy shit,' the research doctor says, after lifting one of Rigel's eyelids. 'He's blown a pupil. Call an ambulance.'

There are two voices in my head, Auntie Violet saying *Indigo, please, what's going on? Is he OK?* And another one, too, the last person I need to hear from right now, and he's saying *what's done cannot be undone.*

No, I think-say. *No, please, leave us alone.* I sink to my knees, tears rolling down my cheeks. Rigel's injuries are serious, that much is obvious from the turbulent flow of the doctor's thought-stream. The doctor's thinking *serious head injury or some kind of stroke.* He's thinking *probably irreversible.* He's thinking *I hope he doesn't arrest because I can't remember when I last had to do CPR.*

I try to go to Rigel's side, but hands hold me back. There are more people in the room now, a clamour of voices. A siren. Running feet. And as I'm pushed into the corridor, into the arms of the vampire who has come for me, the last image I have of Rigel is of his chalky white face, bloody foam bubbling out of his mouth.

TWENTY-NINE:
BILLY

2088

After that, I saw Kat most nights. The nights I wasn't visiting her, she was coming to me . . . in my London apartment. Turned out she didn't need her brother's birthday present to *shift* after all. Turned out she only needed me.

'I don't want you to call me Kat anymore,' she told me after the first week. 'I'm always going to be Aurelia when I'm around you.'

'You're always going to be Aurelia, full-stop.' We were lying in my bed, our discarded clothes on the floor. 'From now on.'

Aurelia flopped onto her back. 'Not in the Cook Islands, I'm not. I can't wait until I turn eighteen and can leave forever.'

'Why wait until you're eighteen? There's no time like the present.' I trailed a finger down her cheek. 'In my world, time is irrelevant.'

'In your world, everything is irrelevant.'

'You're anything but irrelevant.' I kissed her, knowing she was experiencing the same rush as me. Oh, how I'd craved that feeling all those years we'd been apart. Yet now that we'd been reunited, the yearning in the hours we spent apart was worse than ever. 'You are everything to me,' I whispered.

'You have no idea how much trouble I'll be in if we're found together,' she replied, but she was yielding to me, just as I was yielding to her — day by day, hour by hour.

'I won't let anyone hurt you,' I said. 'We're forever, you and me.'

'Forever,' she said, and then it was *her* teeth piercing *my* neck, *my* blood spilling down *her* throat. Our hearts thundered and surged, peaked and ebbed.

I was so happy. So happy, that I was willing to do anything Andromeda asked in return for helping me find Aurelia.

An hour later, I kissed Aurelia goodbye, showered and dressed for dinner. It was two weeks since I'd rediscovered Aurelia, and as far as I was concerned I could live in that happy bubble forever.

But of course nothing ever stays the same. It was time to face up to Andromeda, to discover what my side of the bargain would be.

'You want to *what*?' I asked as a clone set an ostrich omelette in front of me. The omelette was strangely delicious, especially when served with truffle oil.

'You heard me.' Andromeda sucked on her Coke-X. 'I want to go back to 2055. I'll need to hide there, which means I'll need something to stop me from being detected by anyone like us.'

'But why 2055?' Was that an especially good year? I wondered. Was there an equivalent of Woodstock or something?

'Because,' she said patiently, 'it's a good eleven years before the Riva pandemic started. Which means . . .'

'You'll be able to have sex without being infected.'

She glared at me. 'That's not what it's all about. Do you even care about the fate of the human race?' She held up a hand. 'Don't answer that. It's a rhetorical question.'

'Of course I don't care. I'm a complete hedonist.' I leaned forward. 'Let me guess, you want to try and stop the Riva pandemic before it even starts.'

'Yes.' Andromeda prodded a vege nugget with her fork.

'And then what?'

'What do you mean, and then what?'

'What's in it for you?'

Andromeda looked as mystified as I felt. 'OK, so let's say you really don't give a shit . . . consider this. If no one does anything, then the human race will be wiped out within the next one to two generations.'

'You've got those,' I said, waving my knife at a clone, who merely gave me a benign smile and took my empty glass from me.

'Would you like another one, sir?' it asked.

'Please.'

'Clones are not going to help us when we need new treatments for cancer, new vaccines for the next deadly virus,' she said. 'Clones aren't going to come up with new solutions for climate change.'

'Clones aren't going to start wars,' I said. 'And I'm pretty sure AI can solve a lot of the problems you're thinking of.'

'What about art? And theatre, and music?'

'I can time-travel for those. I could even listen to Beethoven play live.' I gave her a slow smile. 'As can you, if you choose.'

'I don't.' Andromeda crossed her arms. 'I found Aurelia for you. Now I need you to fulfil your end of the deal.'

I nodded at the clone as it set my next drink on the table, swirled my straw in the glass. 'I never said I wouldn't. Tell me what you want and I'll make it happen.'

'I need you to transport me to 2055. Not just that, I need you to *hide* me in 2055.'

I gave her a steady look. 'To do that would require hiding your thought-stream.'

'A blocker,' she said. 'Simple.'

'Preferably an implant,' I said, mulling that over. 'Do you know how much grief I'll get if you slip their clutches?'

'Well,' she said. 'You knew that was going to happen sooner or later. And you have Aurelia . . . right?'

'Yes,' I said, a warm glow suffusing me, not just from the Sunset Boulevard I was sipping on. 'Yes, I do.'

THIRTY:
INDIGO

When I wake, I am lying in a soft bed beneath a thick duvet and a grey light is filling the room. Scraps of memories float through my untethered thought-stream. Rigel, his nose streaming blood. Rigel holding me in his arms, his lips on my ear. Rigel, gurgling and fitting, bloody foam bubbling out of his mouth. A man with raven-dark hair, his face altered but his eyes and voice instantly familiar.

Are you surprised to see me? You shouldn't be.

A sob catching in my throat, I sit bolt upright. There is an eerie hush, as if the world outside has been muffled. When I look outside the window, I see why. Snow falling on snow, and beyond that, snow falling on water; a lake. Am I in Norway again? The bedroom is completely different, though, with a low ceiling and wallpaper. It's furnished with a large Turkish-style rug, a dressing table with an oval mirror and a free-standing wardrobe.

What's done cannot be undone.

I cast around for Billy. It doesn't take me long to locate his thought-stream. He's close, but where?

'Right here.' Billy is sitting on the end of my bed, as if he had been there all along. The coat-tails and hat have gone, replaced by blue jeans and a long-sleeved t-shirt with a picture of a band on the front. 'U2,' he says, catching the direction of my gaze, or hooking directly into my thought-stream, most likely. 'They're Irish.'

'We're in Ireland?'

'No, the Scottish Highlands. Same day and month as when we left London, but we've gone back a few years.' He smiles. 'It's 2019, in case you were wondering. I can take you to a castle if you like.'

'A castle?' I can't believe he's talking about taking me sight-seeing when Rigel is dying. Dying? He could already be dead, for all I know. 'Where is he?' I ask, blocking Billy before he can delve any further into my mind than he already has.

'If you're talking about Rigel, then I assume he's been taken to hospital.' Billy's eyes rove over me. 'Don't look so distressed. I'm sure he'll be well taken care of. We recover much faster than normals, hmm?' He stands up and tugs open a dresser drawer. 'I hope you'll find some clothes to your liking in here. Size ten, right?'

'How long will we stay here?' I ask.

'Why, as long as we like. Once we get bored, we'll move on.' So casual, as if I hadn't injected him with deadly venom two months ago. 'Oh, my beautiful moon,' he says, sitting beside me, 'I do hope you're not thinking of murdering me again.'

Acutely aware that I mustn't let my duplicitous undercurrent show — and yet, I have to give him some explanation for my change in behaviour — I say, 'Rigel and Andromeda convinced me that you were evil. I don't know what came over me.' It's not hard to bring tears to my eyes. All I have to do is think about Rigel. 'When the three of us merged our minds, something awful happened. I wasn't even myself anymore. I was completely under their control.' I swallow. 'Rigel's been trying to control me ever since.'

Billy's pupils are huge, his irises yellow, as if he is about to *shift* into wolf form. I feel his thought-tendrils probing at my thought-stream, trying to detect any falsehood in my explanation. 'We need to make you strong enough to resist if that ever happens again,' he says finally.

'I want to be stronger,' I say, and *that's* not a lie.

'I'll help you.' He takes my hand and raises it to his lips. 'But remember this: you are my mate and I can sniff you out from centuries away. Do you understand?'

'I understand,' I whisper, trying not to flinch when Billy curls his fingers around the back of my neck and presses his lips against mine — a slow, lingering kiss, just like the ones he used to always give me.

I'm going to have to be a master of deception to get through this. There's only one person I ever want to kiss again, and now he might be dead.

The Hunter has fallen. No, it can't be true.

Billy draws back. His irises are onyx-dark again, his skin aglow. So handsome. So deadly. 'I love you,' he says. 'But I promise you, if you try to kill me again then you'll wish you'd never been born.'

A shiver ripples through me. There's no response I can give him that won't sound like a lie. Instead, I say, 'Is there a bathroom here? I'd love to have a shower.'

And Billy, ever the gentleman, says, 'Certainly. Come right this way.'

As the water cascades over me, I wonder how long I'm going to be able to fend off Billy's advances. Making sure my block is firmly in place, I mull over my options. What's to stop me *shifting* out of here right now? Would Billy be able to stop me? Maybe he wouldn't be able to stop me, but I know for sure he'll come after me.

You are my mate and I can sniff you out from centuries away. Do you understand?

I reach for the bar of soap and rub it over my breasts, my stomach and down my thighs. It took three of us to defeat Billy last time — me, Rigel and Andromeda. What makes me think I could do this by myself? And where has Andromeda gone anyway?

Squirting shampoo into my palm, I remember the last thing Andromeda said to Rigel and me, right before she left us in nineteenth-century Mississippi: *We'll meet again, all of us, I promise.* A promise — or a prophecy?

The bathroom door opens, making me jump. Billy doesn't knock first. Of course he doesn't. I'm his, or at least he thinks I am.

'Trying to drown yourself?' He's unbuttoning his shirt, unzipping his jeans.

'I'm done,' I say, turning the tap off, even though I've barely washed the shampoo out of my hair. 'It's all yours.'

'Anyone would think you're trying to avoid me,' he murmurs, stepping towards me.

I wrap a towel around myself. 'I'm really tired. I don't know, I think I might be coming down with something.'

'Well, rest up, my darling moon.' He kisses me. 'I've got so much to show you.' As I pad down the carpeted hallway to the bedroom, I feel his thought-tendrils curling around mine, nudging at my block. *If you'll only open yourself to me fully*, he think-says, *I'll give you the world. I promise.*

Shivering, I flee into the bedroom and curl beneath the bedcovers. I *do* feel sick, a creeping nausea that seems to have worsened since I first woke. Not only that, but I feel as if my soul has been invaded. Trying to keep my block in place — Billy seems to have retreated for now — I unfurl my alternative thought-stream, my undercurrent, and begin to scan. I'm looking for *her*, Andromeda, the mysterious silver-blonde girl with the cats-eye ring.

Andromeda, I think-send. *I don't know where you are, or if you're even still alive . . . but we need your help.*

The effort of trying to do that while maintaining a block on my main thought-stream is exhausting, so exhausting that my head does start to hurt. Not only that, but there's a pain in my chest.

'Indigo?' Billy is sitting beside me, having appeared without warning as usual. 'Are you all right?'

I gaze up at him, gasp . . . and pass out.

Voices move in and out of my semi-consciousness.

'Didn't realise he was . . . subarachnoid haemorrhage and massive heart attack . . . no idea, maybe a vasculitis of some sort . . . history of arrhythmias . . .'

My head is pounding, and there's an iron fist wrapped around my heart. I can't breathe. I can't breathe, but my lungs are inflating and deflating and there's something in my throat . . . a tube?

'Hello?' a voice says. Whoever it belongs to sounds older, male, authoritative. 'I've got an eighteen-year-old male, Offspring and BSI operative. We need to arrange transfer to a neurosurgical unit ASAP . . . Well, he probably won't, but we need to at least try . . .'

Can't move. Can't breathe. Can't even open my eyes. Fingers touch my forehead.

'Such a shame,' a female voice says. 'So young.'

He? Where am I? Who am . . . ? Realisation floods through me. Eighteen-year-old. BSI operative. Offspring. I'm in Rigel's body, and he's sick, so sick, but still alive. What's a subarachnoid haemorrhage anyway?

'Great, we'll be on standby,' the voice says. 'Well, no, I think he's screwed, but he *is* Offspring, so who knows?'

Rigel, I think-say. *Rigel, can you hear me?* All I get is a very faint, very distant hum. Desperate, I dive into the closest thought-stream I can find, which appears to belong to the doctor speaking on the phone. From that, I rapidly work out that a subarachnoid haemorrhage is a bleed into the brain due to a burst aneurysm, an outpouching of a brain artery, and that an MI is medical speak for a heart attack.

I work out that Rigel is in a coma.

I work out that Rigel, even if he doesn't die, will likely never walk or talk again.

Rigel, I think-try again. *Rigel, please, you can't abandon me now. I need—*

A thought-vine curls around me and reels me in so fast I think I might vomit.

A syrupy voice pours into my ear. 'Do you have any idea how dangerous that was, my Indigo Moon?'

My eyes fly open. Billy Raven's own eyes are like agate, dark and hard.

'If I were you,' he says, 'I'd stay well away from Rigel Fletcher, unless you want to be meted out a similar punishment.'

'Punishment?' I sit up, unable to stop the tears spilling down my cheeks. 'Why is he being punished? Did *you* do that?'

'No, my darling, I most certainly did not.' Billy reaches out and touches his fingers to my eyelids. 'Now sleep, my beautiful moon.'

'I don't need to—'

'Sleep,' he repeats, bringing his lips to the soft spot behind my ear. The pain is sharp, brief, and then I am sinking, my blood moving like treacle through my veins. 'Remember,' Billy says, as the darkness claims me once more, 'no one will ever love you like I do.'

THIRTY-ONE:
BILLY

2001

We woke to a blindingly bright day, as if the whole world outside our resort apartment had been bleached. White sand, glassy lagoon, and a thin layer of clouds that seemed only to intensify rather than dull the sun's glare.

'This,' I said as we stood side-by-side on the balcony in his-and-hers white flannel dressing gowns, 'has to be my favourite place in the world.' Aitutaki, the jewel of the Cook Islands, was like something out of a dream — the best dream I'd ever had.

Aurelia rested her elbows on the railing. 'Maybe next time we should go somewhere more exotic.' In her time, 2088, she'd only just gone to sleep for the night — or so her parents thought, unaware that their daughter had *shifted* to be with her lover.

'This is exotic enough for me.' I embraced her from behind, nuzzling her neck. 'Where else would you want to go?'

'How long have you got? Greece? The Maldives? Morocco?'

'Too many people,' I said. 'Although I guess if we travel back far enough in time, it won't be quite so crowded.'

'I don't mind a bit of people-watching.' Aurelia turned to face me. 'For someone who's meant to be so relaxed, there's a lot of worry going on in here.' She touched my temple.

Trying to hide my irritation, I released her. 'It's complicated.'

'No one ever has to know you helped Andromeda escape.'

'They're trusting me not to *let* her escape, whether I help her or not,' I said, watching a pair of kayakers glide past below. 'They'll chuck me out on my ear once that happens.'

'So? Who says you need to keep living in London anyway?' Aurelia clasped my shoulders, brought her lips to my ear. 'We can go wherever, *whenever* we want.'

'Of course.' But what if they came after me? I wasn't even sure I completely knew who *they* were. Apart from Miles Newton, I'd only met a few other employees at the Eternity Project, all of them normals.

'I think you're worrying for nothing,' Aurelia said. 'Get Andromeda out of there, hide her in 2055 or wherever it is she wants to go, and we can take off to France or Switzerland or something.' She darted her tongue into my ear and I felt the familiar rush of *her*, only her. Aurelia, my Aurelia, was nothing like the shy girl I'd encountered in Rarotonga only three weeks before.

I wound my fingers into her hair and kissed her roughly on the mouth. Wary of scaring the locals, we moved inside before we *shifted* into panther form, although they might have wondered at the animal snarls they heard floating out of the apartment. But if they couldn't see anything, they'd likely just shake their heads and smile. It was 2001 Aitutaki, and, as far as the resort staff were concerned, Mr and Mrs Raven were on their honeymoon.

Soon, I hoped, that would be true.

'Are you kidding?' Aurelia asked. It was later, much later on the same day; although technically it was now early evening, the last rays of sun bleeding into the horizon.

'Not kidding,' I said from my position on bent knee in front of her. We were on a remote beach on the other side of the island from our resort, our hired bikes propped against a tree.

'But Billy.' Aurelia knelt in front of me, her glossy locks falling over her eyes. 'I'm only seventeen.'

'Time is irrelevant, remember?' I pushed her hair away with one hand, still holding the box containing the ring in the other. It was a three-carat diamond set in white gold, one I'd stashed in my pocket before *shifting* from 2088 to 2001 with her. It was worth a hundred K, which in the grand scheme of things wasn't a lot for someone I was about to spend eternity with. Besides, it wasn't as if I'd been stupid enough to pay for it.

Shifting could come in handy, especially when fleeing jewellery-store security alarms in the middle of the night.

'Quite apart from anything else, if I start wearing that, my parents will be asking where it came from.'

I stood up, snapping the ring box closed. 'Come on, Aurelia. Don't you think it's time you left the Cooks and your parents for good?'

Aurelia rose slowly, her lower lip jutting out. 'I didn't say I never wanted to see them again.'

'I didn't say you shouldn't see them again. But if you're coming with me, you'll have to either tell them the truth or hide from them for the rest of your life.'

'Don't be angry with me,' she whispered.

'I'm not—' I tried to calm down. Aurelia was right. She was only seventeen. As far as she knew, we'd only been together three weeks.

'I just think I need to experience a bit more before I settle down,' she continued. 'You are the first person I've ever kissed, remember?'

'And the *only* person, I hope,' I said, and if she'd blocked me sooner, I wouldn't have seen it. But my telepathic processing had become much more rapid since I'd had the stem-cell procedure. '*What?*' It wasn't an image that flashed up so much as a cluster of sensations — a pair of firm lips, warmly toned skin, a muscular torso pressed against her breasts, the musky scent of male. Another male.

Aurelia leapt to her feet. 'It was only once,' she said quickly. 'I just wanted to see what it was like. It wasn't even good.'

I balled my fists, not even trying to contain my billowing rage. 'You cheated on me.'

'It was just a kiss!'

'Yeah? And what will it be next time? Just a *grope*? Just a *screw*?' I tugged the jewellery box out of my pocket and opened it again.

'Billy, *no*,' she cried, but it was too late. The diamond ring was already arcing over the tangerine-tinged water, twinkling in the dying sun. The splash of the ring entering the sea was distant, almost inaudible.

'If he ever touches you again,' I said, pointing a shaking finger at her, 'then I'll kill him. Understand?'

Aurelia opened her mouth and closed it again. She was still blocking me, but I sensed her own anger bubbling beneath. Anger and indignation, and a tinge of fear.

'Don't you *ever* speak to me like that again,' she said after a long few seconds in which the world seemed to have paused, the sun hovering on the curved rim of the horizon.

I whirled around and stomped up the sand to my bike, flung my leg over the crossbar and start pedalling furiously towards our resort.

Two hours later, I paced the small confines of our apartment. Where the hell had she got to? How much longer was she going to leave me fuming like this?

Aurelia, I thought-sent for about the third time. *I'm sorry. Can we talk about this?* I might as well have been flinging stones against a brick wall. Thinking of that made me remember the diamond ring I'd thrown into the lagoon. Perhaps some lucky snorkeller would come across it tomorrow. More likely, it would be swallowed up by a fish or buried beneath layers of sand on the sea floor, never to be seen again.

Aurelia must have gone home. Where else would she be?

I didn't say I never wanted to see them again.

I lay on the bed, *shifting* within the time it took for my heart to push out one stroke volume of blood. As far as I was concerned, Aurelia's parents were an inconvenience, people standing in the way of our happiness. But I wasn't going to touch them, wasn't going to risk going near her virally optimised father, who'd been using his powers for far longer than I had.

No, I was going to make sure Rua never went anywhere near Aurelia again.

I found him in 2088 Rarotonga, alone behind an abandoned vehicle-charging station. He was tossing a basketball through a hoop fastened to an uneven brick wall.

Rua barely made a sound as I brought him to the ground, a strangled cry that died as soon as I tore his larynx out with my panther teeth. I dragged him into the shadows to finish the job off, feeling my senses sharpen with each gulp of blood that slid down my throat. After that, I crouched beside his body until it was properly dark before dragging him deep into the bush to chew on his bones. Finally, I *shifted* into sea eagle form to drop pieces of him into the ocean, well beyond the reef rimming the island.

No one ever found his remains. There wasn't much left to find.

As for me, after that I was more powerful than ever.

And Aurelia?

Yes, Aurelia. We were in love. Remember that. People will do anything for love.

THIRTY-TWO:
RIGEL

I'm floating deep, submersed in inky blackness. There's pain in my head and in my heart, deep injuries that I don't know will ever heal. Words swirl, confetti-like, through the slow trickle of my thought-stream.

Forgotten your father already . . . not strong enough to fight him in your current form . . . think you can kill a time vampire . . . play him at his own game . . . someone else you need to seek . . . someone far, far worse.

My heart is going so fast, fast and irregular and weak, so weak. But there is another beat weaving through mine, another's breath in my lungs.

Rigel, can you hear me?

It's her, Indigo. How I wish I could respond, let her know I can hear her.

Rigel, please, you can't abandon me now. I need—

Just like that, she's gone, her heartbeat, too.

But no . . . no, if I concentrate, I can just make it out. Slow and steady, a scaffold for my own failing ventricles. It's all I have, the thinnest of tethers to hang on to.

And yet I fear that I am dying anyway, struck down by the very person my father warned me about.

Someone far, far worse than Billy Raven.

THIRTY-THREE:
BILLY

2001; 2088

My human blood meal, namely Rua, further enhanced my talents in all sorts of ways. The most valuable was that I no longer had to concentrate to hide my memories and conscious thought. Instead, I shuffled them all behind the permanent block I'd managed to erect in my rapidly evolving mind, which meant I had gained a very, very important ability: lying.

Of course, I'd been lying to people for years, but it wasn't so easy with virally optimised humans and their Offspring.

'Rua's gone missing,' Aurelia told me, two days after I'd dispensed with him.

'Has he?' We were in Aitutaki once more, sipping piña coladas on the balcony as if we'd never had a blazing argument two evenings before. She'd reappeared several hours after that fight, telling me she'd never kiss another guy again. Knowing that at the very least she'd never kiss Rua again, I'd told her I was sorry, too — for what, I wasn't entirely sure, but she seemed to like the apology.

'Yes. No one's seen him for two days.' Her thought-stream was blue with worry. 'Billy, you — you didn't—'

I clasped her knee. 'What did I tell you?'

'You said if he ever touched me again, you'd kill him.'

'And has he touched you again?'

She stared at me for a moment, then looked away. 'I haven't seen him in over a week.'

'There you go,' I said, ecstatic that she'd swallowed my lie.

'He surfs the breaks in the reef. People think maybe he drowned.' Aurelia sounded sad. I didn't want her to be sad.

I took her hand, raised it to my lips. 'How fraught it must be to be mortal,' I said. 'To always be fearful that death is around the corner. I can't imagine what it would be like to lose you.'

'Or I to lose you.' Her eyes shimmered. 'Promise me that will never happen.'

'I promise,' I said.

The following morning, in my 2088 London apartment, I donned a white shirt, a short-sleeved suit in clay red (the latest fashion) and Nike Air 3000 shoes. In contrast to the previous models of Nike Air, which only *felt* as if one were walking on air (but not really), with these shoes one actually *did* walk on air by means of a feat of physics I hadn't bothered to understand, but which resulted in one gliding at least five centimetres above the pavement. No more stepping in chewing gum, puddles or dog poo, although the former was currently banned in every country apart from the Republican States of America.

I was meeting with Newton and his boss, the founder of the Eternity Project. As much as I didn't really care what happened with the project, another, vainer part of me wanted to make a good impression. If nothing else, my smart dress and good looks turned heads as I glided down the street.

Unlike Newton's office, which was on the sixtieth floor of the Eternity Tower, the director's office was on the ninetieth or penthouse floor. The lift took nine seconds to reach the penthouse level; my stomach took a bit longer.

The lift doors parted, and I stepped onto a shiny tiled floor, white with curved black lines running through some of them. When I swept my gaze across the foyer from left to right and back again, I realised it was a giant infinity symbol, of the type I was taught to use in mathematics: ∞

'You guys are really serious about this eternity thing, huh?' I said.

Newton straightened the cuffs on his jacket. 'I hope you are, too, my friend.'

'Naturally,' I said, turning when I heard footsteps behind me.

'So, I get to meet the man at last.' A bald guy strode forward, extending his hand. 'Billy Raven, I believe.'

'That's me,' I answered, taking in the button in his right ear, the reason why any attempt to read his mind was futile. Newton was introducing me, but I was distracted by a cross-current of communication — Aurelia telling me to *be careful* — and all I caught was the director saying, 'Call me Rudy.'

'Nice to meet you, Rudy,' I said, simultaneously sending Aurelia a *Why?* in a closed-comm that I hoped to hell Newton wouldn't intercept. He had no idea I was sleeping with his sister, and I planned to keep it that way — until both Aurelia and I were at least a hundred years away, anyway.

'Come in,' Rudy said, directing me into an office also shaped like — surprise, surprise — the outline of an infinity symbol. As soon as the door closed behind us, the mind-hums of those nearby — the security staff, the cleaner, the receptionist on the floor below — went silent, as did the more distant ripple of Aurelia's thought-stream. No doubt her *be careful* was a reflex phrase, knowing I was entering a lion's den, as it were.

No matter. I was used to these types of rooms by now, with the alternating waveforms in the walls designed to block all thought-signals from leaving or entering.

After offering me a seat, Gen Eng coffee and a rainbow cookie, Rudy sat behind his surprisingly square desk and tented his fingers.

'So,' he said. 'I guess you know why you're here.'

I crossed my legs and picked up my bone-white coffee cup. 'Andromeda.'

Rudy nodded. 'That's right. You seem to be making some progress with her, at least on the romantic front.'

'Can't keep our hands off each other,' I said, affecting a bored tone.

Newton cleared his throat. 'How about the project? Have you managed to change her mind about that?'

'Yes,' I said. 'Under certain conditions, of course.'

The director broke off a piece of cookie. 'And what might those be?'

'She wants her freedom.'

'As expected,' Rudy said. 'But how do we know she won't run away?'

I flicked a green crumb off my trousers. 'Well, once we're engaged, I guess she will have every reason to stay.'

Newton's eyebrows shot up. 'Engaged?'

'That's right. I have the ring in my pocket.' I sipped on my coffee, which tasted better than I had thought it would. 'It's a stunner, even if I say so myself. A bespoke piece.' Not a hundred grand's worth, like the last one, true, but valuable in a very different way.

'She's willing to let us use her stem cells, then?' Rudy asked, obviously bored with talk of engagement rings.

'Yes, in return for a lifetime of living in luxury with me.' I smiled. 'I assume you'll be happy to make that sort of investment.'

The director pursed his lips. 'We can pay for your rent and all associated expenses if you ensure an ongoing supply of the product. What do you think, Miles?' I didn't need to remove Rudy's blocker to discern that he was thinking perhaps it was all too good to be true. I knew he would be relying on Newton to sniff out any deception on my part.

'Yes, Miles, what *do* you think?' I said aloud, at the same time as I thought-said, *If this goes as expected, you might even have a brother or sister for your first child. And if it doesn't, well, all manner of misfortunes can happen to a woman during pregnancy, can't they?*

'It all sounds very promising,' Newton said slowly, his thought-stream darkening at my not-so-veiled threat. He could order my immediate arrest, of course, but I already knew he'd do anything for his wife . . . and his sister.

Rudy's forehead furrowed. 'Are you all right, Miles? You look a bit flushed.'

'Yes, I'm just— I might have a glass of water.' Newton did exactly that, while I leaned back in my chair, satisfied that my telepathic nudge had been enough to distract him.

'I was hoping she could move into my apartment as soon as possible,' I said.

'Certainly,' Rudy said. 'Once we've secured the next stem-cell donation, that is.'

It was no less than I'd expected. To date, every movement of mine and Andromeda's had been monitored, covert eyes watching us everywhere we went. 'Naturally,' I said. 'I'll talk to her after my proposal.'

'And when will that be?' Newton asked.

I drained my coffee. 'Tonight.'

'Excellent. We shall start making preparations forthwith.' Rudy nodded at the plate on his desk. 'Another cookie?'

'No, thank you.' I stood up. 'I must get going.'

Rudy nodded. 'I'm sure. I hope this has been a mutually beneficial arrangement for you.'

'Yes,' I said, for the first time noticing the framed degree on the wall to my right. *Rudolph Underwood, Bachelor of Engineering conferred 2007.*

As we descended in the lift, I realised two things: (1) either Rudy's degree was fake, or he was at least one hundred years old, although he didn't look any older than sixty and (2) the last time I'd heard the phrase *mutually beneficial*, it had come directly from my own thought-stream to Andromeda's . . . and yet, the words had never left my mouth.

That's when I realised I needed to act soon, and fast.

THIRTY-FOUR:
INDIGO

2019

That evening, Billy takes me to the pub for a meal that I don't have any appetite for. In fact, as the hours pass, I feel more and more nauseated. Stress? Fear? Fatigue? Or maybe I'm merely coming down with a simple case of gastro.

We walk the short distance from our cottage, the icy wind chilling me to the bone. Billy seems impervious to the sub-zero temperature outside, his skin as unnaturally warm as ever when he holds my hand. It's kind of confusing. Aren't vampires meant to be cold-blooded? But then, those are made-up vampires that only exist in books and movies.

I guess they got it wrong.

We sit at a table near a roaring fire, where I order the least gross-sounding item off the menu, along with a ginger beer. Despite my nausea, when the meal arrives I realise I'm starving. I guess I was just hungry.

'Not into haggis, my love?' Billy is tucking into his meal as if he hasn't eaten in days, a foul-combination of offal, mashed potato and something he calls neeps, which appears to be a Scottish word for turnip.

I dip bread into my pumpkin soup. 'Meat is so old-fashioned.'

'Ooh, that was cutting.' His eyes are dancing. Once upon a time, that would have had my breath quickening and my skin flushing. Now it's all I can do not to stab him with my bread knife. What's he really playing at? Could he really still love me after I tried to rip his throat out, then poisoned him to death?

Reining in my contempt — it takes ice to fight a fire — I say, 'You said you'd make me stronger. When's that going to happen?'

Billy pats his lips with a napkin. 'You *are* in a hurry, aren't you? Plenty of time for that.'

'Considering what happened to Rigel, I think it's in my best interests to do it sooner rather than later.' Not only for my own protection from whoever might have hurt Rigel, but if there's a chance that I can somehow help Rigel, then I need to get onto it before it's too late. All I can think about is how he's desperately ill, maybe even dying.

I know he's not dead, though. Not yet. I can still detect his heart underscoring mine, two beats to my every one.

'It's not something you can do overnight,' Billy says, studying the dessert menu.

There's only one way to get his attention, much as I don't want to do it. Steeling myself, I nudge my knee against his under the cover of the table. 'Can we start tonight?'

He gives me a calculating look. 'If I didn't know better, I'd think you were trying to seduce me to get what you want.'

I prop my elbow on the table, rest my fingers beneath my chin. '*You've* already seduced *me*,' I say, injecting a slightly husky tone into my voice. 'Now I want the rest.'

'Well, well,' he says slowly. 'You have the makings of a goddess after all, my beautiful moon.' Reaching beneath the table, he slips his hand up the seam of my jeans. I suck in a breath. *And together*, he think-says, *we'll be able to take on anyone.*

If you love me so much, I think-say, *why did you give me to the cell in Norway?*

Billy hesitates, his thought-stream rippling with regret. *I did what I had to do,* he think-says, *before I figured out how to whole-body shift you away. They were on my case like you wouldn't believe.*

Who was on your case?

Underwood and Aurelia.

Underwood? Why am I not surprised? *And?* I prod, sensing that's not the whole truth.

And, he think-says, slowly, reluctantly, *I needed . . . I thought I needed . . . another sample of stem cells.*

My *stem cells*? I don't know why I'm so horrified. He is a vampire, after all. Why wouldn't he be cashing in on my stem cells, just like everyone else?

My darling moon, he think-says, *I had no idea that you were all I needed. I've made mistakes, and I'm sorry. But you're safe now.*

Somehow I doubt that, but he seems open to my questioning, at least for now. *Do you know who hurt Rigel?* I think-ask as he draws circles on my inner thigh with his thumb, a prelude to what I'm sure will follow once we get back to the cottage.

I have a pretty good idea, yes.

So, who was it?

Someone you need to stay well clear of, he think-answers, but not before I see the name tumbling through his thought-stream.

Aurelia, I think-say. *It was her, wasn't it? She's the one who hurt Rigel. The one who made you.*

Billy's pupils dilate, and for a moment I could swear he is about to *shift* into animal form, his scent musky-wolf, his irises full-moon yellow.

Let's go home, my sweet moon, he think-replies, *and I'll tell you all about her.*

Back at the cottage, Billy stokes the fire in the tiny lounge with wood from a wicker basket on the hearth. I sink onto the couch, watching faux-images moving through the flames: a palm tree, a long face, a four-legged animal — a tiger?

As soon as *that* thought flits through my head, I detect a change in Rigel's underlying heartbeat, a skip-trip before it returns to normal. Regular, but faster, too. But of course. A tiger is Rigel's favourite dream-flow form. Which means—

I send a rapid thought-message, one I hope Billy won't intercept. *Rigel?*

And I hear

The Hunter has—

And I hear

Someone worse than Billy—

Someone worse than Billy? Underwood? No, it must be her, the girl who kissed Billy Quick and said she'd see him in a hundred years.

'Tell me about Aurelia,' I say.

Billy pivots, still holding the poker. For a brief, terrifying moment I think he must have hooked into my thought-stream, that he must have heard Rigel's voice. But he merely smiles and deposits the poker on the hearth before sitting beside me.

'Once upon a time . . .' he says, staring into the fire. 'Is that how one starts a tale like this?'

I don't answer, waiting for him to carry on — and he does, starting with the lonely sixteen-year-old boy who'd recently lost his mother, right through to the girl who left him for dead in the back of a car. 'I found her later,' he says. 'But she wasn't Aurelia, not then. Her name was Kat, and she was a seventeen-year-old girl living in Rarotonga.'

'Kat,' I say, and he gives me a thought-image of a younger, softer version of the girl in the car. 'So how did she become Aurelia?'

'Well, here's the thing.' He throws another log into the hearth, sending sparks flying. 'I created her. And yet, *she* created *me*. A paradox, one I choose to call an Eternity Loop.'

'An Eternity Loop,' I echo, staring into the fire again. The nausea is creeping up on me again. Something I ate, maybe? Another image jumps in front of me. It's no longer flames I'm seeing, but the wind-rippled surface of the Santorini caldera. And our hearts are pounding faster and faster, one-two-three—

Three? I glance at Billy. It's not his heart I'm hearing, I don't think. This third heartbeat is faster, tripping along like that of a small animal.

'Don't worry, my beautiful moon,' he says, pushing me back until I'm lying beneath him. 'Aurelia and I are history, romantically at least. Would *you* like to be the most powerful woman in the world?'

'Yes, but right now I'm going to be sick,' I manage. Billy jumps off me and I run to the bathroom, just in time for the entire contents of my stomach to be forcefully ejected into the loo. Gross. I'm never eating pumpkin soup again. I splash water over my face, turn to see Billy standing in the doorway, his eyes raking over me.

'Hmm,' he says, in a way that has my skin tingling all over, and it's nothing to do with desire. He moves closer, plants his palm on my belly. 'Got something to tell me, Indigo Moon?'

'S-something to tell you?' Did he hear Rigel after all?

Billy tilts his head, like a bird, like a raven. 'Something's different about you. When was your last period, my darling?'

I gape at him. 'My last — a few weeks ago.'

'Hmm,' he says again. 'And yet, I could swear—' He shakes his head. 'I'll be right back.'

Right back? Where's he going? I wait until the front door

slams behind him, then lock the bathroom door (although why, I'm not sure, since he can *shift* anywhere he wants), then turn the taps on over the bath. It's only once I've sunk into the water that I realise Billy is right. Something *is* different about me, something I never noticed when I was in the shower earlier. My stomach is firmer than usual, and it's kind of sticking out. Actually, not just *kind of*. I could swear I wasn't this round yesterday. And my boobs, oh my God, how did they get so big? Not that they were small before, but they've gone up at least a cup size.

It doesn't take long for my brain to join the dots. I'm not stupid. There's only one reason why my boobs and belly would be swelling like that, and I don't think it's got anything to do with my sweet tooth.

'No!' I clench my fists, stare down at my belly again. Billy had said he'd put a baby in me. Oh no, oh no, can this really be happening? And *when* did this happen? I hardly even want to touch it, but I curl my hands around the swelling and hold my breath. Is that the rapid heartbeat I can hear? My parents said they could hear my heartbeat from when my mum was about five weeks' pregnant.

'No,' I repeat, and slide beneath the water. Of course, that does nothing to muffle the sound of the other's heartbeat in my ears, like a clock, no, like a—

Time bomb.

I surface again, just in time to hear a knock on the door, followed by Billy's voice.

'Are you all right, my darling?' I don't need to see him to know what he went out to get. I don't need to take the pregnancy test he's holding in his hand.

I don't have to, because my body has told me all I need to know.

THIRTY-FIVE:
BILLY

2088; 2005

That evening, I took Andromeda out to a floating restaurant for dinner, located on a luxury boat that glided along the River Thames. We were seated in a private booth, a clone waiting on our every need while managing to make itself as inconspicuous as possible. Still, I knew that true privacy was an illusion, knew that there must be a bug somewhere in the room. For all I knew, the bug was in Andromeda, implanted while she was sedated.

But that didn't explain how our thought-speak had been intercepted. At least, I figured it had.

Mutually beneficial. Or was I being paranoid? It wasn't such an unusual turn of phrase.

Andromeda, in a closed-comm to me, said, *You're very twitchy, Mr Raven.*

How's that? I thought-replied.

No need to snap. Stop jiggling your leg, will you?

I stopped jiggling my leg. In comparison to me, Andromeda's movements were languid, her gaze almost sleepy. And yet her thought-stream was anything but slow.

Having second thoughts? she think-asked.

Certainly not. But — please, please, let this closed-comm be working — *I think they're onto us.*

How?

I think they've been listening in on our conversations. This afternoon the director — Underwood — used the exact same phrase I used to you a few weeks ago.

Andromeda narrowed her eyes at me. *What phrase?*

Mutually beneficial.

She pouted, took a long swallow of Coke-X. *That doesn't necessarily mean anything.*

Doesn't it?

Well. Perhaps they've picked up on a snippet of our thought convo. But if they knew our plan, do you really think they'd let us come out like this?

I don't— How would I know?

Andromeda rolled her eyes at me. I exhaled, ran a finger around the rim of my glass. The iced Poison wasn't doing anything to allay my anxiety, which made me long for a stiff whisky, although a dulling of the senses was probably the last thing I needed right then. *Here goes*, I thought-said. Aloud I said, 'You know, I've enjoyed our dinners . . . a lot.'

Tucking a strand of hair behind her ear, Andromeda replied, 'Me, too.'

'And I . . . I hope you can see why the Eternity Project is so important. Why we'd love you to take part — on your own terms.'

'I think I could reconsider. If you think that's the right thing to do.' She gave me a simpering smile.

'I do, I really do.' I pushed my chair away from the table and went down on one knee. *Déjà vu*, except this time I already knew the answer. 'Andromeda, these past few weeks you've shown me what an intelligent, compassionate, beautiful woman you are, inside and out.'

I'm sure, Andromeda thought-said, her thought-stream twisting in a very un-beautiful way.

Keep smiling, will you? I took the jewellery box out of my pocket and opened it. 'Andromeda, will you marry me?'

'Oh my God.' Andromeda clapped her palm over her mouth. 'I — yes. Yes, of course.' She held out her left hand so I could slide the ring onto her finger. The diamond was claw-set and rectangular in shape. Although not as pretty as the one I'd bought Aurelia, it was perfect for our requirements.

'I do,' she whispered, but that's not what I heard.

No, I heard *Now*—

And we *shifted*—

Out of the restaurant and onto a beach, foamy waves thundering onto black sand. Andromeda flipped the top of the ring, took out the black button-like device inside and pushed it into her ear. Her thought-stream disappeared and we smiled at each other, triumphant.

Then the world distorted and blurred and I heard 'You duplicitous bastard!', and I went down hard, my breath knocked out of my lungs.

'Run!' I yelled, right before I *shifted* into crocodile form, the only creature I could think of that might be able to overpower the Newton-wolf on my back. The wolf snarled and tried to bite me, but he was no match for my massive jaws. *Andromeda, quick!* I thought-yelled. *We need to leave before more of them get here.* That's when I remembered that she was wearing a blocker. Shit.

As Newton's blood jetted over my snout, I heard screaming, not just from Miles (and did a part of me feel sorry for him? Maybe, but he didn't scream for long, not once I'd ripped out his throat), but from Andromeda, too.

I *shifted* into human form again, just in time to leap forward and grab Andromeda, who was standing shaking by the rocks. After yanking the blocker out of her ear, I flashed up a thought-image of the first place I could think of and together we *shifted*—

Andromeda and I stood blinking at each other. To our right rose the white walls of Santorini; to our left, the sparkling blue waters of the volcanic caldera.

'Here goes,' I said, taking a cylindrical device out of my pocket.

Andromeda barely flinched as I injected the second, much smaller blocker into the base of her spine. Newton's trouser pockets had provided me with a treasure trove of delights over the past few weeks.

'Welcome to 2005,' I said, glad I couldn't detect the acid whiplash of her thought-stream, the barest flicker of which had reached her facial expression. Lesson number one: never trust a vampire. 'I hope you enjoy your stay.'

The most beautiful prison in the world. And no one but me would even know she was there.

THIRTY-SIX:
RIGEL

Fire. There are sparks in my gut, flames in my chest, an inferno blazing through my thought-stream. Voices fade in and out, in and out.

Hadn't made any further healing attempts as far as we . . . understand you're . . . keep him on the ventilator until you make it over from . . . certainly, Doctor Black.

My damaged brain understands that they, the medical staff, are talking to my mother. Not a medical doctor, not exactly, but she has a PhD in biochemistry, extensive experience in vaccination science, and an advanced understanding of what it takes to heal a dying person.

No, Mum, I'd tell her if I were capable of think-speak. *No. You can't try and heal me. It'll kill you.*

But a subterranean part of me wonders if maybe, just maybe, I might be able to heal myself. Is that even possible?

More flames jump through my dream-flow. More voices, from within rather than without. A woman's voice, familiar but not: *Thin is the line between civilisation and savagery.* Where have I heard that before? And then Billy's voice, dark and syrupy, like molasses: *Something's different about you.* Is he speaking to Indigo? I try to turn my dream-flow towards the voice, but everything is so hazy. I can hear her heartbeat, which is not unusual, but there's another one, too, a faster one running beneath both of ours, two beats to every one of Indigo's.

No, Indigo says.

I suck in a breath. Open my eyes. But all I see is my own body lying on a hospital bed, tubes poking out of my mouth and neck and even between my legs, a catheter to drain the urine from my failing kidneys. My mother is standing beside me, her eyes red-rimmed as a woman in green scrubs tells her it's very unlikely her son will ever regain consciousness. The doctor is using words like multi-organ failure and system inflammatory response syndrome.

'No,' my mother says. 'I don't believe you.'

The doctor touches my mother's arm. 'I know it's not an easy thing to accept.'

Mum shakes her off. 'No,' she says. 'I know it's not true.' If I could speak, I'd tell the doctor not to mess with Violet Black. I'd tell the doctor not to presume they know more than the woman who engineered a vaccine for the M-fever virus, and will likely make a vaccine for Riva, too.

'We'll try for another twenty-four hours,' the doctor concedes. 'But then we'll have to revisit withdrawing life support.'

My mother glares at her. 'Could you leave us alone for a while? Please?'

'Certainly,' the doctor says, her syllables clipped. And after drawing the curtains around the bed, she does just that.

That's when Mum does something really strange. She slips her shoes off, tugs my sheet back and climbs up on the bed beside me, carefully navigating the web of tubes. Then she turns onto her side, facing me, and wraps an arm around my body.

That's when I realise what she's trying to do. I have to stop her. Have to, but my mouth won't open. My limbs won't move. I can't even communicate via thought-speak. If I could I'd tell her, *No, you can't — it's too dangerous. Stop it, stop it!*

The thoughts keep looping around my mind, but there's nothing I can do. My mother is holding me close and I am watching from above, helpless. She's trying to heal me and it could kill her. No, it almost certainly will, because my body is damaged beyond the limits of modern medicine's ability to fix me. No one comes to tell her she mustn't risk bumping my tubes and catheters, that it could be dangerous. As far as the medical staff are concerned, I'm a lost cause, dead meat.

She stays for hours. Hours, and the whole time I'm watching my skin slowly regain its pink colour, even as my mother's complexion turns to putty. A nurse looks in on us a couple of times, but disappears without registering the fact that my mother is the one who is dying.

It's early morning when my mother's implantable defibrillator, her ICD, fires the first time. I know because I feel the jolt in my own chest. I gasp and — *whump* — I'm in my body once more, staring into my mother's glazed eyes.

'Mum, *no*.' I try to push her away from me, but my arms are weak after days of lying unconscious. 'Stop it.' And you'd think the ICD would have the power to save her, but it isn't working. It's. Not. Working. 'No!' My voice is so thin that I know nobody will be able to hear me.

Mum gives me a smile, and I hear a distant sound, almost an echo — *jasmine and snow, sunshine and laughter* — before my vision blurs. Not because I'm passing out, but because I'm starting to cry.

You wait, she think-says. *You'll do anything for your own child. You'll see.* Her thought-stream is thready, ragged around the edges.

'No,' I croak, and my voice is stronger this time, my heart beating so hard it feels as if it's about to explode.

'Is everything— Oh.' A nurse appears at last, her mouth falling open when she sees me clutching my mother's arms. I push Mum onto her back so I can start CPR, my strength growing rapidly even as the last of her life-force flows into me.

'Holy mother of God!' a male voice announces, and then they're dragging me off her and there are more exclamations and calls for *defib* and *adrenaline*, and the last thing I hear before someone rams a syringe into the tube dangling from my neck is *flatline*, and I know it's nothing to do with my heart, and everything to do with hers.

THIRTY-SEVEN:
BILLY

I didn't return to 2088, not immediately anyway. If my instincts proved right, then Rudolph Underwood wasn't a normal as I'd first thought. His eighty-one-year-old university degree meant he must have treated himself to a stem-cell transplant from an Offspring at some stage. If that were true, then it was possible he'd witnessed my termination of Newton, had possibly even been communicating with Newton up until his death.

No, best to lie low for a while. As far as I was concerned, my time in 2088 had been a complete success. I'd found Aurelia and fulfilled my promise to Andromeda, although I hoped she wasn't too grumpy about being permanently ensconced in turn-of-the-century Santorini rather than 2055 New Zealand, trapped in a time spiral. Never mind, that would give her even longer to try and find a cure for Riva or whatever it was she wanted to do about that. Besides, how could she be grumpy about being transported to such a beautiful location?

Also, knowing exactly where Andromeda was could have its uses. I disliked the terms 'hostage' and 'pawn', although she'd flung those at me as I'd *shifted* away from her at lightning speed. No, she was more of an . . . asset. An investment. If need be, I could secure more stem cells off her, or, failing that, feed off her, although the chances of me being able to do that without forcing her seemed pretty slim at that point in time.

For the next couple of weeks, I took up residence in 1999 New York. I didn't even try to contact Aurelia, knowing that could put us both in danger at that stage. Instead, I experimented with my ever-expanding superhuman abilities, which seemed to have come along even further since I'd dispensed with Newton. It had been a gruesome affair, after all, and I couldn't help but ingest rather a large amount of his blood. Of course, every life I took had strengthened me, but Newton's essence had been a magic bullet, an elixir of possibility, or impossibility, depending on how one wanted to view it.

How did I know this?

Trial and error, of course. But mostly, trial and success.

I bought an apartment on my first day. It wasn't hard. Essentially, I strolled up to the one with the best view, knocked on the door and offered the surprised owner a ridiculous amount of money to vacate immediately. *Take your clothes and belongings*, I said. *Leave the furniture and whiteware.* When he hesitated, I upped the price by half a million.

Most people can be bought, I've found, if not with money, then with promises of love.

I even got the owner to leave their Salvador Dali reproduction on the wall, despite it being rather dated. The melting clocks appealed to me, as someone who specialises in travelling through and manipulating time.

Manipulating time? Is that what I'd done when I'd gone to the Cook Islands to find Aurelia? Or was it she who'd manipulated time by coming back to 1988 to find me? We'd created an impossibility, something I'd decided to call an Eternity Loop.

When I wasn't roving around New York indulging in the

usual delights (which mostly consisted of flirting with members of both sexes in bars, although I stayed faithful to Aurelia, and didn't go any further than a chaste kiss on the cheek), I experimented with *shifting* within my new apartment. And yet I seemed to need a constant supply of energy, of life, to keep my powers sharp, honed. Stem cells, I'd learned, were best, followed by Offspring blood. But I was laying low, and vampires can't always be choosers, even time vampires.

If you check the newspapers or search the internet for memorable events occurring in New York in May of 1999, you may find mention of a serial killer they termed, perhaps tongue-in-cheek, 'Vampire Jack'. It was a short-lived killing spree, one unfortunate soul every three nights over a period of twenty days.

Serial killers often have a trademark, and this particular killer's trademark was the bite marks they found on the victims' necks or groins. Thing was, the medical examiner was puzzled, because the bite marks looked as though they came from wild animals that weren't usually found anywhere outside of a zoo: panthers, cougars, cheetahs, wolves.

Why, Mr Wolf, what sharp teeth you have.

Yes. Yes, I do.

And yet, inevitably, living among normals became boring. I needed the company of others like me. More specifically, I needed Aurelia, with whom I hadn't had contact since I'd terminated her brother and hidden Andromeda in Santorini. The urge to be with her, to travel through time once more, eventually overcame all fears I had of being captured and punished by the Eternity Project.

So, on the first of June, I set out to rekindle my relationship with Aurelia once more. It wasn't 2088 that I travelled to, though. Instead, I chose to do something rather different, something potentially very dangerous.

Everyone remembers their first kiss, don't they? Or at least, the first one that counts. Everyone remembers the first time they fell in love.

Imagine if you could do that all over again.

Nineteen-eighties England wasn't a place I'd time-travelled back to before, let alone my family home. How odd it was to return to my bedroom, decorated with posters of Queen and Def Leppard and Billy Idol, how strange to travel into the body of my sixteen-year-old self.

Step aside, Billy Quick. I need to borrow you for a few hours.

Billy Quick was sitting on his bed, listening to Simple Minds sing 'Don't You (Forget About Me)' on his Walkman. As my dream-flow entered his mind, he twitched and gave out a little grunt. Did he know I was there? Surely not. He was still a normal, after all, although deep in the thrall of *her*, Aurelia. I could feel the tug in his gut, the ache in his chest.

If I were in my future body, perhaps a little tremor would have rippled through me then. Because this sensation, this yearning was something I'd only ever felt around Aurelia — but not the young Aurelia I'd met in the Cook Islands, the girl I'd taught to kiss.

But . . . no, surely that was impossible? It was love-lust, as pure and simple as that, an emotion capable of inducing madness in both humans and gods. That was what I told myself, as I took up residence in his hindbrain and waited for the after-school meeting with Aurelia.

How stupid I, Billy Raven, was.

It was Monday afternoon, and a week since I'd met the girl who was going to change the course of my life forever. I fidgeted through all my classes, earning a 'would you please concentrate' from my Chemistry teacher and a 'you'll never amount to anything' from my English teacher.

I *was* concentrating, only not on my classes. As for 'you'll never amount to anything', I had half a mind to return and feast on one of my teachers to see what they thought about that.

I digress.

As soon as the bell rang, I raced out of the classroom, ducking and dodging around the students who were walking at an irritatingly slow pace towards the gates, like sheep or lemmings. Aurelia was sitting on a bench by the riverbank, as I knew she would be. Her blonde locks were scooped into a ponytail, her coat collar turned up against the wind. She stood and turned. For a brief moment I caught the platinum sheen of her thought-stream, and then it was gone, hidden from view.

'Hello, Billy Raven,' she said.

'Hello, Aurelia Nightingale,' I said, *déjà vu* rising and falling like a wave before settling into the Eternity Loop I was starting to know so well. Blood surged through the chambers of my heart. My ears were ringing. I took her hand, noting her warm skin, her roses-and-rain scent.

'Where shall we go?' Aurelia asked.

'I know a place,' I said, as I had eleven years before. I led her down the grassy bank, our feet squelching in the mud, over the rocks and beneath the bridge. *Whump-whump* went the cars overhead. *Thump-thump* went my heart.

Aurelia poked with her foot at a circular arrangement of blackened lumps. 'Someone's had a fire.'

'And a smoke.' I moved closer to her, peering at the tattoo on her neck.

Catching the direction of my gaze, Aurelia said, 'It's a rose.'

'A rose,' I said. 'When did you get that?'

'If I told you, you wouldn't believe me.' She tilted her head to one side. 'What would you say if I told you that where I come from, you taught me how to kiss?'

'I — I don't know,' I stammered. This wasn't going to script, not exactly. But I didn't stop to consider why, because desire-adrenaline was crackling through my veins. She looked so beautiful, even more so than I remembered. And when she said 'Remember, practice makes perfect' and slipped her arms around my neck, I knew that this was it, the moment I could happily relive over and over.

Until I felt the lightning-snap of her thought-stream wrapping around mine, even as she tried to sink her fox-teeth into my throat, even as her thought-voice hissed *Thin is the line between civilisation and savagery*, and I—

Shifted so fast I nearly vomited, first into a raven and then into the smallest animal I could manage, an ant, and then I *shifted* once more, out of 1988 and into the void.

And as I fled through time, Aurelia Nightingale hot in pursuit, the last thing I heard was: *You think this is over, Billy Raven? Believe me, this has only just begun.*

THIRTY-EIGHT:
INDIGO

2019

The following morning, I wake to the scent of freshly brewed coffee and frying bacon. It's enough to make me puke again, something I'll never get used to.

'Don't worry,' Billy says, once I slope into the kitchen, my thought-stream billowing like a storm cloud. 'It's meant to improve after the first three months.'

'Three months? Is that how far along you think I am?'

He deposits a plate in front of me, bacon and eggs on toast. 'Possibly more, but they'll be able to tell us after the ultrasound today. Eat up, my darling. It'll make you feel better, I promise.' He beams at me.

'Ultrasound? Where?'

'In the next village over. It's a short drive away, although we can *shift* if you prefer.' He sits next to me. 'I'm so pleased that you've mastered whole-body *shifting*. It does make life much easier.'

As far as I'm concerned, life has just got a whole lot harder. I'm too distressed and nauseated to argue, though, so I nibble on a piece of toast. Billy is right, eating does make me feel better; my stomach, anyway.

Three hours later, I'm lying on a narrow bed while a woman with frizzy red hair runs an ultrasound probe over my belly.

'There it is,' she says, pointing to the unmistakeable shape of the head and the double lines that make up the spine. 'Looks to be about seventeen weeks. And if I'm not mistaken, there's a ninety percent chance it's a girl.' She takes the probe off and hands me a wad of tissues to wipe the gel off my stomach. 'We can be more definitive with the twenty-week scan. Would you like to book that now?'

'Why not?' Billy says. I swear he hasn't stopped smiling since the second he saw the two blue lines on the pregnancy test stick last night.

As soon as we return to the cottage, I retreat into bed, telling Billy I'm exhausted. It's not entirely a lie, but I also need time to try and work out how this could have happened.

I'm going to put a baby in you, my darling.

I'm seventeen weeks' pregnant. Seventeen weeks, which means I must have got pregnant in . . . what? November? Which is when I first met Billy. Except I'd had a contraceptive injection by then, one I'd asked our family doctor to give me soon after meeting Billy and definitely before we had sex. The doctor had told me it was ninety-nine percent effective. Am I in the unlucky one percent? Billy and I only did it the once. And Rigel and I . . . we only did it once, too, and that was only a couple of days ago.

Wait. It wasn't a couple of days ago, not exactly, because we'd travelled back in time, hadn't we? We travelled back to my bedroom, back to . . .

My heart thuds faster and faster.

'November,' I whisper. *Rigel*, I think-send, even though I know it's futile. *Andromeda. Please, if you can hear me, help me before it's too late.* What did Aurelia do to Rigel? And why?

The door opens. I squeeze my eyes shut, am tempted to pull the blankets over my head, but it's too late. Billy is sitting next to me, pressing his lips to my forehead.

'I'm so looking forward to meeting our child,' he says. 'She's going to be beautiful. I just know it.'

And freezes, his thought-stream morphing from yellow to green to grey.

I'd ask him what's wrong, but within seconds, I have my answer.

'Well, isn't this a lovely scene,' a voice says. My eyes fly open. There's a woman standing in the doorway, a woman with platinum blonde hair and glacial blue irises.

Unlike the last time I saw her, when she was wearing an evening gown, Aurelia is dressed in moleskin trousers, riding boots and a white puffer jacket.

'Aurelia,' Billy murmurs. 'It's not—'

'Time?' She pulls a chair up and sits between us, crossing her slender legs at the knee. 'Oh, I think it is *time*. I've been waiting long enough.'

What is this? Some kind of bizarre love triangle? Is it Billy she's after?

'Oh no,' Aurelia says, which is when I realise my block isn't working, not against her anyway. 'There's a debt to be paid, and Billy hasn't fulfilled his end of the bargain.' She leans towards me. 'Three lives for one. I'm being pretty generous, really.'

I shrink away, my pulse hammering. Billy leaps to his feet.

'She's not ready yet,' he says, his voice hoarse. 'Please, at least wait until the baby is born.' His Adam's apple is bobbing up and down, his eyes wide. *I never meant for this to happen*, he think-sends to me. *I promise you*.

'You murdered my best friend,' Aurelia says, her tone venomous. 'You killed my brother. You took Andromeda . . . and you want me to wait?'

'You have Rigel,' Billy says. 'Isn't that enough?'

'Rigel?' Her tone is venomous. 'The more I fed on him, the weaker his heart became. Much longer, and he'd have been dead.' She lets out a laugh. 'So, I thought I might as well finish him off, especially after he rejected me. Whereas she—' She points at me. 'She just gets stronger, doesn't she? You had a choice, Billy — Andromeda or Indigo Moon — and yet you want to have both of them for yourself. That's hardly fair, is it?'

'Wait,' I say, looking between them. What's going on here? Feeding on Rigel, *what?* 'What's Rigel got to do with you? What have you done to him?'

'Oh, Indigo,' she says, and when I look at her, her face is rippling, changing into the features of someone I used to know, a girl with blonde hair and leaping horse micro-tattoos on her eyelids. The last time I saw *that* girl, she was draping herself all over Rigel at his mother's dining-room table. Huh? Brie is Aurelia? Aurelia is Brie? 'That's right,' Aurelia/Brie says, her voice softer, girlier, 'and now it's time to take you back to where you belong.'

Of course I try to run in the only way that could possibly work — by *shifting*.

Of course, she intercepts me, blocking my dream-flow with guillotine swiftness before lunging towards me and embracing me so hard I can hardly draw breath.

'No,' Billy yells, but it's too late, I'm falling, falling, my vision receding and I am—

Slipping and whirling and falling, over the edge—

And into the Eternity Loop.

THIRTY-NINE:
BILLY

It didn't take much to work out what was going on. Aurelia knew I'd killed her brother, and her friend Rua as well. But when had she found this out? Immediately after the event, or several years later? Was the Aurelia who'd changed me from Billy Quick to Billy Raven the same Aurelia who tried to kill me when I returned to 1988 or an older, wiser Aurelia? Had she been trying to kill me all those years ago rather than change me? But wait, if she *hadn't* changed me, then she wouldn't have met me in 2088 and then . . . There's nothing like an Eternity Loop to make your brain hurt.

What I *did* know was that I needed to do more than lie low for a while. I needed to disappear.

I retreated into 1996, choosing London that time rather than New York. After employing my usual tricks to secure an apartment, I spent my night roaming around bars, using my glamour to seduce woman after woman. The novelty had worn off, though. Not only that, but I sensed that my time-travelling abilities were diminishing, the *shifting* not as easy as it had been at the peak of my powers. Soon, I knew, it'd be time to visit Andromeda in Santorini, to see if I could rejuvenate myself through her. It wasn't a confrontation I was looking forward to. Truth be told, I was a little afraid of her.

Until that night.

Yes, *that* night.

It was a Monday, slow as hell in some cities, especially in the 1990s. Being London, however, the bars, although not packed, were still lively enough. I'd ordered myself a drink and was leaning against a pillar, checking out the talent, when I detected it. Not it, *her*. The hum of her thought-stream was an electrical impulse rippling along my spinal cord. I could smell her, too, although it was a scent that didn't entirely make sense; jasmine and snow.

I turned my head, and looked straight into the eyes of one of her companions, a handsome boy-man with blond hair. Swinging my gaze away, I registered what I'd glimpsed in that split second: a young woman with glossy black hair that hung to her waist, with flawless skin and a curvy figure. A couple of minutes later, I saw her jogging down the stairs, flanked by the blond boy and a red-haired girl of around the same age — heading for the dance floor, according to the wide-open thought-streams of her companions.

As for *her* thought-stream, that wasn't quite so open. I'd already figured out by then why she was having such an effect on me. She was an *other*, most likely a time-travelling Offspring. Excitement coursed through me, but I made myself linger a little longer, finishing my drink before going to find her.

Within ten minutes, she was beckoning for me to join them, her lips curling up in the most delicious way. Jasmine and snow. Sunshine and laughter. Oh, how I wanted her, and I hadn't even spoken to her yet.

In fact, it was she who spoke first. 'What's your name?' she asked, her mouth so close that I could feel her breath in my ear.

'Billy,' I said. 'What's yours?'

'Indigo — Indigo Moon.'

I smiled at how perfectly her name suited her, hinting at

beauty and intrigue. 'Have you ever been into orbit, Indigo Moon?'

'I never left.' She let me take her hand, pirouetted beneath my raised arm. 'Do you like to dance?'

'Depends.' The music changed, Oasis singing 'Wonderwall'. 'Where are you from, Indigo Moon?'

'Your future,' she answered, confirming my suspicions that she, too, was a time-traveller.

'Funny you should say that,' I said, as the boy-man, Griffin, grabbed her from behind. It was all I could do not to deck him. I tolerated him pawing her for a couple of minutes before reclaiming her and spinning her around the dance floor, showing off the dance moves I'd learned over the years.

Within the hour, we were on Tower Bridge. A few minutes after that, I kissed her for the first time, and knew I'd never need to go looking for Aurelia again.

FORTY:
RIGEL

My eyes fly open. I'm lying on a bed in a smaller room. Smaller, but still in a hospital. I can tell by the Observation Robot to the left of my bed, by the medicinal smell and electronic ID circling my wrist. I can tell by the thought-streams I'm picking up on as I cast my dream-flow out, probing, seeking, hunting. I could have sworn that was thought-speak I heard just now. Was that my mother? Could everything that happened just now have been a nightmare?

But no. No, that didn't sound like Mum. And Mum is . . .

I sit up, the awful realisation hitting me with tsunami-force. Try as I might, I can't find my mother's thought-stream. Not only that, but I've already picked up on the nurses' conversation down the corridor.

A miracle and a tragedy . . . doesn't make . . . Medivac . . .

Medivac? I sit up. Am I being airlifted out of here? Yet when I look out of the window, it's the familiar spire of the Sun Tower I see rather than the Tower Bridge or London Eye, and I realise I've been transferred already.

I look down at my body, noting the saline-filled tube snaking into the IV in my arm. Have they been sedating me all this time? How long is *all this time* anyway? How long has it been since Mum . . . No, no, she can't have died.

Panic strafing through me, I extend the reach of my dream-flow, trying to find the only person I trust and send out a rapid, semi-hysterical *The White Wolf has fallen, oh God, Indy, I need you, please, I can't handle this on my own.*

She doesn't answer. A sob catching in my throat, I shove the covers aside and stand up, swaying when the room spins around me.

'Rigel, sit.'

I look up, and straight into my uncle's eyes. His tone may have been curt, but his thought-stream is running blue and deep; sorrow and helplessness, and beneath that, an anger I've only glimpsed on a few occasions.

'Get away from me,' I say.

'Rigel . . .' Rawiri moves towards me.

I stumble back, sitting with a thud on the bed. 'No. I mean it,' I say, my voice cracking. 'I don't want anything else to do with the BSI, which means I don't want anything to do with *you.*'

'What makes you think the BSI has anything to do with your mother's death?' Rawiri asks, while think-saying in a closed-comm *Don't answer that question aloud, OK? I've got news to share with you . . . but not here.* 'Look,' he continues, 'Fox is staying with me. When you're well enough, I'd like to take you home as well.'

I stare at him for a moment, then say, 'I don't want to stay here another second.'

'Well, they might want to observe you for a bit longer.'

'No,' I say, ripping the electro-dots off my chest, followed by the IV button on my wrist. Ignoring the thin line of blood trickling down my arm, I say, 'Mum did a really good job of healing me, in case you missed it. So well that it killed her.' My voice begins to shake. '*I* killed her.'

'No, Rigel, it wasn't your fault.' My uncle grabs a wad of tissues from the box beside the bed and presses them over the hole in my wrist, where the IV button used to be. 'It was your mother's choice to make. Parents will do anything for their children.'

'How would *you* know?' I snarl, the jagged edges of grief cutting into me.

'I haven't experienced it myself,' he says grimly, 'but I've observed it many times, believe me.' He sits beside me. 'I'll see if I can get clearance for you to come home.'

'Don't bother.' I slide out of the other side of the bed, ignoring the spinning in my head. 'I'm self-discharging. No one's going to arrest me for that, are they?'

'No,' he says. 'They're not.'

It's not until we're in a Zuber, destination Rawiri's apartment, that I learn that Indigo has gone missing.

'Has anyone made even the slightest effort to look for her?' I'm pacing Rawiri's lounge, casting sideways glances at my brother, who is curled up in a ball on the couch, listening to who-knows-what on his earphones. Fox's eyes are red-rimmed, his face gaunt. Hardly a surprise when we've lost both parents within the space of three months.

'Of course they have.' Rawiri's glancing at my brother, too, and I realise this is a conversation we should be having away from him. Massaging my temples, I go to have a shower, resolving to delve deeper once Fox is in bed.

It turns out that's impossible. Now that I've returned, Fox doesn't want to leave my side. He's never been this clingy before. Again, no surprise.

'Are you sure you're not tired?' I ask him around ten-thirty, when my own eyelids feel as though they have uranium sewn into them.

Fox, whose eyes are glued to the e-screen, mumbles, 'I don't want to go to sleep.' His thought-stream is ragged and pale. He's been having nightmares, I realise, is waiting for me to go to bed as well so he won't have to be alone.

My heart lurching, I say, 'Hey bud, I'll be right here, OK?'

Fox glowers at me. 'I'm not going to bed yet.'

I hesitate. *Look*, I think-say, deciding the truth might be the best strategy, *I need to talk to Uncle Rawiri. Alone.*

My brother leaps up. 'Stop it!'

I gape at him. 'Stop what?'

'Treating me like a little kid. I'm sick of it. I'm nearly fourteen, Offspring like you. Have you even asked if *I* can help? No, everyone just keeps shoving me aside like I'm some kind of liability.' He points at me. 'And don't make fun of me for using that word. I'm *not* stupid.'

'You're far from stupid,' Rawiri says, going to clasp his shoulder, but Fox shrinks away.

'I want to know what's going on. I want to know why both my parents are dead. I want to know where Indigo is. I want to know who's next.' He's shaking, his cheeks glistening with tears. 'I want—'

'Hey,' I say, my own eyes welling. 'Hey, I get it. I do.' I put my arms around him. *And I promise you*, I think-say, making sure Rawiri can hear us, *that we won't hide anything from you. But we might have to ask you to keep some secrets, OK?*

I can keep a secret. Fox's thought-stream is sparking, fiery. Somehow that's better than the half-dead version I was seeing before. *If you need me to, I'll keep it until the day I die.*

That won't be happening, Rawiri interjects. Our uncle crosses his arms. *Let's take this conversation to the basement, shall we?*

It's a while since I've been in Rawiri's basement, over a year. The gaming chairs, four of them, are still there, perfect for a Virt Real experience. There are no headsets required, considering the whole room acts as a giant headset, by way of a technology that Rawiri designed himself.

Something's different from when I was here last. It's not until I sit in one of the gaming chairs that I work out what it is.

'Super-quiet in here,' I say, once Rawiri has closed the door behind us.

Just how I like it, he think-says, and I realise he's installed blockers in the walls; the alternating magnets that the BSI are so fond of. *But I can't speak for the absence of hidden mics, so we should talk like this.* He cuts Fox a worried glance.

Relax, Fox think-says, thudding into the chair beside me. *I've taken a vow of silence.*

As per Offspring rule number three, I think-say, if only to reassure our uncle.

Rule number three: An Offspring's promise is binding . . . until death.

Rawiri grunts. *That's meant to make me relax?* he think-asks, but his hue has softened. He feels sorry for us. That's the last thing we need right now.

Tell us what you've got, I think-say, unable to wait any longer.

Our uncle passes a hand over his forehead. *What I'm about to tell you is something that goes all the way to the heart of the BSI*, he think-says. *To tell you the truth, it's got the potential to blow them apart.*

What have you found out? Fox think-asks.

So, he says, *last night I broke the law. At least, I broke a BSI law.* He jumps up and crosses to the drinks fridge in the corner. *Coke-X, anyone?*

'*No*,' Fox and I chorus.

Well, you know where they are if you change your mind. Rawiri flips the tab on a can and sits down again. *I have to admit, this Riva business is giving me the shits. Thought I'd travel forward thirty years, see if it was as bad as all the predictions would have us believe.*

And is it? I think-ask.

Yes and no. I mean, mostly yes. For a start, there are clones everywhere, doing all the menial jobs, and non-clone young people are a rarity. But that's not what was really interesting. He gulps on the Coke-X. *I navigated to the BSI building. And what do you think I found?*

A black hole? Fox think-suggests.

Good guess, Rawiri think-answers, his sarcasm a match for my brother's. *But no. Anyway, the building was there, with the BSI symbol and everything. But when I* shifted *inside — as a fly, mind you, because I didn't want to call attention to myself — who do you think I came across?*

Deciding I need a drink after all, I jump up and grab a Coke-X out of the fridge. *Yourself?*

Rawiri tilts his head to one side. *Actually, no. But what I did find was the office of the director-general. There was a different name on the door, which was no more than I expected. Underwood would be dead or retired by then, I would have thought.*

You would have thought, I say, the cogs starting to turn in my brain.

Well, here's the thing. I shifted *in there, a fly on the wall, and the new boss — a woman — was talking to a colleague. It almost looked as if he was physically in the room with her, but then I realised it was a projected image from some kind of video link, that this colleague was beaming in from London. And guess who it was?*

Dad? Fox think-asks, looking crushed when our uncle shakes his head.

I'm guessing it wasn't you, I think-say.

It wasn't me, no. It was someone she called Rudy. And he looked like this. He's showing us an image, one that makes my mouth drop open. It's *him*, Rudolph Underwood. He's got the same shiny bald head, the same lined features.

He should look heaps older than that, I think-say, chugging the rest of my drink.

He should look thirty years *older than that*. My uncle drains his can, too, and crushes it. *Which made me think that someone has been playing with someone else's stem cells. The stem cells of someone who is already immortal.*

Someone like me or Indigo, I say. *Right?* Unbelievable. When did Underwood do that? Hang on — what if he's already done that in our present time? No wonder he was so eager to get a sample off me. What if he can *already* read our minds? And if so, what other secrets has he already extracted from us?

My uncle doesn't say anything, but I can tell from his thought-stream that he's already thought of all these possibilities, and more.

He nods at my can. *Want something a bit stronger?*

My mood coal-black, I say, *Why not?*

And Fox think-says, *I bet you anything this Underwood dude knows where Dad is.*

My little brother is smarter than I gave him credit for.

FORTY-ONE:
BILLY

2065

Let me make this clear: I was in love with Indigo Moon. If it hadn't been for Aurelia, we could have had a fine life together.

I should have been more careful. But love addles the brain; opens one up to mistakes.

I'd been laying low, trying my best to keep my mind blocked whenever I wasn't utilising my telepathic talents. Problem was, once I'd found Indigo, I couldn't resist the urge to know where she was and what she was doing every minute she was away from me. And when she was with me, how tempting it was to communicate in thought-speak, to mind-mine her for information on her family and friends, to take her on time dates. New York, LA.

Jesus, LA. I can hardly bear to think about what happened in LA.

I'd taken Indigo shopping on Santa Monica Boulevard, and had blown a cool ten K on clothes, shoes and accessories for the awards evening. How beautiful she was, so fresh, so unspoiled. What a stunning couple we'd made at the awards, not to mention the parties before and after, enough to turn heads and stir jealousy in men and women alike. I couldn't remember the last time I'd felt so content.

That was, until I glanced across the room and saw the only person who could ever hope to match Indigo's allure. She was wearing an elegant dress the colour of blood, her blonde hair cut into perfect layers. It's hard to say what I felt then. Nostalgia. Regret. And thick, overwhelming fear. I sculled my Champagne and prepared to whisk Indigo away after citing an upset stomach or whatever it would take to convince her we needed to get out of there *right now*.

But before I could even open my mouth, I smelt her, roses and rain, and heard her no-longer girlish voice. 'Billy Raven, I thought it was you! Where have you been hiding?' How had she moved so fast?

Well, Aurelia think-said, *I* am *superhuman, after all*.

'Aurelia.' I tried to keep my voice steady. Was she going to take me out right then, destroy me in front of everyone? Steeling myself, I kissed her on each cheek before slinging a protective arm around Indigo's waist. 'Aurelia, meet Indigo. Indigo, this is Aurelia.'

'Lovely to meet you,' Aurelia said aloud, and in another closed-comm to me, *And where did you meet* this *fine specimen, Billy?*

None of your business, I shot back, and suddenly it was as if Aurelia and I were the only ones talking, the only ones moving forward in time.

How did I know this? Because the whole room had stilled, as if someone had hit pause on a movie. Out of the corner of my eye, I saw a wine glass frozen in mid-air, having slipped out of someone's hand half a second before.

'You seem to have developed a taste for Offspring,' Aurelia said, circling Indigo, whose own glass had halted halfway to her lips.

'Leave her alone,' I said through gritted teeth.

'Leave her alone?' Aurelia trailed a tapered fingernail down Indigo's arm. 'Oh, I don't think so.' She was rummaging through Indigo's mind, I could tell. Jesus, what was Aurelia going to do now? Erase Indigo's memory banks? Tell Indigo all about my past with her? Turn Indigo into a vegetable?

Aurelia dropped her hand. 'Do stop panicking, Billy. She's got potential, hmm?'

'I don't know what you're talking about.' My ears were ringing. Nausea gripped my gut. What was going on? And how had Aurelia managed to stop time?

'Billy, Billy.' It was *my* arm Aurelia was touching now, her fingers unnaturally warm. 'Don't sound so surprised. You have debts to repay, after all.'

'Debts?'

'Let me see. Quite apart from the slaying of my brother — more on that later — you've robbed the Eternity Project of one of their greatest assets.'

'I assume you're talking about Andromeda.'

Aurelia tapped her chin. 'Very good. Now tell me, what's to stop me dragging you into 2088 and having you tried for rape, murder and abduction? They have interesting ways of dealing with virally optimised criminals and Offspring, although vampires could require special attention, I imagine.'

Desperate to escape, I did the only thing I could think of, but was arrested mid-*shift* by a blinding pain in my skull, the equivalent of being whacked by a virtual hammer.

Don't even think about it, Aurelia purred. *Or you get to watch your girlfriend being tortured before we harvest her.*

Stop it, I think-pleaded. The pain in my head eased, leaving a dull, unpleasant ache. I squared my shoulders, looked around the room.

'What do you want?' I asked, my voice strained.

'Why, it's simple,' Aurelia said, and pointed at my second love. 'I want her.'

FORTY-TWO:
INDIGO

When I come to, I'm lying on my side in an unfamiliar bed, the light in the room telling me it's either early morning or early evening. When I try to sit up, it's as if I have a weight on top of me.

Oh no. The heavy thing isn't on top of me, it's inside me. How did my belly get so humongous? When I cup the bulge, it moves in an alarming way.

'Oh!' I could swear that was a foot . . . and there's something else nudging under my ribs. Another foot? A head?

'Good morning.' A figure bustles in and, seconds later, the tinted windows clear, revealing a dawn-pink sky. 'How are we feeling?'

Moving like a stranded whale, I manage to sit up by swinging my legs over the side of the bed. The woman standing by the window is dressed in a nurse's uniform, her hair tied up in a bun, her mouth and nose covered with a mask.

'How's baby this morning?' the nurse continues, as if we've met before. 'Has she been moving?'

I nod, still trying to process what's going on. The nurse's accent is Kiwi, which means I'm most likely in New Zealand. From the mask, I'm picking that the Riva pandemic has really taken off, as predicted. Either that, or I'm infectious in some other way.

The nurse moves forward and snaps a cuff around my arm,

which starts inflating. 'Any more bleeding?'

Bleeding? I gape at her. 'From where?'

'Down below, of course.' Her brow wrinkles. 'Unless you've been having bleeding elsewhere?'

'No. I mean, no, I don't think so. I don't remember.' I cast my eyes around the room. I'm obviously in a hospital, but which one? I get my answer when I look more closely at the nurse. Her uniform is turquoise, with the lyre emblem I'm used to seeing on Auntie Violet's work shirts. The nurse's badge tells me that her name is Teva. I've been returned to the Apollo Foundation, then — by Aurelia, no doubt.

'Let's have a peek, shall we?' Teva suggests. From the direction of her gaze, I realise *exactly* where she wants to peek. If only I could read her thought-stream, but — surprise, surprise — she's wearing a blocker. So much for that.

'You don't need to,' I say. 'I'm not bleeding.' At least, I don't think I am, but how long have I been out to it? Months, if the size of my stomach is anything to go by.

'Yes, but I need to assess your cervix. If you're about to go into labour, then best to know sooner rather than later, hmm?' With that, she makes me lie down again and proceeds to examine me down there. 'OK, no sign of anything happening yet,' she says a couple of minutes later. 'But remember, you're on strict bed-rest, OK?'

'Why?'

Teva gives me an are-you-nuts? look, which is fine, because I'm starting to wonder if I'm going crazy, too. 'I'm sorry, I thought someone would have told you by now,' she says, as if it was my fault for not paying attention. 'The longer you keep baby inside, the more chance we give her lungs to mature. Even a few more days makes a difference at this stage, although baby may need to come out sooner if your blood pressure doesn't behave.' She takes a penlight out of her breast pocket and shines it in my eyes. 'Do you have a headache? Blurry vision?'

'No.' At least, I didn't before she tried to blind me with her torch.

'No other signs of pre-eclampsia,' she says under her breath and strolls towards the door.

Desperate for more morsels of information, I ask, 'Um, so how many weeks am I today?'

Teva pauses. 'Thirty-four weeks and two days.'

'And,' I grab her sleeve before she can leave, 'I know this sounds dumb, but I can't remember the date. I really need to know the date.'

'It's the eleventh,' she says, and when I give her a blank look, 'of June. Now, try to get some rest.'

As soon as the door locks behind her — and from past experience, I know that 'locked' is the right word — I start seeking with my thought-stream, but I can't hear anything, anyone. The walls are blocked, too, then. Again, no surprise, but it's incredibly frustrating.

Feeling another kick, this time aimed at my bladder, I jump, then burst into tears. I've never felt more helpless. Somehow my life has been fast-forwarded several months and now I'm locked up, waiting to give birth — and then what? Will Aurelia swoop in to claim me and the baby? What will happen to me after that? And what has happened to Rigel?

Realising I'm busting to go to the toilet, I clamber out of bed again and waddle to the bathroom. Is going to the toilet OK when you're on strict bed-rest? How would I know? After peeing for what seems like forever, I stare at myself in the mirror. My cheeks appear fuller, my hair longer and lusher. And although I feel enormous, it's really only my stomach that's sticking out, my arms and legs are as skinny as ever. The thing inside me is moving again, and it's the strangest sensation. When I peer down, I'm sure I can see the outline of a foot.

'Who are you?' I whisper, and detect an answering ripple that's nothing to do with the physical movements inside me. The walls may be blocked, but suddenly I can detect the only other thought-stream in range, and it's clear and bright and so beautiful I almost start crying again. There are no words from her, but I'm getting shapes and sensations, and a pink glow that can only be — what? Warmth? Comfort? Love? There's her heartbeat, too, strong, sure, steady. There's her essence, her dream-flow, almost fully formed.

I sink onto the tiles. What's Rigel doing? Is he still alive, and, if so, does he know I'm here? Where did the last four months go?

'Goodness me, are you all right?' A woman with golden hair crouches beside me. 'Don't worry, Miss Moon,' she says. 'You're safe here.'

I look up — and gasp. It's Laura, the woman from the Norwegian cell, the woman who stole my stem cells and threatened to Erase my brain. 'Get away from me!' I shout. 'Get away!' I hit out at her, even though I know it won't do me any good.

I feel a sharp pain in my neck, hear a murmur of voices and then—

Nothing.

FORTY-THREE:
RIGEL

After the revelation about Underwood, both Fox and I are busting to find out more. But our uncle makes us go to sleep first, as if that's even remotely possible, before reconvening in the games room the following morning.

Where shall we start? Rawiri asks. He's sitting in his gaming chair, which has a harness for when things get really wild, like when he flips upside down.

We need to find Indigo and Dad, Fox think-replies.

Obviously — but where do we start? I swing my chair around to face Rawiri. *When was the last time you talked to Dad?*

The day after he left here. He'd just reached London, and you'd just got yourself into a spot of bother. . . remember?

Oh . . . yeah. How stupid I'd been, dared into *shifting* into a tiger by my friends and setting off a manhunt. Not only that, but I'd attracted the attention of the BSI. Yet rather than punishing me, they'd recruited me.

It was bound to happen sooner or later, my uncle says, in tune with every wave and eddy of my thought-stream. *The recruitment, I mean.*

Could have recruited me, Fox think-mutters.

Ignoring him, I think-say, *Did Dad know they were going to do that?*

Yeah. Rawiri's thought-stream angles away from me, but I reach for it, not willing to let it go.

You argued about it?

Kind of.

Why was he against it?

My uncle clears his throat. *He said you were too young, but I got the sense that wasn't the whole story. When I said that we needed your assistance to help flush out a time assassin, Johnno said, 'All right then, but just so you know, there may be more than one.'*

I frown. *You already knew about Billy Raven when you recruited me?*

Of course we did. Why do you think the Black Wolf was in London? Rawiri think-asks, referring to Dad by his BSI alias.

Seriously? I stand up and pace around the room, pausing next to the shelf with the weirdo figurines my uncle likes to collect, including some of his own gaming merchandise — such as the creepy teal-eyed children of the Plague, with their spiral and Rod of Asclepius tattoos. *I thought you said he was flushing out a cell.*

The cell, yes, Rawiri think-mutters. *One he'd stumbled across when he wasn't meant to be looking, you know what I mean?*

I come to a halt. *Do you think Underwood has something to do with the splinter cell that captured Indigo?*

I think Underwood has everything to do with the splinter cell. My uncle's thought-stream is grey and scalpel-sharp. Mine is glowing red. The Norwegian splinter cell had harvested Indigo's bone marrow without her consent, saying they wanted to use her stem cells to cure infertility. Underwood had taken a sample of my bone marrow, too, saying he needed it for safe-keeping.

And look who's stopped ageing, I think-say, remembering the debriefing we had just after Indigo, Andromeda and I had killed Billy Raven the first time. Indigo had said *he told me that the splinter cell wanted a supply of organs and stem cells for anyone who's willing to pay the price. I think they wanted to sell my cells to normals who want to live forever.*

Trying to curb my rage, which is threatening to trigger a *shift* into tiger form or something more deadly, I think-say, *Did Dad say anything else?*

Rawiri exhales. *He said, 'It is just an illusion here on Earth that one moment follows another one, like beads on a string, and that once a moment is gone, it is gone forever.'*

Slaughterhouse-Five, Fox think-says, knowing as well as I do how Dad loves that book. *What's that supposed to mean?*

I shake my head. What are we missing? I wonder. Why does our father keep referencing the Vonnegut book as though it's some kind of manual or holy text?

Fox drums his fingers on his knee. *Maybe he means that we can go back in time, try and fix what's already happened.*

Maybe, I think-say, although something tells me it's not that simple. *But . . . We could travel to that day, the last day you spoke to him.* I'm directing this to Rawiri. *Do you think we can do that?*

And my uncle says, *Yes. Yes, I think we can.*

We're still in my uncle's games room, but it's three months ago, November 2066, and we're staring at past-Rawiri through our compound eyes. Past-Rawiri hasn't noticed the trio of flies on his ceiling. He's too focused on the thought-conversation he's having with my father.

With my father. I can't believe I'm hearing Dad's voice, the voice of the person he was before his dream-flow got ripped out of his physical body.

He's too young, my father is think-saying. *I'd rather keep him out of this whole mess.*

We need him, my uncle think-answers. *This Billy Raven guy is more powerful than anyone we've ever come across. And we know that an Offspring's abilities are more developed than ours.*

My father's thought-stream glows purple. *We have no idea what Rigel is capable of.*

That's exactly my point. Rigel is nearly eighteen, and if we don't act soon, Raven will slaughter more of us.

If the information we've been given is correct, that is. My father is thinking about the intel the BSI members were sent by encrypted message just over a week ago; intel that Camilla Chase had told them came from a source she couldn't reveal. <mark>Time assassin . . . goes by the name of Billy Raven, age indeterminate, behaviour dangerous and unpredictable.</mark>

If the intel is correct, Raven is taking the abilities of others and making them his own, past-Rawiri think-says.

Which is why we need to be even more cautious, my father think-says. *Rigel would be a prize catch.*

Raven is threatening the futures of all our children, my uncle think-says, even though he doesn't have any of his own. Not that I know of, anyway.

My father think-sighs. *All right, then*, he think-says. *But just so you know, there may be more than one.*

More than one what?

More than one person to worry about, if you can call Raven a person. Look, I've come across something really— He breaks off.

Are you going to let me out of my misery? my uncle asks, once it's clear my dad isn't going to finish his sentence.

All I can say is, be careful who you trust. That's when Dad quotes the line from *Slaughterhouse-Five*, the one about it being an illusion that one moment follows another one. *I've got to go, OK?*

Speak soon, past-Rawiri think-says, and as one, present-Rawiri, Fox and I think-chime *Now*, and follow the contracting arc of my father's thought-stream to its source, like iron filings to a magnet, simultaneously *shifting* and appearing—

Inside the carriage of a magnet train, which is hurtling through the countryside. My father is sitting facing forward, although his gaze is on his I-Bio rather than the view outside. I'm guessing we're in France from the signs on the inside of the train, although I suppose we could be anywhere in Europe. There's something strange about the signs, though, something I don't get a chance to figure out, because at that moment a door at the end of the carriage opens and a bald man in a suit enters.

Remember, my uncle think-tells me, *we're merely observers.*

Observers, I think-echo, my compound fly eyes fixed on the stranger, who isn't a stranger at all. *Easy for you to say.*

No. Rawiri's thought-stream is colourless, the hue of helplessness and regret. *No, it's not.* I've worked out what's weird about the signs. At least one, an advertisement for the theatre, has *2088* on it. So my father was time-travelling after all. And Underwood hasn't aged. One. Bit.

'Hello, Black Wolf,' Underwood says, sitting opposite my father and straightening his cufflinks. 'In a hurry?'

'Not at all,' Dad says.

Rawiri, as if sensing what I'm about to do, think-says *Don't*, but I can't help it. I need to find out what happened. I blink, realising I'm looking through human eyes once more — my father's eyes. The minute the words 'Not at all' leave my father's lips, there is an agonising pain in our skull, and I'm travelling with my father this time, not just travelling but being sucked into a spiralling vortex—

And I hear a voice, Billy's, say, *Didn't anyone ever tell you that curiosity killed the big bad wolf?*

Prick, my father think-gasps and hits out, but there's nothing to hit out with, his dream-flow body gone. There's nothing to see, only darkness flowing through us, no colour, no light. The spinning gets worse and worse, until I feel as though I'm going to throw up. What a relief that would be, but we have no body, no form. That's when I realise that Billy has reached out from who-knows-where and ripped Dad's dream-flow from his body; just as Audrey did the same to my mother all those years ago.

Hold on, I tell myself, even as the pain rips through us. How can there be such agony when we have no physical form? How I wish I could let Dad know I'm with him, but I can't let Raven know I'm here. Not yet. There has to be another way, something else I can do.

I need to find my father's body. I need to retrieve his dream-flow from the time slip or time spiral or whatever the hell this is, and reunite them once more. There's only one way I can think of to do that. It's not as if I haven't done it before.

If only you'd left well enough alone, Raven think-says, and I sense a glimmer now, so faint and brief, like a lighthouse in a storm. It's time to leave my father, as hard as that is, and make the leap—

Out of my father's dream-flow and into Raven's.

If I'm in luck, he won't even know I'm there.

The next thing I know, I'm looking straight into Billy Raven's eyes — handsome, slick, debonair — at least to the outside world. How could Indigo have let him anywhere near her?

'Well done,' Raven says to his mirror-image, before leaving the office. It's a short walk down the shiny corridor to his destination, a door with a plaque on the outside that says *Rudy Underwood, Director-General*. It's an image I remember from when Rawiri showed it to me, an image from 2088. No wonder I'm feeling so disorientated.

'Come in,' Underwood calls out before Raven has raised his fist to knock.

'Show-off,' Raven says, loping inside.

'You've been doing the same for the past century or so, sneaking around other people's thought-streams like a dog on heat.' Underwood leans back in his swivel-chair. On the wall behind him is a massive painting that at first glance looks like a stained-glass window, but is actually a replication of a DNA sequence coded in multiple different colours.

Raven perches on the edge of the desk. 'Fun, isn't it?'

'May I remind you that in some cultures, sitting on desks is considered to be a filthy habit?' Underwood points at the stool in front of the desk.

'This reminds me of the dunking stool they used to use for witches,' Raven says, transferring his butt.

'Is that what you do in your spare time? Travel back to scenes of torture?'

'I don't need to travel anywhere for that.' Raven takes a paperweight off the desk, a fake eye suspended in glass, and peers through it. 'Don't you want to know what I did with your Black Wolf?'

Underwood tents his fingers. 'If you can promise me that he's gone for good, then that's all I need to know.'

'Fine. He's gone for good.' Raven sets the paperweight down. 'What are you going to do with the body?'

'Use it, of course. Virally optimised stem cells fetch a high price on the black market.'

'Speaking of prices . . .'

Underwood gives us a look that has me wondering if the eye in the glass paperweight is real after all. 'Your debt isn't repaid yet, Mr Raven.'

'What?' Raven angles forward. 'I stopped Black Wolf sniffing around your splinter cell, didn't I? And gave you a supply of stem cells for another century or so, at a guess, although admittedly his powers of regeneration may be slowed a little without his dream-flow.'

'That's hardly enough to make up for letting our prize catch escape.' The director-general's voice is like a slamming door. 'The Black Wolf is no replacement for Andromeda, as you know. Females' stem cells are much more potent, especially when they're from second-generation Offspring.'

Raven sighs, picks at his fingernails. 'So what do you want, then?'

'I want you to bring me someone else.' Underwood presses a button on his desk, and the wall to his right lights up. Raven's shock mirrors mine, or maybe it's the other way around, I'm not sure. In the photograph, Indigo is laughing at something or someone out of the field of view, her Smart-Glasses sitting on top of her head, her expression more carefree than I've seen in months.

'I can find you someone else,' Raven says.

'No, Billy,' Underwood says, stretching out the vampire's name as if it's chewing gum. 'I want *her*. Indigo Hoffman is her name, although she also goes by the name Indigo Moon. She's Offspring, and if you get her in time, we'll be able to retain her fertility before the Riva virus really takes hold. Will there be a problem with that?'

I sense Raven's Adam's apple bobbing up and down, feel his fists clench beneath view of the desk. 'No,' he says. 'Not at all.'

If only I could get Raven to *shift* into wolf form so that we could tear Underwood's throat out. But I can't. Not yet. I have other work to do.

'Excellent.' Underwood waves a hand, and the screen blinks off. 'Once you've brought her to us, then we can discuss how we can use your talents in other ways, for which you will be compensated most generously.' He glances up. 'Well? What are you waiting for?'

I'm not sure if Underwood hears the low growl in Raven's throat, any more than he can detect the duplicitous twist of Raven's thought-stream. They're blocking each other, after all.

'Your wish is my command, director,' Raven says, standing up and giving Underwood a mocking bow.

'Piss off, Raven,' Underwood says, his tone bored, and Raven does just that.

At least, *Billy* thinks he does, because at the moment Raven enters the corridor I make my move.

'For God's sake, Raven,' Underwood says when I return, closing the door so he can't hear the actual Billy Raven's footsteps receding down the corridor. 'What do you want now? Three singing virgins? A partridge in a pear tree?'

'Nothing so difficult,' I say, sitting on the stool and crossing one leather-clad leg over the other. 'I require a piece of information so I can keep the Black Wolf's dream-flow safe.'

'And what would that be?'

I pick up the paperweight, contemplate chucking it at his head and think better of it. 'Where have you stowed his body?'

Underwood's lips twist around each other like snakes. 'Why,' he says, 'it's right here. Want to have a look?'

FORTY-FOUR:
INDIGO

It's the afternoon of the same day, a day where I've been poked and prodded and sampled. Laura tells me I fainted in the bathroom before, but I know she's lying. I haven't spoken to her since she sedated me. What's the point?

Teva tells me that I'm having an ultrasound next, as if I need one when the baby is moving all over the place. I could tell them that there's nothing wrong with the baby. I can tell from her thought-stream.

Oh man, I'm still reeling, still trying to figure out how this could have happened. How could Rigel and I have conceived a baby from time-travelling back to November? But nothing else makes sense. I wasn't pregnant before we did that, I'm sure I wasn't. For one thing, my belly was a whole lot flatter, and my boobs weren't the size of melons. I've also had two periods since then. And now I'm castigating myself for being so careless. But how could we have expected *this* to happen? It's as if time is messing with us rather than the other way around, as if it's seized on the opportunity to—

Hang on, hang on. What if this was *always* meant to happen? What if I hadn't met Billy last November? Would Rigel and I have got together and accidentally conceived a baby anyway? Maybe Rigel was right, and time is a god after all, trying to set things right.

Exhausted, I turn on the e-screen and swipe through the

channels. The Riva pandemic is proving almost impossible to contain, especially when no one gets that sick. What do most teenagers care about fertility? I settle on an old movie instead, one that always used to make me laugh.

It doesn't make me laugh now. I can't concentrate. All I can think of is how I can try and get a message to Rigel, if he's still alive. *That* thought makes me want to cry, but crying's not going to get me out of here. I turn the e-screen off and sink into the pillows, closing my eyes. I can't hear any thought-streams, because of the alternating magnets in the walls. I can't hear any thought-streams, but I can hear something else.

I frown, then get out of bed, which is another mission that ends up with me in tears again, mostly because I can't believe that my body has betrayed me like this. My body — or time? Or is this something that Billy and Aurelia have engineered between them?

'Stop it,' I whisper, touching my fingers to the wall. I close my eyes again. Perhaps I'm imagining it, but I can feel the force of the magnets. Not only that, but I'm picking up on the gaps, the split seconds when the polarity changes. Holding my breath, I stand very still, waiting for the next gap and — there. It's fleeting, like a flicker of a flame, but in that split second I heard the hum of other thought-streams. Hope sparks within me.

If I can detect others' thoughts in the gaps between the magnets, then perhaps I can send messages, too. Even better, perhaps I could—

The door slides open, making me jump.

'Hel-lo.' It's Teva, accompanied by a woman pushing a trolley. 'Laura's here to do your ultrasound.'

I shoot Laura a venomous look. Laura gives me a saccharine-sweet smile in return.

'I'm sure you're dying to see your baby,' she says. I don't answer, know there's no point in resisting. Besides, I'm curious to see what the baby looks like now, because what I saw in Scotland looked like a frog.

What I'm not expecting is to see a full-on face, with eyelids and a nose and lips that could almost be smiling.

'Isn't she beautiful?' Teva says. Scared I'll start crying again, I merely nod, my gaze fixed on the images on the screen.

Laura pushes buttons, moves the probe lower. 'Everything looks perfect.'

'No cause for bleeding, then?' Teva asks. I don't know why she's fixated on that. I haven't had any bleeding as far as I can remember.

That's the problem, though. My memories appear to have a big hole in the middle, one that is four months long.

'No cause for bleeding.' Laura lifts the probe. 'The doctor will be along shortly.'

I tug the sheet over me. 'To do what?'

'Check up on everything else,' Teva says. 'You want the best outcome for you and your baby, don't you?'

I'm guessing we might have different ideas of what the best outcome might be, but I wait until Laura leaves the room before saying, 'Can't I be on bed-rest at home?'

'People have trouble sticking to the rules at home, we find. Best to stay here.' She gives me an unconvincing smile.

I cross my arms. 'Can I have visitors?'

'Unfortunately, we have a strict no-visitors policy at the moment, with the pandemic.' She straightens an invisible wrinkle in my bedclothes. 'Is there anyone in particular you'd like to speak to?'

'My boyfriend,' I say. 'And my parents.'

'Well, I'll see what I can arrange.' She takes my blood pressure again and frowns.

'What's wrong?'

'It's a bit higher than I'd like,' she says, pressing a couple of buttons on the machine. 'Have you got a headache?'

'No,' I lie, because all I want is to be left alone. It's no surprise I've got a headache after all the stress I've been through.

'Would you like a cup of herbal tea? A snack, perhaps?'

'No,' I say, staring out of the window until she gets the hint and leaves. Where is Rigel? Why hasn't he come to see me yet? Why haven't my parents come to see me, or even tried to contact me? Do they even know I'm here?

My back is aching. I wriggle around, trying to get comfortable before finding the least uncomfortable position and trying to focus on the e-screen again. But it's no good. The news is too depressing, especially as it's mostly about Riva and how the human race is about to become extinct. I turn it off and tune into the magnetic current again, listening for the gaps when it changes polarity. I can't hear anything, though, no matter how hard I try. It shouldn't be a surprise — why would they let me escape a second time — but I'm disappointed anyway. The e-screen is really crappy anyway, the image blurry. No wonder this headache seems to be getting worse by the minute.

My disappointment is turning to frustration, frustration to fury, when I hear a knock on my door.

'Good afternoon, Indigo. I'm Doctor Keira McMahon.' The doctor is wearing a mask and green-rimmed glasses with square frames. Although she appears middle-aged, with greying hair and a voice to match, the contents of my gut are curdling.

'I know who you are,' I say, and she lifts her chin.

'Really? I don't think we've met before.'

I stare at her. The last time I saw her was in Scotland, right before she spun me into the Eternity Loop.

I'm not here to kill you, Aurelia think-says. *Can't be losing our incubator, can we?*

I block her so fast that she hisses. 'Don't touch me,' I say. 'Don't come a step closer, or you'll be sorry.' My dream-flow is tight with fury, my vision coming and going. I've heard of seeing red, but this is ridiculous. My headache has progressed from an annoying ache to a pounding in both temples. I don't think I've ever had one this bad.

'Relax,' Aurelia says, for the first time looking slightly rattled. 'We can't have you bursting a blood vessel on us, can we?'

I'm so stressed at that suggestion — what does she know that I don't? — that I lose control, my dream-flow unspooling so fast I don't have time to stop it. The next thing I know, I'm plastered against the window, my compound-moth eyes taking in the view below of Auckland harbour.

'Very pretty,' Aurelia says. 'But *shifting* isn't going to save you now.'

At that moment several things happen at once. Waiting until I detect another gap between the magnets, I *shift*, reaching towards the outer arm of the spiral spinning in the periphery of my dream-flow and grasping it tight, right as a massive cramp grips my belly, right as Aurelia think-screams *Stop her, right now!*, as I think-call *Blood Moon! Blood Moon!*, and then I'm hurtling into yet another Eternity Loop, time's fugitive, destination—

Unknown.

FORTY-FIVE:
RIGEL

Underwood takes me to a room in the basement level, one containing a giant tank that's a lot like the ones at the aquarium my parents used to take me to as a kid. I'd gaze at the seals and sharks, my chubby hands pressed against the tank, my breath fogging the glass.

There are no seals or sharks in this tank, though. I stare, wordless, at my father's naked body, which is suspended in a liquid that wouldn't normally be compatible with life.

'Liquid nitrogen,' Underwood says. 'It's minus 196 degrees Celsius in there.'

'You froze him?'

'We did. Of course, we had to inject a cryo-preservative into his veins first,' Underwood nudges his own jugular, 'as otherwise we'd have run into issues with ice crystals forming in the cells. Pleasingly, there have been no signs of deterioration.' He checks a digital read-out on the side of the tank. 'The only issue is that we've stopped his cells from dividing, which means there is only a finite supply of stem cells to draw on.'

'You're worried about running out.' My voice is flat, my heart racing. I can't quite get my head around this. My dad has either been here for a couple of days or twenty-two years, depending on which timeline we're operating from — yet another Eternity Loop, another time-travel violation.

'Yes, although we've been very careful to take only what we need. The cells divide well when transplanted into another person, but for some reason we've been unable to clone them in the lab, so we keep having to come back to the source.'

'What will you do when you run out?'

Underwood taps his chin. 'That's where you come in. Presumably, once his dream-flow is restored, then the Black Wolf's cells will be able to start dividing once more. We'll need to warm him up before you retrieve his dream-flow, and we'd need to move him to a maximum-security facility. And of course, once you've brought us Indigo Hoffman — or Moon, as she likes to call herself — then we'll have another renewable energy source, one that will also address the fertility issue.'

I gesture at my father. 'What about him? Is he infertile, too?'

'Unfortunately, yes. Riva has been circulating for longer than anyone realised.'

'So how do you know that this Indigo girl is fertile?'

'Because,' Underwood says, 'she has already proven herself to be so.' He opens up his thought-stream and I gape as the truth rushes in.

'No,' I say.

'Yes,' the double-crossing, conniving, murderous BSI director tells me, 'the young woman you let slip through your fingers — the young woman you were so keen to seduce — is Indigo's daughter.'

'Andromeda,' I say through numb lips, trying to block him from my thought-stream, which is making a bunch of rapid-fire realisations and conclusions. 'But . . . that's impossible.'

'On the contrary, Mr Raven,' Underwood says, 'as you know, with Eternity Loops and dualities, almost anything is possible. If we get Indigo Moon into our possession, then all is not lost. In fact, we have everything to gain.'

'So you're going to do *that* to her?' I nod at the tank as if it's a small thing, nothing much to do with me.

'Oh, no. No, that won't do. Besides, I'm not sure we can prevent the inevitable, not if we want to keep our main prize.'

'What do you mean?' My head feels as though it's about to split open. There's an echo starting up in there, one that won't leave me alone.

Don't touch me, I hear Indigo say. *Don't come a step closer, or you'll be sorry.* Who's she talking to? Is Billy Raven with her? Whatever, it sounds like she's in trouble.

Underwood's teeth, when he smiles at me, are whiter than I remember. 'Unfortunately for her, Indigo Moon is merely the vehicle,' he says. 'A means to an end. Because I'll tell you this: once Andromeda is born, we'll ensure she receives the care and upbringing she deserves. And in doing so, we will ensure the preservation of humanity. Not just that, but we will herald in a new race. We'll create a race of superior beings, superhumans with the enhanced abilities that we've been cultivating since the first M-fever experiments began.'

'But what about In— This Moon girl?' I ask. I'm getting a signal now; the panicked flurry of Indigo's thought-stream, the rapid swirl of blood through two hearts.

He shrugs, so off-hand that I want to punch him. 'You win some, you lose some.' His eyes glitter at me. 'If it weren't for Andromeda's father, Andromeda wouldn't be alive at all. What a terrible choice, but what would *you* do?'

'What would I do?' What *am* I going to do? What have I already done?

'If you had to choose whose life to save — the mother or the child — what would you do?'

I gulp, trying to focus on him when all I can feel is a visceral tug deep within me, along with a massive cramp that nearly doubles me over.

'I would save them both,' I say, my eyes watering.

'That won't be an option,' Underwood says as the pain in my gut amplifies, as I realise Indigo is calling me, screaming *Blood Moon! Blood Moon!* and the twin heartbeats are thundering in my ears, both as rapid as each other.

'I'll find her,' I manage. 'I'll bring her to you.' What would Raven say at a time like this? 'Now if you'll excuse me, time is of the essence,' I blurt, then *shift* in the direction of the heartbeats, think-calling *I'm coming*, and I don't know if she can hear me, don't know if she's capable of meeting me, but I know this: if I don't find her soon, she'll be dead.

FORTY-SIX:
INDIGO

I'm lying in a puddle on hard, rocky ground and it's dark, so dark. I'm not sure what's worse, the pain in my head or the pain in my belly. The pain in my stomach is coming in waves, accompanied each time by a tightening in my belly. I may be young and inexperienced, but I'm not so naïve that I'm blind as to what's going on. I'm in labour, and there's no one to help me, no one who can stop this happening.

I moan and twist, trying to get comfortable, but it's impossible. I can't see very well, partly because of the lack of light, and partly because I have blurry spots in my field of view, but I think I'm in a cave. Where have I *shifted* to, and when? And how is Rigel ever going to find me?

The contractions are getting stronger and closer together. I don't think I've ever been in this much pain before, and I'm all alone. Can I *shift* again, get out of here? Where to? Back to the hospital, where they'll know what to do? To Santorini, where Andromeda can call an ambulance or a doctor? But what if she's not there?

After the next cramp-contraction-whatever-it-is eases, I detect the third heartbeat again. That's when I know he's coming and I get the sense that the air is bending or warping or I don't know what. Next thing I feel a hand on my shoulder, lips on my forehead and I can't speak can't cry can hardly breathe and my brain is foggy, and Rigel is saying, 'Hold on Indy — please, you have to hold on, we need to get help.'

But there's no time no time no time; no way that we can stop this, the inevitable. Another knife-like pain tears through my belly, and my head is about to split open and my heart is going *whump-whump-whump*, and I'm fading, I'm fading—

I need to tell him before it's too late. 'Brie is Aurelia,' I pant. 'And Aurelia is . . . Brie.'

'What?' Rigel says, at the same time as I hear Andromeda say, *I'm so sorry, Indigo. I'm so, so sorry*, and I understand that she's very, very far away and also very, very close and that's when I realise what she's been keeping from me all this time.

'Andromeda,' I gasp. 'Her name's . . . Andromeda.' And my heart is fluttering, moth-like, in my chest, and as the colours burst behind my eyes, yellow-green-purple, I rise above the cave, above the trees, and my eyes are full of moon and I'm setting my path, flying high and I know this is it, I've done my part and now I'm—

Going home.

PART II

FORTY-SEVEN:
RIGEL

———

'Here.' Indigo's mother places the baby in my arms. 'She's just been fed.'

'Huh.' I stare down at my daughter. My daughter. Our daughter, mine and Indigo's. Except Indigo died before Andromeda drew her first breath. Three weeks ago, the longest three weeks I've ever lived through.

If you had to choose whose life to save — the mother or the child — what would you do?

I would save them both.

That won't be an option.

I hadn't even known how little time we had. While I held the baby, waiting for her to suck in a breath, a blood vessel in Indigo's brain had burst. I could have saved her, could have healed her, but those precious few seconds I spent waiting for my daughter to breathe had cost Indigo her life. Eclampsia, according to the doctors who'd examined her lifeless body, caused by a massive increase in blood pressure. Her kidneys had failed. Her brain had failed.

I have failed. No matter how often I try to go back in time, to travel back to before it all happened, it never changes. It's as though my healing powers are drawn like a magnet to the baby rather than Indigo; as if time and fate are conspiring against me, against *us*. Or maybe I'm just doing it wrong. Maybe I'm just not smart enough to figure it out.

'Rigel,' Auntie Harper whispers, tears streaming down her cheeks. My thoughts have been flowing through to her, un-restrained. There's no point in trying to hold them in. They're threatening to drive me insane as it is.

Maybe I already am. Insane, I mean. Who wouldn't be after losing both parents and their girlfriend, the mother of their child, within a few months of each other? Although a few months is debatable, because somehow I've lost four months while I was time-travelling. It's winter outside, the trees stripped bare, the sky grey and close.

'You healed her,' Harper says, stroking the sleeping baby's downy hair. 'She started breathing because of you.'

'I never asked for that,' I mutter and push the baby back at her. The baby hiccups and starts crying. I block Harper, block the baby, and turn my head away. After a short time — but no time is short anymore — Harper leaves with the baby, closing the door behind her.

I stare at the BSI symbol on the door, that fucking Rod of Asclepius. I stare at it for ten seconds, maybe less, before picking up the glass beside my BSI-issue bed and throwing it at the door.

'I'm never healing anyone again!' I yell. 'Never, never, never!' I yell *never* until the door opens, keep yelling it as the needle goes into my arm, as the sedative infiltrates my thought-stream, pulling me down and under. It feels like drowning.

I wish I could drown.

I wish I were dead.

FORTY-EIGHT:
RIGEL

There's only so much you can take before you go crazy. I think I've reached my limit.

Today I wake up long enough from my sedation to ask where Rawiri is. I haven't seen him since I returned from the cave with a barely breathing baby and a newly deceased girlfriend. Can it really be four weeks since that happened?

The nurse gives me a blank look. 'Rawiri?'

'Rawiri Sullivan.' I'm sitting up in bed, poking at the unappetising food on my breakfast tray. Nothing tastes good anymore. 'He works here.'

The nurse shakes her head, but I know there's something she isn't telling me. If only I could read her mind, but she's wearing a blocker, just like everyone else who works in here.

'Where's Rawiri?' I ask Auntie Harper when she arrives with the baby.

'Oh.' She puts the baby in my arms and sinks into the chair. 'There was a . . . complication.'

'What sort of complication?'

The baby obviously senses my tension, because she starts crying. I freeze, as usual, because I have no idea how to soothe a crying baby and don't even want to try.

Harper takes the baby from me and jiggles her until she stops. 'He collapsed in the basement room of his house a few months ago, right around the time you disappeared,' Indigo's mother says. 'They had to use explosives to get in because Rawiri had sealed the room off.'

I twist the blanket between my fingers. 'So now what? Is he sick?' Or worse? Did they blow him up as well?

The baby starts fussing again. Harper takes a dummy out of her pocket and plugs it into the baby's mouth. 'He's very sick, but it's nothing to do with the explosives. They just blew off the lock with those. It looks as though he had a period without oxygen. He's alive, but there's no one there — you know what I mean?'

'As in, he's a vegetable?' When will this end? Is everyone around me cursed? Am *I* the curse?

'Well, I wouldn't like to put it like—' My aunt sighs. 'Sort of. He's breathing for himself and moving all his limbs, but he can't talk or do anything for himself.'

It doesn't make sense. Rawiri had the body of an eighteen-year-old, the ageing process arrested the minute he became virally optimised. How often do eighteen-year-olds have strokes?

'No one knows why it happened,' she says. 'Not even Fox, who was in the house at the time.'

'I bet,' I mutter, hoping my suspicions are wrong, that the BSI haven't used one of the Eraser devices the splinter cell had threatened Indigo with in Norway. I massage my forehead. There's something weird going on with my brain, too, something I'm only registering now that my sedation has fully worn off; now that I'm four weeks down the track from the worst thing that ever happened to me.

'Your brain scan was fine,' my aunt reassures me, obviously receiving my unblocked ponderings.

I could tell her what I think of that, which is that the brain scan doesn't know shit. Instead, I block her and watch her get a bottle out of the huge bag she's brought in, which is overflowing with nappies and baby wipes and tiny jumpsuits. Will a brain scan show the gaps in my memory? *Are* there gaps in my memory, or am I imagining that? I don't think I am. All I can remember is that one minute I was planning to shape-shift into Billy Raven's form, so I could try and find out where Dad's body was, and the next, I was in a cave delivering a baby. How did that happen?

'I think you should feed her,' Harper says, once she's exchanged the dummy for the bottle.

'I don't know how.'

'It's not rocket science.' She dumps the baby in my lap, making me support her head with my elbow while holding the bottle at a forty-five-degree angle. 'I know you've had a big shock, but, believe me, feeding them only gets harder. You might as well do it while it's easy.'

I bite my lip, trying not to focus on the baby, but now she's snuggled in my arms, gazing up at me with her blue-black eyes, I can't take my gaze off her.

'And I know you've been otherwise distracted,' Harper says, digging in the humungous bag, 'but it's time you gave her a name. I've been calling her Baby Doll, but I don't think she'd be too happy about that when she's older.'

'Indy named her,' I say, trying to keep all emotion out of my voice.

Harper starts. 'What? Why didn't you tell me that before?'

'I don't know. I guess I only just remembered.' And why is that, when those were the last words Indigo ever said to me? 'Andromeda,' I say, feeling a massive *whump* in the centre of my chest, and suddenly I can't breathe. Andromeda? Did Indigo merely like the name? Or — no, surely not? Because if the alternative is true, then it's almost too much to twist my tired brain around. Can the baby in my arms really be destined to grow into the Andromeda who helped us defeat Billy Raven in nineteenth-century America? Is that why the grown Andromeda helped us, because otherwise she might not have been born at all? Did she know Indigo was ultimately going to die from the time she very first met us? How could she not have?

'Oh Rigel,' my aunt says, sitting beside me and taking me into her arms, baby and all, 'it's going to be all right. Let me take you home. I'll give you as much help as you need. And Fox would love to see you, huh?'

I try not to look at Andromeda, try not to let her in, but it's impossible. Her dream-flow is fluttering, like a butterfly learning to spread its wings, and it's golden and new and innocent. And it's at that moment that I fall in love for the second time, and I know I'd do anything to protect this child, our child.

So why do I still feel so empty inside?

Harper's wrong. It's not all right. It will never be all right. But I know if I don't leave here, then I won't be able to *shift* again. I won't be able to travel. I won't be able to see Indigo, to hold her the way I did before everything went wrong.

'OK,' I say. 'OK. Let's go.'

FORTY-NINE:
RIGEL

Living at Auntie Harper's isn't much different from living at BSI HQ, considering the country is still in lockdown, still battling the invisible Riva virus. Sleep is almost impossible, although I guess I must be getting snatches of it in between waking to the baby crying and lying awake, going crazy with what I could have or should have done differently over the past few weeks. What if we hadn't time-travelled back to November and accidentally conceived a child? What if Indigo hadn't fled from Apollo when she did? If she'd stayed at Apollo, the doctors would have been there when she went into labour, would have been there to detect and stop the bleeding . . . wouldn't they?

And when I'm not doing that, I'm . . . well . . . reminiscing, I suppose you'd call it.

I know it's wrong, illegal even, if the Black Spiral rules still hold true.

Truth is, I can't help it. It's the only time I feel remotely alive, remotely like who I used to be.

Over the course of the next few weeks, I travel back to several good memories of hanging out with Indigo — in jungles, Indigo in one of her eerily beautiful giant moth forms; bringing down a deer when hunting as tigers in India; in my SUV after throwing our orca bodies around in the surf at Piha.

I return to that last one a lot. It was a couple of months before Indigo began time-travelling, before all the craziness started. We're lying shoulder-to-shoulder in the rear of my SUV, stars in our eyes and laughter in our lungs.

We should go to South America again, I say. *You could be a white witch*. Indigo says, *Is that meant to be an insult?* And I say, *It's a type of moth*, because I know how this script goes, know we'll end up play-fighting until I nearly kiss her. But I don't. Why didn't I? I guess I chickened out, scared she'd laugh at me, scared I'd ruin our friendship forever.

'Crap, look at the time,' I always say at the crucial moment, when kissing her could have changed everything. It's at that point that I always return to the present, because I don't want to disturb the arrow of time any more than we already have.

Sometimes I wonder why I bother. It's not as if things could get any worse.

I return to that other memory all the time, though, the one where Indigo and I were in her bedroom, mucking around when we were meant to be studying. But no matter what I do, kiss her or not, make love to her or not, nothing changes. Indigo is still dead, along with half my family. I still have a baby. I'm still in a black hole, unable to escape the gravity of consequence.

Are some things always meant to be, while others are alterable? Is there anything I can do to change where I've ended up? Poisoning Billy with taipan venom clearly didn't work . . . or did it? I haven't seen him since we did that.

At least, that's what I think until the day in the park.

On the day Andromeda turns six weeks old, I go to the park with Harper and Fox. We're all wearing masks, apart from Andromeda, who of course is too young. I'm pushing her pram and she's looking up at me, and when she smiles I get a yellow glow inside — one that mirrors her thought-stream, glittering up at me like a gold ribbon. Sometimes, at moments like this, I think that perhaps things aren't so bad after all. But then I'm reminded of how Indigo and my parents are dead and how Rawiri might as well be, and the black comes rushing in again.

'I don't see what the point of doing any schoolwork is,' Fox says, kicking his feet through the leaves. 'Once I turn eighteen, I can join the BSI anyway. They're not going to care whether I can write an essay or do algebra.'

'It doesn't hurt to exercise your brain,' Harper says, but her tone is vague, as if her heart isn't in it.

Andromeda gurgles and gives me another smile. I wonder if she can tell I'm smiling back at her behind my mask. Can she detect the hue of my thought-stream, or will she be like me and Fox, unable to read others' minds until she hits puberty? Will the next generation always be stronger than the last?

'Hey.' Fox nudges me. 'Remember that tree?'

I look up. In front of us is a Moreton Bay fig, its branches snaking along the ground and curling up into the sky.

'The fairy tree,' I say. We used to play for hours in this tree, pretending we were in a magical world while our parents read books or, in my dad's case, pretended to read a book when really he was draping it across his face while he was napping.

'I'm going to climb it,' Fox says, breaking into a jog. 'Come on,' he yells over his shoulder. 'What are you waiting for?'

Harper inclines her head at me. 'Go on,' she says, obviously picking up on my sudden urge to do the same as Fox. I follow him, running up to the tree and clambering into the branches. We could *shift* into any animal we choose, but we don't. Instead, we climb higher and higher, until the ground is far below us. It's colder up here, the wind whistling through the branches.

I peer down. Harper is wandering slowly along the path, pushing the pram, probably because Andromeda is crying. Not that I can hear Andromeda from here, but I'm getting the blue ripple of her distress, although by now I'm learning to distinguish her cries. This one is pure boredom.

Turns out babies get bored all the time. Who knew?

'So,' Fox says, swinging his legs, 'how's the time-travelling going?'

'I don't want to talk about it.'

'I'll bet you don't.'

'Piss off, will you?' If we weren't several metres off the ground, I'd be shoving him about now.

Fox shrugs. 'You're not the only one, you know', and when I narrow my eyes at him: 'Well, you can hardly tell me off.'

I sigh. 'Where have *you* been going?'

'Back to before,' he says, his tone melancholy now, the belligerence gone. 'When we were still a family. Like when we went on that holiday to Vanuatu, remember that?'

'Of course.' I'd got really sunburned when snorkelling and Fox had got stung by a jellyfish, but it was still one of the best holidays we'd ever had.

'Maybe you could have healed my arm, if you'd known.'

'I was only fourteen, so probably not.'

'You could have tried, though.' He leans forward slightly, and I suck in a breath.

'Don't fall. I don't know if I can fix a multi-trauma.'

'Fancy words. You should become a doctor.'

I huff through my nose. 'Then I really *would* be dead, after all that healing,' I say, and we both go silent for a moment, remembering Mum.

'Do you think things will get better?' Fox asks.

'I don't know. Maybe you should go into the future and take a look.'

'Yeah?' His eyes shine at me. 'Do you dare me?'

'No, I don't,' I say, an eerie sense of *déjà vu* washing over me as the edge of a memory slides into view then disappears again.

'Have *you* ever travelled into the future?'

'No, I— Wait.' I press my fingers into my forehead. 'This might sound weird, but do you think you could mine my memory?'

He frowns. 'For what?'

'For Indigo . . . you know.' I shake my head. 'My memories are really patchy around then. I'm missing something, I know it.'

'Right . . .' Fox gives me a contemplative look, even as I feel him delving into my mind, into my thought-stream and beyond. 'That's weird,' he says after half a minute or so. 'It's like there's a blurry spot in there.'

'In where?'

'In your memory, duh. Right around that time you're talking about.'

'Huh.' Have the BSI managed to erase part of my memory, the way I'm pretty sure they've erased all of Rawiri's?

'I can see when you were with us in the games room, after Mum died,' Fox says, 'and then . . . Oh.' His thought-stream clouds. 'That's horrible.'

I don't say anything, just block him so he doesn't have to see the scene in the cave, although from his expression, I figure he got the gist of it.

'Sorry. I didn't mean to show you that.' I frown at him. 'Hey. You've got one, too.'

'Got what?'

'A blurry spot.' In his temporal lobe, or more specifically in his hippocampus — which is, I know, where memories are stored.

Fox's eyes widen. 'What are you suggesting?'

'Take a look for yourself.' I grip the branch, letting my suspicions flow to him. 'They've erased our memories.' Selectively, in our case, rather than a whole-brain procedure as with Rawiri; I guess we'll never know whether Rawiri's total memory erasure was intentional or a mistake, something that could easily have happened to Fox and me. I sift through Fox's memory banks again, trying to get past the blurry spot. Fox winces. 'Sorry,' I whisper.

He grimaces, obviously realising what I'm attempting to do. 'Just do it, will you?'

'Not here. I don't want you to fall.'

'Later then.' He looks down. 'Hey. Who's Auntie Harper talking to?'

I follow his gaze . . . and freeze. Harper is standing a couple of metres away from the base of the tree, one hand on the pram handle, the other raised to shield her eyes from the sun. She's chatting to a strikingly good-looking guy with dark hair and skin that almost shimmers in the sunlight.

'What?' Fox asks as I scramble down the tree, a growl rumbling deep in my throat. 'Who's that?'

Stand back, I think-say. *I don't want you to get hurt.*

And Raven think-says, *Wait.*

FIFTY:
RIGEL

I scoop Andromeda out of the pram and hold her close. Her tiny heart thrums against my chest, like a hummingbird.

'I've killed you once,' I tell Billy Raven. 'What makes you think I won't try again?'

Behind me, Fox has assumed his namesake, and is slinking around us, his eyes bright. Harper, too, is coiling, ready to *shift*-strike.

'Relax,' Raven says, his hands up, as though he is truly afraid of us.

'She's dead,' I spit at him. 'Are you satisfied now?'

'No.' His voice is a whisper. 'I never wanted that to happen. I was in love with her. I needed her.'

'In love with someone who poisoned you?'

'Unfortunately.' He spreads his hands. 'I've come to offer my protection.'

'To who?'

'To her.' He inclines his head and Andromeda lets out a squawk. 'Aurelia is still out there, you know.'

'If I see her,' I say, my voice icy, 'I'll kill her, too.'

Fox paces around us, his teeth bared. *Why are you protecting her?* he think-asks. *What's in it for you?*

Billy's eyes are on Andromeda. 'It's only natural for a parent to want to protect their child,' he says.

'Are you kidding?' I feel like spitting at him. 'She's not related to you.' Of course, Billy had no idea about me and Indigo going back in time and hooking up just before Billy came on the scene. When he met Indigo, Billy knew he was her first and only lover; but that was then.

'I wouldn't be so sure.' For a moment, I worry he's going to snatch her away from me, but he stays where he is. 'But let's not quibble, hmm? I figure she's safer with you than me. And as for Aurelia, if I can deprive her of all she ever wanted, then I guess you could say I've succeeded in my . . .'

'Revenge?' I say.

'Love and revenge.' Harper gives out a bitter laugh. 'That's what makes the world go around, huh?'

'I don't believe you,' I tell Billy.

'I never lied to Indigo,' he says. 'All I ever wanted was for her to love and need me the way I loved and needed her.' His thought-stream curls around us, retracts again. 'I've hidden Andromeda from the view of others like us,' he says. 'Until she learns to project her own dream-flow, anyway. After that, my friend, it's up to you.' His outlines are becoming less distinct, his substance fading.

'Where are you going?' I ask.

'Nowhere and everywhere,' he says, and then he's gone, like a hallucination or a bad dream.

'What a load of bollocks,' my brother says, having *shifted* back into human form.

I gather my jacket around Andromeda. 'He's deluded if he thinks Andromeda's his,' I say, rattled at the thought that Raven could return any time to claim her. But if he'd wanted to do that, he would have done so by now . . . wouldn't he? And I'm remembering something Indigo had told me after escaping Billy for the second time: *I think he really did love me, even though he had a weird way of showing it*. I guess Raven probably isn't lying about that. I clear my throat. 'I suppose only time will tell.'

'Time has a lot to answer for,' Harper says.

'It sure does.' I gaze down at my daughter, whose thought-stream is slow and undulating, the flow of sleep. And all I can think is: *Maybe his protection worked. Andromeda grew into an adult, didn't she? But then why did he lock her into a time spiral? Was he trying to protect her, even then?*

I wonder what the adult Andromeda is doing now, if she's still trapped in 2005 Santorini. Or maybe that's another timeline, another future.

'Come on.' Fox tugs on my sleeve. 'We've got work to do, remember?'

'Work?' Harper asks. 'What sort of work?'

I shiver, grip the handle of the pram. 'Do you think you can look after Andromeda for an hour or so?'

'Of course,' she says, and we exit through the gates. The wind has picked up, and the leaves are swirling, red-brown-gold. When I squint, I can almost convince myself that there is a shape in there, like a bird, like a phoenix.

Phoenix, I think, which was my father's nickname, once upon a time. Phoenix. Johnno. Black Wolf.

Fox swings his eyes towards me, and I know he's getting the images, too, flowing from my blurry memory to his: a man floating in a tank. A man with a tattoo above his eyebrow. A man who is our father.

'Got to go,' I say, pushing the pram at Harper, and Fox and I *shift*—

Away from the park and into Rawiri's games room.

'At least the blockers are working,' Fox says, after shutting the door behind us. No chance of locking it — the explosives have ruined that — and the BSI could force their way in anytime they want anyway, so what's the point?

'The magnets.' I sink into one of the gaming chairs. 'I didn't even know they were there.' I rub my forehead. Or did I? Just another hazy memory, one I can't quite grasp the edges of.

We were in here, Fox think-says, sitting beside me. *All three of us.*

Playing a game? I think-ask, then, *No. We weren't playing a game.* I reach for the other memory again, the one with Dad in a tank.

Fox's thought-stream nudges mine, and we merge them, the whole greater than the sum of its parts. Memory fragments glimmer at us, gold nuggets in a stream.

Yes, I think-say. *Yes, yes.* Fox and I haven't been in this room since Rawiri got sick and Indigo died, but now we're here, it's all coming back. My father and the train. Underwood, the slimy bastard. Raven. The stem cells. And Dad, cryogenically frozen in a tank, his dream-flow trapped who-knows-where.

'Pricks!' Fox jumps to his feet.

Ssh, I think-say.

I'll kill them, he think-replies.

Believe me, I want to do that, too. But first we need to find Dad.

Fox glowers at me. *How are we meant to do that? Find Billy Raven and ask him to set Dad free?*

I stand up too and start pacing around the room. *No*, I think-say. *No, we need to stop Billy Raven being created in the first place.* I grab two cans of Coke-X out of the drinks fridge and lob one at him. *We need to break the Eternity Loop.*

Fox catches the can. *The Eternity Loop?*

The one involving Billy and Aurelia, I think-say, showing him what Indigo had found out. *A boy called Billy Quick kisses a girl who says she'll see him in a hundred years.*

So it's not enough to just kill Billy, then? Fox sucks on his drink, lets out a burp. *You need to kill her as well, correct?*

Fox is right. We can't close an Eternity Loop unless we address both ends of it. It's the only thing I can think of that could possibly bring someone back from the dead . . . and the only thing that will enable us to kill Billy and Aurelia. But how are we meant to do that? I pick up one of Rawiri's creepy mini-figs, a Child of the Plague with its teal-coloured eyes, and turn it between finger and thumb.

I don't think we can do this without Indigo, I think-say.

Then don't, my brother think-replies.

FIFTY-ONE:
RIGEL

I'm staggering backward, my hand clamped to my nose, which is streaming with blood.

You could have warned me that you were coming, past-Indigo think-says. I've just arrived in her room in the London BSI, and she's socked me one, thinking I was Raven.

It hurts just as much as last time.

Look, I think-say, settling into and taking control of past-Rigel's thought-stream, *we need to get out of here, fast.*

You think that's going to stop Raven coming for me? Indigo's grabbing a flannel from the bathroom, and oh, my chest is aching, hearing her voice again.

Maybe, I think-say, showing her where I want to go. *Quick, I'll tell you why when we get there . . . OK?* Without stopping to ask her permission, I wrap my arms around her and we *shift*—

Back to November 2066. We're hanging out in her bedroom, eating chips and pretending to study. The disorientation this time is brief, for me, anyway. There's Indigo lounging on the bed in her tiny shorts and bikini top, her lips twitching, on the verge of laughter as always. The old Indigo was never serious. It's so tempting to let this scene play out again, to feel the warmth of her body, to love her the way I've not been able to since the last time we left this room.

But I can't, because I know by now that it'll always end up the same way.

'Indy,' I say, and she sits upright, her smile fading. The Indigo from the BSI compound has settled into November Indigo's brain, and she's waiting for me to tell her what is so urgent. 'Look,' I say, 'I think we've figured out this Eternity Loop thing.'

'We?' Indigo fiddles with her necklace, a black spiral pendant she's worn ever since she was thirteen. 'Who's we?'

'Me and Fox.' Do I tell her? No, how can I tell Indigo that she's dead in my present?

'Are you all right?' Her expression has changed from intense to concerned.

I turn my head, swipe my wrist past my leaking eyes. 'Damn allergies.' I inhale, steady my voice. 'Aurelia created Billy, right? And Billy created Aurelia.'

'That's right.'

'So, we can't kill one without killing the other. They'll just keep creating each other again. It's like those toys where you hit one peg and the other one pops up, do you get it? We have to break the Eternity Loop so we can kill them for good.'

Indigo's thought-stream flickers and flares. 'That makes sense, I guess. But how are we meant to do that?'

'I've got an idea,' I say, at the same time as Fox think-says, *Can I come now?*

Soon, I think-reply, standing up and crossing over to Indigo. She doesn't protest when I clasp her hands, doesn't protest when I pull her closer.

'Whatever happens,' I say, my voice trembling again, 'remember that I'll never stop loving you.' Her lips are as soft as I remember, her jasmine scent intoxicating.

'I love you, too,' she whispers. It's all I can do to resist what could happen next, what did happen next in another past, another time.

'Indy,' I say, kissing her again before dropping her hands. 'We can't do this alone.'

Her forehead wrinkles. 'Uncle Rawiri?' she asks, then shrieks, clutching her chest. 'Jeepers, Fox! Is scaring the hell out of people hereditary in your family or something?'

Fox is sitting on the end of her bed. 'That's not all that's hereditary,' he says, obviously pleased that his time-travel skills are sharp enough that he's managed to find us.

'So,' Indigo says, transferring her glare to me, 'what's the plan?'

'Simple,' Fox says. 'Rigel and I kill Billy, and you kill Aurelia.'

Indigo chews her thumbnail for a moment, then says, 'No.'

'No?' Frustration simmers in my gut. 'What do you mean, no?'

She squares her shoulders. 'I got us into this mess, and I'll get us out. Leave Billy to me. You can take Aurelia out.'

'Deal,' Fox says.

'No,' I say. 'I don't want you anywhere near him, do you hear me?'

Indigo's gaze locks with mine, and I could swear the air is distorting around her, as if she's about to assume moth form. 'For a moment there, I thought you were trying to tell me what to do,' she says. 'But maybe I was wrong about that.'

The silence stretches out for long seconds. I'm the first to break eye contact.

'Fine,' I say. 'You take Billy, we'll take Aurelia.'

Later, as time's arrow points towards midnight, Indigo travels counter-clockwise, *shifting* across the world to 1988 London, while Fox and I travel clockwise, jumping forward twenty-one years to Rarotonga. Within a nanosecond (but relative to what, exactly?), we're crouched in a coconut tree, peering at the lagoon through our gecko eyes. The sand is bone-white, the lagoon baby blue. In the distance, I see a line of surf, the waves crashing against the reef.

Perfect, Fox think-says.

Perfect, I think-echo, my gut grinding with anxiety over what's happening with Indigo. But I can't think about her now. I need to focus on my target.

Our *target*, Fox think-says, and as one we expand our dream-flow, searching for her.

We're not looking for Aurelia, though. We're looking for a seventeen-year-old girl called Katerina, affectionately known as Kat. On we flow, skittering across the benign hum of the thought-streams of several islanders and tourists, over the mountain in the middle and down Muri Beach to a sprawling single-level dwelling with a wraparound balcony.

There, Fox think-says as our dream-flow hovers overhead. Her parents are nearby, but not in the house, I don't think. Shopping? At work? We *shift* again, into a pair of mynah birds sitting on the roof of a house in which a teenage girl sleeps, oblivious to what is about to occur.

Here goes, I think-say, and fly onto the sand below. There's no one else around, at least not that I can see. I focus on the image in my memory-banks, that of an olive-skinned man with dark eyes and hair. I've *shifted* into Billy Raven before, well enough to convince Underwood — but can I do the same with Kat? I'm hoping I can, since she's only met Billy the day before.

Taking a deep breath, I move around the side of the house. I'm tuned into her now, into the undulating flow of her sleeping thought-stream. Not for long, I think, raising my fist to rap, softly, on her window.

Kat, I think-say. *It's me. Billy.*

Nothing happens. My heart racing, I step away.

Try again, Fox think-says, right before the window opens and a blonde-haired girl pokes her head out.

'Oh,' she says, and smiles. 'I thought we were meeting at lunch-time.'

'Couldn't wait,' I say, trying to conceal my shock at her appearance. Of course Indigo had told me about Brie/Aurelia in the cave but it's another thing seeing the spitting image of Brie, apart from the colour of her eyes, and the absence of tattoos on Kat's eyelids.

Kat hesitates, then smiles. 'Well, you might as well come in,' she says, moving aside so I can clamber over the windowsill and onto her bed. All she's wearing is a singlet top and underwear that hardly cover anything.

'Cute teddy bear,' I say, before realising that doesn't sound very Raven-like. Or does it? How would I know?

Kat doesn't seem to notice, because she climbs onto my lap and winds her arms around my neck. 'I can't stop thinking about what happened last night.'

'Me neither,' I say. I don't know exactly what happened between her and Billy last night, but I can hazard a pretty good guess from the way she's kissing me. I draw away, and she pouts.

'Don't you want to?'

'I do,' I say, in a Raven-syrupy voice. 'But what about your parents?'

'They're at work. The resort never sleeps.' She strokes my arm. 'Mum will be home after two, Dad probably not until around seven tonight. Lots of time.'

'I like the sound of that.' I pass a hand over my forehead. 'Man, it's hot already. Let's go for a swim.' I smile at her, my gut twisting with dread. As much as I hate Raven and Aurelia and what they've done, I don't know how I'm going to bring myself to murder this girl. She seems so young, so innocent.

Kat sighs and stretches her arms above her head. 'You really know how to keep a girl hanging on, don't you?'

'You have no idea,' I say.

FIFTY-TWO:
INDIGO

When I appear in the doorway to the bedroom, the scene is exactly as I saw it in Billy's memory: a moody, dark-haired teenager is sitting on the bed, listening to music on flimsy-looking headphones.

The boy glances up and jerks in surprise. 'Blimey!' Billy Quick jumps off his bed. 'Who are you? How did you get in here?'

'Relax,' I say, closing the door behind me. 'Sorry to crash in on you like this, but I asked your dad if you were home and he showed me to your room.'

'Right . . .' Billy doesn't look as though he believes me.

I give him a friendly smile. 'Aurelia and I thought you might want to come to a party.'

'Aurelia?' He swallows. 'How do you know her?'

'She's only my best friend.' I swivel, taking in the posters on his walls. 'Oh, hey, Queen's my favourite band.'

Billy stands up. 'Where's Aurelia?'

My heart skitters. What if I can't pull this off? What if he refuses to come with me? If only I could shape-shift into Aurelia's form, but it seems that talent isn't something I share with Rigel. 'She's still getting ready, wants to look her best for you. I said I'd come get you, meet her at the bridge.'

'Oh. Right.' He glances down at his band t-shirt. 'Do I need to get changed?'

'It's a party, not the theatre. You look fine.' I affect a laugh. 'Come on, we'd better get going. We don't want her waiting by the bridge all by herself, do we?'

Billy grabs a denim jacket off the floor. 'OK, let's go. Do I need to bring anything?'

'Nah,' I say, letting him lead me down the hall, past the lounge with its flickering TV.

'See you,' he calls out to his dad, who is slumped on the couch. There's no response, which makes me wonder if Billy is going to question me about getting his dad's permission before, but he doesn't.

We exit the house and stride down the darkened street. Billy regards me from beneath lowered lids. 'What's your name?'

'Uh, Sarah,' I improvise.

'Aurelia never mentioned you.'

I snort. 'Typical.' I don't know how I can sound so carefree when I'm feeling anything but. I don't think I've ever murdered anyone in cold blood before. The last time we killed Billy Raven was an act of self-defence, an act of desperation.

This is desperate, too. And yet somehow I can't match the quiet, reserved boy strolling beside us with the Billy Raven I know — the suave, sophisticated, self-absorbed, cunning vampire who wants to have me for his child bride.

'Where's the party?' Billy asks.

'Over that way,' I say, gesturing vaguely across the other side of the river, which is flowing fast and black beneath the bridge. 'Hmm, doesn't look like Aurelia's here yet. She's probably getting changed *again*.' I stroll up the footpath, glancing over my shoulder at him. 'You seem to have that effect on her.'

'I do?' Billy thrusts his hands into the front pockets of his jeans. 'What else has she said about me?'

'Now *that* would be telling. Best friends should keep each other's secrets.' I loop my arm through his, sticking my other hand in the pocket of my duffle jacket. 'She said you were the hottest guy she'd ever kissed, though, and now I can see why.' Billy's thought-stream is flaming with embarrassment, the exact opposite of the cold, hard metal of the blade beneath my fingers.

Can I really do this, slit his throat and leave him to die? But what's the alternative — being Billy Raven's prisoner and baby factory for the rest of my life, which, being Offspring and all, could mean eternity?

Once we reach the apex of the bridge, I halt, and turn to face him. 'Is Aurelia the first girl you've ever kissed?'

He blinks at me. 'That's pretty personal, don't you think?'

'Just wondered.' I can tell from the twist of his thought-stream that I'm making him nervous. Not just that, but he's finding me curiously alluring. No surprise, I guess, since his future self is in love with me.

Which, I'm hoping, will play in my favour for what I'm about to do next.

After making a show of checking for any passers-by — the only people around are a man walking his dog on the riverbank below, and an occasional car going over the bridge — I say, 'Want to see what it's like to kiss another girl?' I tilt my head to one side. 'If nothing else, it'll be good practice for you.'

Billy swallows, flicks his eyes sideways. 'She'll kill me if she finds out,' he says, which probably isn't too far from the truth.

'She'll never know. This is just between us, me and you.' I turn my face up. Billy barely hesitates before leaning in to kiss me. That's when I start to have doubts about my plan. How am I supposed to get in the right position to slit his throat? What if

I miss? He's at least twenty kilos heavier than me and will over-power me easily.

No, I think, as the kiss deepens and Billy makes a noise in the back of his throat, desire colouring his thought-stream purple, no, I need to try something else.

Wu: Have you ever tried to control the thoughts of others?

Me: As in take over their thought-streams?

That's when I know what I need to do.

FIFTY-THREE:
RIGEL

Kat takes me to the other side of the island, saying there'll be less chance of us being spotted by her parents. We use an e-moped, Kat driving, me sitting behind her, my arms wrapped around her waist. I wonder if she's spotted the mynah bird overhead, tracking our progress.

Good work, Fox think-says in a closed-comm. I'm too terrified to answer. What if Kat, or even worse, Billy, hears us? We'll be shredded before we've even begun.

After parking in a secluded cove, we wander along the sand hand-in-hand, stopping every now and then to kiss.

'When will you teach me how to *shift*?' Kat asks, after a kiss that goes on for far longer than I'm comfortable with.

'Soon,' I say, peeling my shirt over my head. I walk backwards into the water, grinning at her. 'Maybe I can teach you how to *shift* in here. Ever wanted to be a dolphin?'

'Yes!' She strips down to her bikini and runs in after me. We horse around for a while, splashing each other and snatching kisses. It takes a long time to get out anywhere beyond our knees, the lagoon stretching out for ages, but eventually we're in chest-deep water.

'So, when are you going to show me?' Kat asks, looping her arms around my neck, her legs around my waist.

'Soon,' I tease, pulling her out deeper, deeper. The roar of the waves against the reef is so close now. 'Like this,' I say, then *shift* into dolphin form. *Just concentrate on the animal,* I think-say, swimming around her. *Coil down your dream-flow.* I *shift* back again, give her a smile. *See?*

Kat laughs, her delight spilling into my duplicitous thought-stream. How well can she swim? I wonder. Well enough to save herself once I take her out beyond the reef? Not if I drag her out far enough, considering she doesn't know how to *shift* into animal form yet. That's when I notice something is different about her, something I'm sure wasn't there before.

'Oh Rigel,' Kat/Brie says, batting her tattooed eyelids at me. 'Did you really think I wouldn't notice your arrival?'

Quick as lightning, she *shifts* and lunges. I jump backwards, but it's too late, and her shark jaws have clamped down on my arm. At first I'm too shocked to react, and then the pain hits me, an agony beyond anything I've ever felt. And I can't even look at it, at the place where my arm used to be, and I'm trying to get away from her, to *shift*, but I can't move, can't think—

And then the water starts churning, and Fox think-screams *Get out, get out!* I start kicking with my legs, trying to put distance between myself and the sharks: Kat and Fox. My head is whirling, and the water around me is turning red. Blood is coming out in arterial spurts and I know there's no one to save me, no paramedics, no mother, nothing I can use as a tourniquet.

I go under and come up again, choking. The sharks have moved out further, beyond the reef. If only I could — just — float but I—

Bob up and down, up and down, swallowing more and more water each time.

And as my brother battles it out with Aurelia, two sharks in a life-and-death battle, as my life-blood jets into the ocean, I realise I've lost everything.

The Hunter has fallen, I think-send, weakly, faintly—
And slip beneath the water for the last time.

FIFTY-FOUR:
INDIGO

'Gosh,' I say, breaking off the kiss before Billy's hands can wander any further, 'that's made me feel all weak at the knees.' Groaning inwardly at my soppy turn of phrase, I step backward before sinking onto my butt.

'Are you all right?' Billy's breathing is rapid, his voice thick.

'I'll be OK. I just need to recover. Wow.' I lean against the railing, knowing I'll need to keep my body safe for what I'm about to do next. 'Can you see her?' I tip my head back, closing my eyes so I can focus on the rhythm of his thought-stream.

'Uh, no.' I hear the scrape of shoes on gravel as he turns to look for the girlfriend he just cheated on. Rapidly, I coil down my dream-flow and—

I'm looking through his eyes, down towards the riverbank, where the man with the dog is no longer visible. Beside me, the girl Billy Quick only just met is slumped forward, as if unconscious. I hover in his midbrain for a moment, watching him crouch beside her, watching him touch her shoulder.

And — *now*. I extend tendrils into his thought-stream, commandeering and changing its direction. Billy rises up, crosses to the railing.

There she is, I think-whisper, and of course, he has no idea where this thought-voice is coming from, no idea what is compelling him to climb up on the railing. *Aurelia, she's there, can't you see her? She's fallen in the river, and she can't swim.*

And Billy *can't* see her, but he's panicking now, desperate to save the girl he's been obsessed with since the day he first met her. He clambers over the railing and dives into the river—

Headfirst. I barely have time to *shift* away again, barely have time to reclaim my own body before he strikes the rocks below with a sickening thud.

And as I jump up, ready to run down to check that he's dead, *really* dead, I hear *The Hunter has fallen*, and something else, a scream. It's *her*, Aurelia, oh no — and as I try to *shift* towards them, towards Rigel, everything begins to warp and spin and thud.

Die, you stupid cow, die! someone else screams, and it's Fox, and I realise the thudding sound is their heartbeat, Billy's and Aurelia's, and it's going faster and faster, so loud that I think my eardrums are about to burst, until it becomes one continuous, overwhelming noise, until all I can do is curl into a ball on the ground, clutching the sides of my head as everything begins to spiral and collapse in on itself, and the last thing I hear before everything goes black is—

What's done has been
What's done has been
What's done has been
Undone.

And just like that, the Eternity Loop collapses.

FIFTY-FIVE:
RIGEL

Indigo and I are driving out to Piha beach in my SUV, just the two of us. The sky is dark and moody, the late afternoon drizzle coating the windscreen.

'You honestly have the worst music taste ever,' Indigo is telling me, and I'm rolling my eyes at her, the way I always do when she tells me that my taste in music/girls/basically everything is crap.

'Listen to this,' she says, tapping on her I-Bio. Next thing, Neon is playing through the speakers. She's singing 'Love Triangle', which naturally Indigo knows all the lyrics to because Neon is Indigo's *favourite musician ever*. Indigo joins in, singing 'this is true love', while I start warbling 'this is true shit'. She thumps me on the shoulder and I nearly lose control of the car, which for some stupid reason has both of us cracking up instead of freaking out that we nearly crashed.

'You suck,' Indy says, once our giggles have subsided.

'Not as much as this song,' I say, when Neon launches into the first verse of 'You're My Reason'.

'You should listen to the lyrics sometime.'

'I have, and they make me want to remove my eyes with forks. Thanks.' I coast into the carpark and kill the engine. 'Race you.'

As we run towards the waves, Indigo takes off with a sudden burst of speed, having *shifted* into a greyhound. *Cheat*, I think-say, leaving my *shift* until I've launched into the surf, by which stage Indigo has assumed the form of an orca as well. We jump and twist, dive and churn through the salty foam until even my whale-self is exhausted. Then we cruise back in, *shifting* into human form once we're close to shore.

'That was awesome,' Indigo says, once we've tramped back to the SUV and wrapped towels around ourselves.

'The best,' I say. We sit in the rear of the SUV, passing a thermos of orange tea between us as the stars wink into the sky. And maybe we didn't need to drive all the way out here — we could have *shifted* instead — but then we wouldn't get to do this.

We lie down, a blanket draped over us, and gaze through the sunroof. There are so many stars out now, constellations and the Milky Way and a razor-sharp crescent moon. The universe looks so cold, but our body warmth is mingling, Indigo's shoulder and hip touching mine.

'We should go to South America again,' I say. 'You could be a white witch.'

'Is that meant to be an insult?'

'It's a type of moth.'

Digging her elbow into my side, Indigo says 'I *know*', and I nudge her in return, which turns into a tickling war, and that's when *it* happens.

'Say mercy,' I say, pinning her down, and she's staring up into my eyes, and I hesitate, because I don't want to ruin everything, but something tells me I may never get another chance.

'Never,' she whispers, and that's when I kiss her.

The rest, as they say, is history.

EPILOGUE:
ANDROMEDA

I bounce up and down on my bed. 'Tell me a bedtime story.'

Grandad lingers at the door. 'What sort of bedtime story?' He thinks he's got away with tucking me in, a quick kiss on my forehead, but I've got news for him.

'You know,' I say, as my parents' laughter drifts in from the lounge. 'The one about Grandma Violet.'

Grandad, as always, can't resist. 'All right,' he says, sitting on the end of my bed. 'But straight to sleep after that, OK?'

Ignoring him, I say, 'What was she like when you met her?'

Fingering the tattoo above his eyebrow, Grandad says, 'She was fierce and smart and beautiful, just like you.'

'And she could fly like a bird and run like a wolf . . .'

'She could fly *as* a bird and run *as* a wolf,' he gently corrects. 'As will you, when you're old enough.'

'I can't wait!' In five years, I'll be thirteen, old enough to start *shifting*. Will I be a moth, like my mother? A wolf, like Grandma Violet? I quite like the idea of being something different, like a spider or a whale. 'And tell me,' I say, 'how she cured the whole world.'

'Nearly the whole world, yes.' He leans against the wall. 'Once upon a time, there was a terrible virus called Riva. People who caught it become infertile, which means—'

'That they can't have babies.'

'You've heard this story before,' Grandad says, a smile tugging on his lips. From the lounge, I hear Mum shout 'Primo!' which means she's won the game they always play when Uncle Fox and Great-uncle Rawiri are over.

'Please . . .' I beg, so Grandad continues.

'Your Grandma Violet made a cure for the Riva, or she nearly did. Of course she died before she could finish it, but—'

'But her lab team carried on her work and she got the biggest prize in the world.' I spread my arms wide.

'The Nobel Prize, yes.'

'But why did she have to die?' I ask, and Grandad's eyes grow sad.

'Because your grandma was a healer, and yet it made her heart very weak. She was told she should never heal anyone again. But one day, not long after the Riva epidemic started, Fox accidentally *shifted* into the middle of a road and got hit by a car. His injuries were so severe that the doctors wanted to turn off all life support. But your grandma—'

'Healed him and died because her heart stopped.' I twisted my sheet between my fingers. 'I wish we could go back in time to stop Uncle Fox being run over.'

'I do, too, but it's far too dangerous. The time-travel laws say that we must never do that again.'

Grandad looks so sad that I climb onto his lap and give him a hug. 'I hope you never die.'

'I hope so, too, Andi.' He ruffles my hair. 'Now. It's late. Off to sleep, hmm?'

I pull the covers to my chin, waiting until Grandad reaches the doorway before saying, 'Can you send Uncle Fox in next?'

Grandad waggles a finger at me. 'What did I say?'

'Uncle Fox!' I say, and Grandad says 'I'll see if he's available' in the tone that always makes me giggle. While I wait, I tune into the thought-streams of my family in the lounge. I know it's kind of naughty, but ever since I realised I could read minds a year ago I haven't been able to resist.

'Well,' Mum is saying, 'I think it'd be a travesty of justice if he *ever* gets released.'

'Relax,' my father replies. 'The BSI have their own way of dealing with criminals and, believe me, he's never going to see the light of day.' Now this story is one I don't completely understand, not yet. All I know is that Grandad and Rawiri are heroes, just like my grandma, because they got an evil guy called Underwood locked up not long after my Grandma Violet died. I don't know what *illegal procurement of stem cells* and *exploitation of minors* is, but it sounds evil.

'Almost as evil as time vampires?' Uncle Fox jogs into my room and sits on my bed with a thud.

'I wasn't listening,' I say, my cheeks going all hot.

'Sure.' He tickles me, and I giggle.

'Tell me about the vampires.'

He arches an eyebrow at me. 'Are you sure you won't be too scared to go to sleep?'

'Of course not. They're not real, right?'

'Nope,' he says. 'They're not real. But this is the sanitised version, OK?'

'What's sanitised?'

'Let's just say I removed the boring bits.' He stands up to turn off my light. 'Once upon a time . . .' he says, stretching out beside me. 'Is that how a story begins?'

'Yes,' I tell him, lying back and closing my eyes. 'That's how it begins.'

ACKNOWLEDGEMENTS

The quotes 'Billy Pilgrim has come unstuck in time' (page 84), 'And I asked myself about the present: how wide it was, how deep, how much was mine to keep' (page 84) and 'It is just an illusion here on Earth that one moment follows another one, like beads on a string, and that once a moment is gone, it is gone forever' (page 216) are from *Slaughterhouse Five* by Kurt Vonnegut. Copyright © Kurt Vonnegut Jr. 1969, published in Great Britain by Jonathan Cape 1970, Vintage, 1991, 2000. Reprinted by permission of The Random House Group Limited.

Thank you to my beloved family and friends, most especially my husband Grant and children Lachie and Maisie. Thank you once again to Nod Ghosh, who provided critique on the early part of this novel, and to my publisher, Harriet Allan, and my agent, Nadine Rubin-Nathan of High Spot Literary. Thank you also to the rest of the amazing team at Penguin Random House, and my readers, without whom this book would not be possible.

READ THE ENTIRE
BLACK SPIRAL
TRILOGY

Wise, tough, heart-breaking, funny, this compulsive love story is about facing your demons.

Fifteen-year-old Rebecca McQuilten moves with her parents to a new city. Lonely but trying to fit in, she goes to a party, but that's when things really fall apart.

I couldn't tell anyone what had happened. Especially since I was the new girl in town. Who would want to believe me?

Things look up when she meets gregarious sixteen-year-old Cory Marshall.

'You're funny, Becs,' Cory said.
'You have no idea,' I said, and clearly he didn't, but I was smiling anyway. And after that, he was all I could think about.

Cory helps Rebecca believe in herself and piece her life back together; but that's before he shatters it all over again . . .

A moving novel about learning to find happiness in the face of uncertainty and discovering a love that transcends the boundary between life and death.

Seventeen-year-old Alex Byrd is about to have the worst day of her life, and the best. A routine blood test that will reveal her leukaemia has returned, but she also meets Jamie Orange.

Some people believe in love at first sight, and some don't.
I believe in love in four days.
I believe in falling.

Both teenagers have big dreams, but also big obstacles to overcome.

'Promise me you won't try to die,' I said. 'Ever.'
'Promise me you won't either,' he countered.
'It's not really something I can control.'

A moving story about unconventional love, bullying and being true to yourself.

'I wish I wasn't the weirdest sixteen-year-old guy in the universe.'

Felix would love to have been a number. Numbers have superpowers and they're safe — any problem they might throw up can be solved.

'If I were a five, I'd be shaped like a pentagon . . . there'd be magic in my walls, safety in my angles.'

People are so much harder to cope with. At least that's how it seems until Bailey Hunter arrives at school. Bailey has a stutter, but he can make friends and he's good at judo. And Bailey seems to have noticed Felix:

'Felix keeps to himself mostly, but there's something about him that keeps drawing me in.'

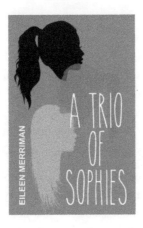

A missing girl, a secret diary and unsettling revelations . . .

Today is the first of September, the first day of spring, and it's been sixty-four days since I last saw Sophie Abercrombie. It's been sixty-four days since anyone saw Sophie Abercrombie.

The prettiest Sophie.
The missing Sophie.

As Sophie MacKenzie — Mac — confides to her diary, she last saw Sophie Abercrombie kissing James Bacon, their English teacher. Mac has passed this on to the police, but there is plenty she knows about James Bacon that she has kept to herself. She hasn't even told Twiggy, the third Sophie in their once tightknit threesome.

The Trio of Sophies is no more.

PRAISE FOR EILEEN MERRIMAN

Pieces of You

'. . . the kind of book you want to read in one sitting because it is so breathtakingly good . . . It feels utterly real. It does not smudge the tough stuff. It is kaleidoscopic in both emotion and everyday detail . . . Eileen writes with such a flair for dialogue, for family circumstances, for teenage struggles and joys. This is the kind of book that will stay at the front of my mind all week and longer — I recommend it highly.' — Paula Green, *Poetry Shelf*

'. . . could well become one of the biggest local YA books of the year. It's intelligent, literate . . . pertinent, witty when it needs to be, thought-provoking and relatable.' — Dionne Christian, *NZ Herald*

'Merriman's acute observation and awareness of teen mentality comes to the fore. It all feels very real and fresh.'
— Denis Wright, *The Sapling*

Catch Me When You Fall

'My best pick for 2018 for young adults, the standout for me . . . it's kind of heart-wrenching and really real and quirky and a great teen read for girls and boys.' — James Russell, *Radio NZ*

'This book . . . is interested in life and death struggles, and the way that these struggles interact with the more everyday agonies and ecstasies of coming-of-age . . . The story is well paced and absorbing . . . effective in its depiction of the desperation inspired by love and fear of loss.' — Angelina Sbroma, *NZ Books*

'When it comes to the medical details, the story pays impressive attention . . . the story doesn't only focus on Alex and her physical sickness but also on Jamie and his far subtler mental illness . . . well written and cleverly expressed.' — Madeleine Fountain, *NZ Doctor*

Invisibly Breathing

'. . . more than just a book to be read, but gripping literature which both celebrates love and also exposes society's harmful behaviour towards love that is not considered "conventional".
Rating 5/5 stars' — Faga Tuigamala, *Tearaway*

'. . . dialogue is crisp and convincing and their characters are well drawn . . . a gripping account of two young men on the brink of manhood, uncertain and deeply involved emotionally, facing the reactions of their family and friends . . . It is a moving story, well told.' — Trevor Agnew, *Magpies*

'It's a clever book. Ingenious chapter headings, smart sentences, inventive glides of plot and relationships. It's very contemporary, veined with phones and txts and Twitter and *Grand Theft Auto V*. There's a stadium-sized cast of kids, and Merriman gets their blitheness, erratic fuses, invulnerability-cum-fragility spot-on . . . her book is bloody good.' — David Hill, *NZ Books*

A Trio of Sophies

'I absolutely endorse this in a Young Adult Section, or High School Library. It could just save a life — and no I'm not being dramatic. It was a book that fifteen-year-old me needed to read, and that twenty-seven-year-old me is glad to have . . . Absolutely worth the five stars. And the late bedtime.' — Krystal B, *Goodreads*

'Fast-paced and unpredictable, *A Trio of Sophies* will keep readers on their toes and caught up until the last page. And if it's your first Merriman book, it certainly won't be your last.'
— Sarah Pollok, *Weekend Herald*

'This is a page turner make no bones about that . . . Much to enjoy in this novel. Best New Zealand YA novel of the year so far. Don't miss it, you will kick yourself if you do. The ending will make you think.' — Bob Docherty, *Bobsbooksnz.wordpress.com*

Violet Black

'With a light touch, Merriman invites us to examine heavy questions about right and wrong, indoctrination, the rights of the individual versus the rights of society, all without sermonising . . . *Violet Black* marks the beginning of a thrilling sci-fi adventure with sparks of romance and humour to light up the dark twists and turns of The Foundation. Merriman is a gifted-storyteller.' — Rachael Craw, KidsBooksNZ

'This was the first book by Eileen Merriman I have read and it did not disappoint. I can't wait to explore more of her work. The story was engaging right from the start, pacey, and scarily close to current events! . . . Overall, this was an enjoyable, easy, fast read with sufficient twists and a great first book for anyone looking to expand their reading into dystopian fiction. This is definitely a book that will hook teen and adult readers looking for a high octane, quick read in.' — Molly Molving-Lilo, *Magpies*

'Merriman . . . has always been particularly strong at writing death and loss and shock. Here she makes her protagonist, Violet, hurt like hell and she makes us hurt with her. There are giddy highs, too — a new love, those psychic powers of course, the satisfaction of teens outsmarting their elders. It's very bloody sinister in parts; lots of sedation and trippy dream elements; that and the whole "team of extraordinary kids training for a mission" thing reminded me of Veronica Roth's *Divergent*. Except *Violet Black* is much better written.' — Catherine Woulfe, *The Spinoff*

'I would recommend this book for anyone who enjoys a good sci-fi or fantasy adventure, a thrilling dystopia or an against-all-odds story; a fast-paced opening to a trilogy or a mystery novel. If you've ever dreamed of being recruited by a secret agency, or fighting bad guys, this book is for you. This is a stunning book which I would recommend for readers aged 12–15.' — Sasha Maclean, *Hooked on NZ Books, Read NZ*

Black Wolf

'Eileen Merriman has created a gripping plot with complex issues presented with plausible medical and psychological details . . . The result is a fast-moving, multi-layered story with characters you care about.' — Trevor Agnew, *The Source*

'Action-packed from beginning to end, prepare yourself for a gripping, and sometimes terrifying story of a futuristic world on the brink of destruction. . . . Will everything fall to pieces? Hooked from the start, this was a question I found myself asking very often throughout my read of *Black Wolf*. Or actually, I was probably more like *when will it fall to pieces?* Merriman takes you on a rollercoaster ride with climate change, science and romance all playing their part. . . . *Black Wolf* was an engrossing story with interesting characters and a fast-paced and dynamic plot. For anyone 14+, who enjoys a lot of drama!' — Savarna Yang, *Hooked on NZ Books, Read NZ*

'With more detailed coverage of characters from book one, a deepening plot and a startling new setting, *Black Wolf* is engrossing. While it could be read as a standalone novel, it would be more sensible to read in order, especially to understand the science fiction elements. Despite the insidious machinations, Merriman leaves an overarching impression of fun. While Violet and Phoenix are defending their own lives, inversely they also seem to be enjoying their escapades.' — Jessie Neilson, *Kete.co.nz*

Black Spiral

'This is the best Sci-Fi series and futurism I have read since *The Arc of a Scythe* series . . . It is the final in the series and ties up all the themes and plot lines in a satisfactory ending but leaving food for thought. . . . An extremely thought provoking series that is compulsive reading. Don't miss this series you will kick yourself if you do.' — Bob Docherty, *Bobs Books Blog*

'I adored reading the first two volumes in Eileen Merriman's Black Spiral trilogy. My words grace the back of the third volume: "Characters matter, dialogue matters, real-life detail matters, significant issues matter and you are always held in the grip of a perfectly pitched narrative . . . This is YA fiction at its life-crackling best." This appraisal also applies to the third and final volume, *Black Spiral* because it resonates and grips on many levels. Like the first two books, it is exquisitely crafted at the level of both sentence and architecture . . . I couldn't put the book down . . . Novels as good as this offer retreat, reinforcement and uplift. Glorious.' — Paula Green, *Poetry Shelf*

'The third and final book in this excellent Young Adult trilogy from Eileen Merriman. . . . A gripping finale to this series and an author to watch out for.' — Ann Kilduff, *Rotorua Daily Post*

'*Black Spiral* is the final book in the Black Spiral trilogy and brings the series to a thrilling conclusion. . . . *Black Spiral* takes the trilogy to a deeper level while still being a suspenseful, page-turning read. The characters are well-drawn, the plotting first-class, and the story lingers in your mind long after reading the final page. It's aimed at the young adult reader, but older readers will also enjoy these futuristic books.' — Karen McMillan, *NZ Booklovers*